ENDORSEMENTS FC

The
Enchanted
Mirror

Sheila Reeves Rigby:
Author of *Life's Mysteries – Your Key to Understanding*
"Occasionally, we hear stories of very ordinary individuals who unwittingly become caught up in leading extraordinary lives.

The stories of Dian Fossey and Joy Adamson, whose lives became irrevocably involved with their animals, come to mind.

This is such a story.

David and his sister Tracy J Holroyd (widely published author of children's works) tell the compelling story of dolphins Duchess and Herb'e as seen through the eyes of the boy who trained them. The authors' inimitable style of writing immediately engages the reader, making the book increasingly impossible to put down.

This book proves beyond doubt that telepathy is not only a phenomenon between humans, but also between humans and animals.

I can't wait for the second instalment!"

Simon JR Adams, BSc, BVMS, MRCVS:
Zoo & Wildlife Veterinary Adviser
"This important story highlights not only the incredible psychic bonding possible between Man and Dolphins, but also draws the reader's attention to the major animal welfare implications of keeping wild dolphins in captivity merely for the commercial purpose of entertaining parents and kids.

After reading this revealing story, hopefully the public will realize the true cost to these beautiful wild creatures. The only way to prevent their suffering is to appreciate this, and then decide if they really truly wish to attend Dolphinaria, and so support and perpetuate this form of 'entertainment show'?

As a wildlife vet, I have no doubts that whenever possible, Dolphins need a free life in the wild, to fulfil their complex welfare needs.

Watching them pursue their elaborate and often playful free-swimming lives is the real entertainment!"

Professor Brenda Cooper:
Literary Critic
Commenting on David C Holroyd's winning entry for the Manchester Evening News Literary Competition – A Piece of Your Life (Deliver Us from Bobby! Chapter 11)

"*Deliver Us From Bobby!* is an original piece of life writing. It uses the outlandish device of a mal-contented Californian sea lion called Bobby to tell a story of male aggression and territoriality, as played out in a small mining town.

It is told in the first person and demonstrates the level of violence potentially unleashed over a contested parking place. This has the ring of truth as two men, our self-critical narrator being one, are ready to fight to the death over the spot.

The teller is even more culpable, having erased Bobby from his consciousness, so intent is he on combat. What ensues is as hilarious as it is serious. This wonderful piece of life has a beautiful ending, which suggests that a capacity for loyalty and empathy could be the flip side of male aggression."

The Perfect Pair

The Enchanted Mirror

David C Holroyd

and

Tracy J Holroyd

Matador
9 Priory Business Park,
Wistow Road, Kibworth Beauchamp,
Leicestershire. LE8 0RX
Tel: (+44) 116 279 2299
Fax: (+44) 116 279 2277
Email: books@troubador.co.uk
Web: www.troubador.co.uk/matador

ISBN:
SB: 978 1780882 352
HB: 978 1780882 369

British Library Cataloguing in Publication Data.
A catalogue record for this book is available from the British Library.

Typeset in 12pt Bembo by Troubador Publishing Ltd, Leicester, UK
Printed and bound in the UK by TJ International, Padstow, Cornwall

Matador is an imprint of Troubador Publishing Ltd

FOREWORD FOR

by William Roache, MBE

This is a remarkable and heart-warming true story of dedication, devotion and love, overriding normal barriers and allowing one young man to make extraordinary achievements with two dolphins, and to have close contact with many others.

There is a move afoot to classify whales and dolphins as non-human beings. That to kill them would be murder. This indicates the high intelligence, understanding and feelings that these animals have… they have a soul.

What David found through his love and understanding of dolphins was a natural means of communication. It was two way, and the dolphins wanted the contact, enabling them to learn quickly and enjoy the thrill of performing. To David this was just a natural way of doing things - as indeed it is to the animal kingdom - and David developed his telepathic communications and his psychic abilities through working so closely with these wonderful animals.

This is a moving story, beautifully told, carrying the reader effortlessly through the joys and heartbreaks of one young man's selfless devotion as he struggles to bring out the best in his dolphins and achieve the impossible.

I read the book in one sitting and was often near to tears, but there was an overriding feeling of joy.

NOTES FROM THE AUTHORS

This is a story well known to those who work in the dolphin industry: a tale that over the passage of time has taken on an almost mythical quality. It tells of a young boy who took the dolphin world by storm, creating 'The Perfect Pair', two dolphins who worked in absolute unison, eventually achieving the much-revered somersault routine – a shadow ballet of exquisite grace and beauty.

However, the tale of their 'psychic trainer', as he became known, sent shivers down the spines of fearful managers, who deemed the boy's total control over his charges as dangerous to Company interests. So, 'The Perfect Pair' and their special trainer were deliberately written out of dolphinarium history… until now.

Because of this book – based on official dolphin logbooks, long since thought destroyed – the dream team is no longer consigned to marine folklore, but reborn, allowing Duchess and Herb'e to once again weave their magic. An enthralling story for those too young to remember… and a shameful reminder for those too old to forget.

David C Holroyd

There are literally hundreds – if not thousands – of academic works written about dolphins. This is certainly not one of them, for within these pages dwells a graphic story of the plight of the commercial dolphin.

However, there are also heart-warming tales of the trainers and handlers who work with them. *The Perfect Pair: The Enchanted Mirror* is an immensely personal account of a young boy's first love – a special love that takes him on a mystical journey deep into the world of the dolphin, effectively casting him into a reality that constantly questions man's overall appraisal of these very special people of the sea. It tells of a mind 'connection' – a psychic bond so strong that it enables the boy and his dolphins to become Europe's top performing team... the best of the best.

No one reading this book will ever view a dolphin in the same light again.

Tracy J Holroyd

ACKNOWLEDGMENTS

We would like to thank the following people for all their help and support during the writing and production of this book:

Marion Ibbotson and Paul Goodier, who passionately shared our dreams, but never saw our project completed. We will always remember your love and support, and hope you enjoy this read in Heaven.

Our fantastic Mum and Dad, Barbara and Ronnie Holroyd, who endured so much neglect during the writing of this book... please forgive!

William Roache, MBE, whose warm enthusiasm, celebrity and excellent foreword helped propel us towards a wider audience.

Simon JR Adams, BSc, BVMS, MRCVS, Zoo & Wildlife Veterinary Adviser, for his enthusiastic encouragement, advice and endorsement. Also, for his unwavering belief in our project and his efforts to spread the word.

Sheila Reeves Rigby, author, for her valued feedback, warm encouragement and wonderful endorsement... and, more importantly, her friendship.

Professor Brenda Cooper, Ursula Hurley and Peter Kalu, judges of the *Manchester Evening News'* prestigious 'A Piece of Your Life' writing competition, for kick-starting our dream.

Deanna Delamotta, *Manchester Evening News'* Features Editor, for her enthusiasm, support and excellent newspaper coverage.

Our beloved cousin, Antony J Reid of Reid Design & Illustration (www.reiddesign.co.uk), for his advice and digital origination of the book's graphic layout. Also, for enhancing our somewhat faded photographs and drawings. But, more importantly, for his delightful eccentricity and fabulous sense of humour!

Don and Irene Campbell for their ever-cheerful support and Don's marvellous photographs.

Shirley Swaine for her wonderful photographs; also, for permitting use of her father's phenomenal close-ups… thank you, too, Edgar Swaine.

William M Johnson, author, for lifting us up when we were down.

Chris Lovett for his friendship, support and invaluable introduction to Simon.

Barbara and Vince Meehan for their input and friendship over the years.

Henye Meyer, author, for her valued support, guidance and friendship.

Our dear cousins, Pamela and Albert Morris, for their introduction to the US publication, *The Union Jack*, along with *The Union Jack's* owners, Ron and Jeff Choularton, for their excellent publicity.

Steve Suttie, former manager of Salford City Radio, for his vision in creating the 'Twisted Ear' drama production group, which started it all.

Jill Bowyer and Ian Rothwell for their continued friendship and support, and for giving us valuable airtime on their radio shows.

Our lovely cousins, Patricia and Annie Clark, whose enthusiasm helped to pass the word Stateside.

Anna Ganley, Sarah Baxter and Nicola Solomon of 'The Society of Authors' for their professionalism, encouragement and invaluable advice.

Staff members of Salix Homes Ltd, Salford for their interest; especially Debbie Broadhurst and Georgina Dalton for securing us welcome publicity.

Finally, the many friends and family members, too numerous to mention, who have supported and encouraged us. Thank you all: we love you.

CREDITS

Cover photograph of *The Perfect Pair:* Edgar Swaine.

Cover font: *The Perfect Pair* – created and designed by David C Holroyd.

Digital origination of the book's graphic layout and enhancement of our somewhat faded photographs and drawings: Antony J Reid of Reid Design & Illustration – www.reiddesign.co.uk

Inside photographs: Don Campbell, Vince Meehan, John Rock, Edgar Swaine and Shirley Swaine.

Line drawings: David C Holroyd.

❦ PROLOGUE ❧

"And now, ladies and gentlemen, it's time for Duchess' highball, the only trick that Duchess performs alone. Normally, as you've already seen, she works as a team with Flippa. Now, at twenty-three feet, this is the highest highball in the country – an exceptional achievement for Duchess – so, if you have cameras, this is the time to use them. If you want a real good shot, you're welcome to come down to the front of the dolphinarium. All I ask is that, once the trick is performed, you go straight back to your seats. Oh, and, by the way, you could get very wet. You have been warned."

Good old Dan, he's really giving Duchess' highball a big build-up, milking the trick for all it's worth, although I have a feeling that all his flannel is for nothing, because today's the day. I just know it. Today's the day when Herb'e parts with his most treasured possession – his secret.

Dan lowers the microphone and waits as the photographers in the audience navigate through rows of people and down the long steps leading to the pool. I have just rounded off the dolphins' last trick with a feed and a long blast on the whistle, and the audience has responded enthusiastically. It's a great feeling.

Today, we have a good house – especially for the time of year – nearly six hundred people, maybe more. The whole building echoes with excited chatter, and the crowd's delight at being so close to real, live dolphins is reflected in bright smiles and eyes that follow Duchess and Herb'e everywhere they go.

Herb'e? Well, that's Flippa's real name. Flippa is only a stage name, adopted to satisfy the expectations of the public, who visit a dolphin show *wanting* to see a *Flippa*, just like in the movies. And what the public want, they get.

The sun streams through the skylights, reflecting off blue water. Today, my *enchanted mirror* is sparking electricity. Duchess is already mentally preparing; I feel the tension building in her. This is Duchess' big moment, her cameo performance. I indicate to Herb'e to move out of the way and, as usual at this point, he meanders off to a corner of the pool, where, hopefully, he'll dilly-dally around until the trick is finished.

Dilly-dally around? Who am I kidding? The radio's on. I can hear the static echoing in my ears. He has invoked a silent *connection*. I can literally feel his nervous excitement as he scurries around inside my head, preparing me mentally, fine-tuning me, so that when it happens, I'll have crystal clear reception.

"I know your game, Herb'e. You've got me hooked, and you're slowly reeling me in."

The frequency is wide open, but he's still not saying anything. He doesn't want to spoil the moment.

Cameras jostle for position over the safety barriers, then become still. The hum of conversation ceases. There is silence.

Duchess is bobbing in the water just before me, watching me intently. I take a breath, signal for her to momentarily hold her position, then throw out my right arm.

"Go!"

She dives.

To execute this trick, Duchess needs to pick up considerable speed. She usually does two laps of the pool, circling faster and faster, building momentum, tension, energy, then on the third lap she shoots out of the water missile-fashion, climbing higher, higher, higher, until she can reach the ball and bash it with her 'nose'. This done, she free falls into the water, showering everyone in the first two rows of the dolphinarium.

Now, every living thing in the place holds its breath – even Herb'e, as he watches assiduously from his corner. The atmosphere is charged. Just beneath the water's surface, Duchess speeds... lap one... building nicely... lap two... almost ready...

Suddenly, Herb'e shoots across Duchess' path! At these speeds, a collision could be catastrophic, and Duchess has to swerve to avoid him, twisting her body awkwardly. She thrusts her head out of the water, glares at him, then dashes towards me, bobbing her head frenziedly and literally screaming with rage.

"Look what he's done to my trick! Look what he's done!"

I stare helplessly. I know what's coming. He's spoiled Duchess' trick deliberately so that he can outdo her. There has always been rivalry between the dolphins, but this intentional act of sabotage has been a long time in the planning. I glance at Dan, who is also staring goggle-eyed at the dolphins, microphone drooping in his hand.

Then, unbelievably, Herb'e takes up lapping the pool, just as Duchess had been doing moments earlier, a dark figure just beneath the water's surface, travelling faster and faster... building speed, momentum, energy... lap one... lap two...

Dan and I continue to watch breathlessly. The audience watches, silent and confused. Only Duchess doesn't watch, her eyes fixed firmly on me as she continues to remonstrate.

But I see only Herb'e. I have an inkling... a faint hope... it's coming... it's going to happen.

Herb'e arcs out of the water, rising higher, higher, higher... and suddenly everything goes into slow motion. He starts to spin and, as I watch, I will his body around, lifting him, turning him, mentally spinning him through the air.

"That's it, Herb'e, go for it!"

I'd been working on this trick for months, but getting nowhere. So exhausted, so frustrated and disappointed had I been at our failure, I'd actually given up. And now Herb'e's doing it: he's doing the trick I've always dreamed about, the trick that will put my dolphins – and me – at the top of our field in Europe.

As he completes a full one and a half forward somersault, splashing back into the pool and drenching me with water, I stand frozen. The trick replays in my mind, still in slow-mo, whilst the realisation of what he's just done fully sinks in.

Herb'e has given me – and the audience – a trick never before seen in Britain! I can't even be sure that it's been seen in Europe. He has somersaulted through the air and seized the crown for us all.

It's also startlingly clear that he knows what he's done, and has planned it to make the biggest impact: first, ruin Duchess' starring moment; second, blow everyone away with something even bigger… even better. I'd thought he just didn't understand. Now, I know that he's been prevaricating – and extorting fish out of me for months and months and months!

Irrelevant now. My chest is thudding, and my mind feels like it's reeling through a wormhole. I start to blow the whistle, one blast for every piece of fish.

Herb'e resurfaces and shoots towards me, his gleeful dolphin voice echoing as I bombard him with fish and loud excited whistles.

Whistle – fish! Whistle – fish! Whistle – fish!

Suddenly, I think, Signal, signal… what you doing, Capello? You need a signal! Think! And the Roman salute leaps into my mind. I tightly curl the fingers of my right hand, then throw my arm across my chest, rapping my shoulder with my fist. Once, twice, three times.

Whistle – fish! Salute! Whistle – fish! Salute!

Two whistles – two fish! Salute! Two whistles – two fish! Salute!

Three whistles – three fish! Salute!

Herb'e catches his reward deftly, laughing noisily at his own cleverness and the treasury of food raining down upon him.

Duchess screams even louder, *"What are you doing? What are you doing?"* She's confused. All she can hear is the whistle blowing and Herb'e's triumphant cries as fish pour into his open mouth.

"Why are you feeding him? Why are you feeding him? He ruined my trick!"

As my left hand showers Herb'e with fish, my right hand reaches sympathetically for Duchess. *"I know, girl, I know. I'll tell you in a minute."*

I don't speak verbally, but with my mind, because that's the way you speak to dolphins, the way you *really* speak. The *connection* – the one I talk about, the one the managers scoff at – is white-hot now.

It's always there, the *connection*, even during the calmest times: the conversation between me and my dolphins that happens only in our minds. The only downside is that it always leaves me drained. I can't count how many times I've staggered off stage, exhausted by it. But this time, it's different: my mind is racing, my body numb to everything except the tingling of my nerves. I'm on a rush, higher than I've ever been. But I am not alone. There are three of us on this ride: Duchess, Herb'e, me. Three minds, three conversations: a conference where everyone's shouting at once. It's chaos, but the sort of chaos that kick-started the universe, chaos with intention, chaos with order.

"You've got to show Duch, Herb'e."

"But HE RUINED MY TRICK!"

"I know, Duch... I know... I'll tell you..."

And Herb'e's laughter.

All doors are slung open. We're in the loop. His glee, her anger, my excitement.

I drop to my knees, extending arms and pulling them both into an embrace, holding them: comforting her, congratulating him, relishing the feel of their warm, wet faces against mine.

Then, somewhere a million miles away, I hear the bewildered murmurings of the audience. The audience! I'd completely forgotten about them. Glancing up, I take in the bemused expressions, the shaking heads. They haven't a clue what's happening. They waited for a highball. They didn't get it; and now they aren't going to get it. And what's more, I don't care. I couldn't give a damn, because I've got something better... *we've* got something better!

Dan is watching us, Duchess, Herb'e and me, arms hanging loosely by his side, confusion in his eyes. He doesn't know what's happening either, and though he should be calming the crowd, covering for the turmoil, he just doesn't know what to say.

I struggle for breath, my voice little more than a gasp. "Tell them that they've just seen a full one and a half forward somersault, never before known in the UK, nor probably in the whole of Europe."

Dan lifts the microphone to his mouth, his words reverberating throughout the dolphinarium, a meaningless confusion of noise inside my head.

My mind is already back with Duchess and Herb'e.

The crowd ceases to exist.

The compère ceases to exist.

The show is ruined, but that doesn't matter.

Everything is in shadow; but we three are cocooned in a light, blinding in its brilliance.

Dolphin heads nodding, shaking...

Dolphin voices shouting, celebrating...

We're on a rollercoaster, flying away on Herb'e's laughter... flying so fast that I can almost feel the drag as we whizz back in time to where it all began...

❦ 1 ❧

Mum first spied the advert whilst lying on the sofa, browsing the pages of the *City News*: a job with a difference, appropriately framed in bold, black lines.

Like most '70s teenagers, I'd been skulking in my room, listening to records, playing air guitar and singing to my reflection in the mirror – my reflection and a crowd of screaming groupies! It was thirsty work, so I briefly interrupted my performance to nip downstairs for a glass of milk. As I walked through the door, Mum waved the newspaper and announced, "There's a job here that would be ideal for you."

"Yeah?" I smiled blankly, then trotted off into the kitchen to pour my milk.

Mum followed me, rattling the paper in my ear. "Yes, they're looking for strong swimmers who'd like to work with dolphins."

Now she had my attention. "Dolphins?" I repeated, craning my neck to read the ad over her shoulder. "Doing what?"

"Presenting them in shows."

"Wow…"

I could understand why Mum felt the job would suit me: I'd been a powerful swimmer from being a small child, competing at the highest levels in town galas. I had a strong affinity with animals, loved the sea and loved fish. I loved swimming with fish in my snorkel and mask; loved *being* a fish, wearing an Aqua-Lung and flippers; and loved watching fish as they explored their compact world within my magnificent tropical fish tank. In fact, the only thing I didn't love about fish was eating them! But, of course, I knew that a dolphin wasn't a fish – it was a mammal. Fab!

Theoretically, I'd make an ideal candidate. But there was one huge drawback: I was apprenticed to Dad in the sign-writing business and, if I got the job, I'd have to leave him. I didn't think I could do that.

"Well?" Mum persisted. "Will you apply?"

"It sounds terrific… but I don't think so. Wouldn't be fair to Dad, would it?"

Mum frowned. "Your Dad wouldn't stand in your way if that's what you wanted to do."

"No… I guess not." But he would be hurt, I thought. And I didn't want that. So, I shrugged my shoulders, retrieved my milk and wandered back upstairs to resume my gig.

And that was that – for me, at least. Not for Mum. Next morning, she called the number and left my details. Well, for the past eighteen years, she'd cooked my meals, washed my laundry, made my bed, lain out my clothes and generally cosseted me, so why shouldn't she apply for a job on my behalf? Only one thing: she forgot to mention it to me, so when I received the message calling me for an interview, it came as a complete surprise.

Within days, I found myself languishing in a queue of around two hundred interviewees at the local zoo. We hung around for hours waiting to be seen, exchanging life histories, gossiping about the advert and fantasising about escaping the dull routine of suburban life. Most of us had only ever seen a dolphin in photographs or on TV, but we'd all heard a treasury of tales about these friendly sea-dwellers.

To be honest, up until then I hadn't actually thought about dolphins, or what working with them might entail. Instead, my head had teemed with unrealistic visions of white sands and palm trees stretching as far as the eye could see; crystal waters abundant with brightly clad fish; never-ending sunshine. It was almost as good as being a rock star!

My turn came at last, and I was ushered into a small, plain room, where three men were sitting behind a table, armed with pads and pens. As I lowered myself into the chair opposite them, they put me in mind of the three wise monkeys: *See No Evil, Hear No Evil, Speak No Evil.*

One of them, a small, dark-haired man with black, beetle-like eyes, introduced the panel. His name was Rogers, and he was head of the dolphin project. Next, he introduced a Mr Blair, head zookeeper, and finally Mr Philip Haynes, veterinary surgeon – world-famous veterinary surgeon, I would later learn. Both men greeted me with a nod and a smile, but the vet in particular struck me with the warmth of his presence.

Then, the interview began in earnest.

"Why did you come to this interview?" Rogers' first question seemed abrupt and almost aggressive.

"I think I could do this job."

"What makes you think that?"

Taken aback, I glanced at the other two men. Haynes nodded encouragingly, a slight smile playing about his lips.

"I'm a strong swimmer – I've swum in competitions. I love animals, and my pride and joy at home is my tropical fish tank. I think I'd be good working with dolphins."

Haynes' smile widened. "Have you ever seen a dolphin, David?"

"Only on telly."

"So, what makes you think you'd make a good presenter?" Blair interjected.

"Well, I'm confident with people, and I'm a good talker."

"Who says you're a good talker?" Rogers again, cool and snappy.

"Everyone."

"So, have you worked with animals before?" Blair asked.

"No, but I have a dog. His name is Butch."

"Ah, so you *are* experienced in handling an animal. Excellent!" Haynes again. This almost felt like a good cop, bad cop scenario. "How would you feel about leaving home?" he continued. "If we were to offer you the job, you'd eventually be working at one of two pools, both some distance away."

"Well, I've never been away from home before, but if that's what it takes, I'll do it." I felt somewhat surprised to hear myself saying that: home had always been a loving and secure place, which I'd never previously imagined leaving.

The interview lasted for about fifteen minutes, during which time the head man remained brusque and critical, whilst the vet tried to be encouraging and friendly. It felt as if he was trying to shield me from Rogers' icy probing, and I sensed strongly that he liked me.

I underwent a second interview about two weeks later: the same three men asking pretty much the same questions. But when the telephone call came inviting me for a third interview, I began to get seriously excited. My name was now on a shortlist of only six people, which meant I stood a good chance of getting the job. Suddenly, that vision of a tropical ocean paradise lay within my grasp and, with it, Hollywood-style glamour, fame and fortune.

For the next two days, I continued working with Dad, lettering vans in dank workshops, a bright spark of anticipation warming the pit of my stomach. But on returning home on the second evening, Mum greeted me with a devastating message.

"They've been on from the zoo, David. They've decided to offer the job to someone else."

"Oh." I stared at her blankly as she went on to explain that I'd only narrowly missed out. It seems it had come down to a choice between me and an ex-naval diver and, in light of his professional experience, they'd decided on him.

As she broke the bad news, I could see the hurt in Mum's eyes. She knew how disappointed I'd be, and felt my pain as acutely as I did.

That evening, I ate dinner unenthusiastically, retreating early to bed to lick my wounds. I felt as if I'd missed the chance of a lifetime: bright lights, exotic adventure and playboy lifestyle. From now on, it would be hard work and sombre suburban days after all.

I struggled to settle back into a routine, the intense disappointment leaving me frustrated and dissatisfied.

But I didn't suffer for long. Two days later, Mum took another call: the panel had reviewed its decision and decided to take me on, along with the diver.

I couldn't believe it: the job was mine! I couldn't think why they'd changed their minds, but strongly suspected that the vet, Philip Haynes, had had something to do with it. Whatever, I'd arrived, and the excitement left me breathless.

High! Low! High! My emotions were in turmoil, and this was only the beginning. Had I only known then how much more frenzied this shredding of my nerves would eventually become.

I was to be packed and gone within the week to a training pool in North Liston, a small shire mining village. There, I would meet my dolphins, and undergo a course in presenting.

Whilst I was preparing to leave – or, more accurately, whilst Mum was preparing me – the Company's publicity machine kicked into action, and the story of my success hit the newspaper: *David Lands a Dream of a Job*. I read about myself with glee, relishing my first taste of a future bathed in fame and publicity.

Days later, I was stepping onto the train from the busy platform of City Railway Station. Farewell suburbia, farewell mundanity: hello North Liston, doorway to exotic adventure.

North Liston… where was that again?

❦ 2 ❧

Just over an hour later, I disembarked the train at North Liston Railway Station, my excitement already dampened. The vehicle of my great escape had propelled me relentlessly across a landscape that grew greyer, bleaker and more dispiriting by the second. Disconcertingly, I was the only passenger to alight at the station, which had only two platforms and one shabby station house. The only other person around was a short, stocky fella dressed in full stationmaster regalia and grasping a silver whistle. He bustled towards me, appraising me with sparkling grey eyes, set in a heavily lined face. I could see him taking in my skinny purple granddad shirt, blue split flares, platform boots and shoulder-length hair.

'E's not from round 'ere!

"Are you from this 'ere marina?" he demanded breathlessly.

"Yeah, I am."

A callused hand grabbed mine and gave it an enthusiastic shake. "Pleased to meet yer, lad! Please to meet yer! It's a grand thing fer our village is this marina, a grand thing!"

I couldn't help smiling. This 'ere marina was supposed to be a closely guarded secret: dolphins were new to the UK, and a training pool was *unheard of*, and should have stayed that way. But I was to find out later that this 'ere marina had been the worst kept closely guarded secret ever: for months, the whole village had been awaiting our arrival with breathless excitement.

"You couldn't by any chance tell me where Jim and Ida Butterworth live, could you? That's where I'm staying."

"Jim and Ida? Aye, lad, that I can – they're not five minutes from 'ere! But be warned, the 'ouses where they live are kinda funny."

"Funny? How do you mean?"

"Well, they're built arse-uppards, so to speak."

I gave him a puzzled look.

"The backs of the 'ouses face directly ont' road, instead of t'other way round. Still, yer shouldn't 'ave any problems finding Jim and Ida – just look for the 'ouse with the battered old pit bull on the step. Yer can't miss it – it's the spittin' image of Jim."

Except, never having met Jim, I didn't know what he looked like yet. Still, the dog should be easy enough to spot – there couldn't be that many battered old pit bulls lounging on steps around here. Or could there?

I couldn't help but wonder just what sort of place I had come to when you could throw a couple of names at the stationmaster and instantly get directions. Insular? Close-knit, certainly. Probably a real backwater.

I left the station and headed across a croft towards the main road. There, just before me, stood the training pool: an old, red-bricked building with a bell tower and steps leading up to a double swing door. The stationmaster had told me that, if I turned left here, Jim and Ida's place would be less than fifty yards away.

I hesitated, uncertain whether to go straight to my digs or to investigate the pool. Decision made, I crossed the road, climbed the steps and pushed my way into the pool building.

I found myself in a dark, dampish lobby that smelled strongly of chlorine and salt. Ahead of me was a glass-panelled office, where a young man was sitting at a table, poring intently over a file. As the door slammed behind me, he turned a pair of startlingly blue eyes to look at me, then – spotting my suitcase – broke into a friendly grin and dashed from the office, hand extended.

"You must be David." He had a slight American accent.

"Yeah…" I looked at him hesitantly.

"Rob Briers," he explained, vigorously shaking my hand. "Been expecting you! Come in, come in! I'll make you a brew and show you around."

I was parched after my journey, so the offer of a brew sounded heaven-sent. But I soon realised that I wouldn't be seeing a teapot any time soon because, part way through our journey to the kitchen, Rob got distracted into giving me a full tour of the pool building.

Leading me down a dimly-lit, meandering corridor, he explained that the pool had once been a public swimming baths. Each time he reached a door, he threw it back to show me what was behind: kitchen, male changing rooms, stairs leading up to the female changing rooms in the bell tower.

Halfway down the corridor, there was a set of double swing fire doors leading to the pool itself: a mass of water, framed by white tiles and flooded by daylight pouring through glass panes in the roof so that it shone like a mirror.

Despite being antiquated, with its stone floors and shabby furnishings, the building gleamed. Everything was clean to the point of being pristine, and I learned later that this was down to Rob, who had an almost obsessive desire to keep everything nothing short of sterile.

So, when I first spied the scruffy wooden hutch located at the rear of the pool, I couldn't help but feel curious. Enclosed by a wire mesh fence, it looked desperately in need of a good paint job, and totally incongruous in its pristine surroundings.

"What's in there?" I asked, pointing.

Rob's smile faded, his face twisting into something that wouldn't disgrace a gurner champion. "Smelly and Worse," he growled.

Smelly and Worse? Who on earth were they? I didn't get chance to ask because, as we neared the hutch, two tiny figures shot through its doorway, hissing and spitting. Penguins! Two little penguins; flippers flaring and squaring up to us like gladiators going into battle.

Actually, they were Humboldt penguins – I recognised them from pictures I'd seen in a book. I leaned towards them to get a closer look, but Rob placed a warning hand on my arm. "Don't put your hands over the mesh. In fact, don't put your hands anywhere near them!"

I grinned. He had to be joking: how could these two tiny creatures be a threat?

He read my thoughts. "Believe me, these things are vicious. They'll have you, given half a chance." His eyes flickered back to the penguins and narrowed. "I hate them."

I backed off, but not before catching the dreadful odour emanating from their hutch. "They don't smell too good, do they?"

"That's because all they do is shit all day," Rob replied. "You drop a fish in one end and, within minutes, twice as much comes out the other. All they do is shit, shit, shit all over my lovely clean pool!"

Clearly, he hated the poor little fellas with a ferocity that seemed unreasonable. Trying to lighten the moment, I quipped, "Which one's Smelly and which one's Worse?"

Not one of my better ideas. Rob threw me a dirty look and snapped, "How do I know which one of these shittin' things is which? Why would I even care? I hate them!" He paused, then reiterated vehemently, "I hate them!"

I didn't pursue it: Rob just seemed to be getting more and more worked up, and I didn't want to get off on the wrong foot. But, as we walked away, I couldn't help wondering what the big deal was. After all, they were only two little penguins.

Little did I suspect that I'd just met what would soon become my foremost antagonists: two little nightmares who would pursue and haunt me throughout my entire working life with the Company.

I was somewhat disappointed to find that there weren't any dolphins at the pool, although Rob explained that this was because their transport had been delayed. Other than Rob and the penguins, the only other person there was my fellow trainee, the ex-naval diver, Matt Bannister – a small but powerfully-built teenager with whom I would work and share a room at Jim and Ida's.

It all seemed very subdued and unexciting: a sleepy shire mining village where we were the biggest thing to happen in ages. Long streets of terraced houses set against a backdrop of bleak moorland and overshadowed by the black umbra of the pit, squatting at the top of the hill.

No sands, no palm trees – and not a dolphin in sight. And by the time I'd arrived at Jim and Ida's, having lugged my suitcase past windows dingy with coal dust, yet another shred of my dream had been carried away on the breeze.

❤ 3 ❤

The back door of the squat terraced house where Matt and I would live lay ajar. An aged pit bull, heavily scarred and wearing a studded leather collar, reclined on the stone step. It rose as we approached, eyeing us in a way I didn't quite like. Suddenly, a gruff voice from behind the door growled, "Gerrin!"

Lowering its head, the dog gave us an unpleasant look, then sloped inside. We followed uncertainly, ready to drop our cases and run at any moment.

We needn't have worried. When we stepped through the door, it was into a world of glorious warmth and mouth-watering aromas: roasts, puddings, stews… The kitchen in which we found ourselves might *look* uninspiring, with its sallow walls, lino covered floors and battered furniture, but the range and hearth, which stretched the entire length of one wall, promised previously undreamt of delights.

Working the range was a thin, timid-looking woman. She wiped her hands on her apron as we entered, turning to look at us with weary, careworn eyes.

"Mrs Butterworth?" I asked. When she didn't reply, I explained, "David Capello and Matt Bannister from the training pool."

She nodded in silent acceptance that her lodgers had arrived.

"'Ow do." It was a statement, not a question, and I recognised the gruff voice that had summoned the dog.

Jim Butterworth sat in an armchair behind his wife, warming his feet in front of the open fire whilst his boots dried on the hearth. He was a thickset chap, with no neck – his physique no doubt moulded by years of digging coal in the pit – and his grey face was etched with dusty-looking grooves.

The pit bull had settled by his feet, and as I looked again at dog, then back at man, the stationmaster's words sprang into my head: "It's the spitting image of Jim!"

I could see exactly what he meant. Like Jim, the dog was heavily-built and had no neck; like Jim, its face was deeply furrowed. In fact, the dog looked so much like Jim, it was uncanny; the only difference being that the dog had a much healthier colour: a ruddy coat that contrasted favourably with Jim's unwholesome pallor.

And that, as they say, was that. Neither Jim nor Ida spoke much; Jim seemingly comfortable in his own silence, and the hard-working Ida appearing excessively timid.

Forsaking her range for a few minutes, Ida showed us to our room – a sparse, dingy retreat – then gave us a quick tour of the house: functional and sober, with the same yellowish walls, lino covered floors and tired-looking furniture as we'd seen in the kitchen. The dark cast of coal dust seemed to be everywhere, so the whole house looked faded.

Only one place was off-limits, apart from Jim and Ida's bedroom, of course, and that was the parlour. No one was allowed in there but Jim. That was where he went to get some peace and quiet, and to read his paper. If we wanted to hang out downstairs, then it would have to be in the kitchen.

After we'd finished the tour and unpacked, Ida seated Matt and me at the sparse, wooden table with Jim, and served the first course of our dinner. She placed a huge ceramic dish before me, which nursed the biggest Yorkshire pudding I'd ever seen: golden-brown and drenched in rich gravy, aromatic with the heady scent of beef… And it was *all* mine – we actually had one each.

I stared at this culinary masterpiece, salivary glands working overtime, scents of what would follow caressing my nostrils; then I stared at Ida.

"Well, tuck in, then!"

Tiny, pale, tired and nervous: I was looking at a genius…

❦ 4 ❧

With no dolphins, there should have been very little to do work-wise. However, Smelly and Worse were truly as bad as Rob had painted them to be.

Each morning, after eating one of Ida's glorious fry-ups, Matt and I would make our way to the pool, where our first job would be to clean up after the two penguins.

Smelly and Worse definitely had a bowel problem, and appeared to spend every night looking for secret places in which to deposit their stinking white puddles of dirt. In fact, there was so much of the stuff, I half wondered whether Rob hadn't got another half-dozen penguins hidden away somewhere. With annoying regularity, it was deck scrubbers, bleach and bucket upon bucket of scalding hot water.

After shifting Smelly and Worse's mess, we would begin general cleaning: scouring sumps, filters, buckets, walls, windows and sinks, closely watched by Rob, who would later meticulously check every surface for smears and misses.

And we learned. We learned about dolphins, filtration systems, water maintenance and every other conceivable aspect of running a dolphinarium.

But it wasn't all work. There was plenty of time for swimming, drinking tea and indulging in Rob's favourite pastime: trips to the pub...

We were now celebrities and, as the locals bombarded us with invitations, the parties never seemed to end. Warm, generous and curious, the people of North Liston lapped up Rob's flamboyant storytelling, longing to be part of the novelty that had arrived in their quiet, hard-working village.

In his stories, Rob constantly referred to something called *The Perfect Pair*: two dolphins so close that they literally work as one. In the dolphin business, the quest for *The Perfect Pair* was like the search for the Holy Grail. Even the Florida dolphin catchers tried to play their part, scanning schools for dolphin couples who swam and leapt in harmony. Little did I realise then that this quest would soon become *my* obsession.

In the meantime, we lived in a glorious state of irresponsibility. But not for long. We'd been at the pool for only a few weeks when Rob received a telephone call. As he called us into the office, the look on his face immediately told us that something was wrong.

"We've got a problem, lads, a bad problem." Rob took a breath: this was a momentous announcement.

"We're getting a sea lion!"

❧ 5 ❧

Matt raised his eyebrows. "A sea lion? I've never seen a sea lion before – not a real one, anyway."

He wasn't the only one; I'd never seen a real sea lion either, and I wasn't sure I wanted to. My job description said I was employed to present Atlantic bottlenose dolphins. No mention of sea lions.

Rob's face was etched with dismay. "You'll wish you hadn't seen this one either. They're rotten, vicious things." He paused dramatically. "You two had better sit down."

This was the cue for Rob to spin one of his colourful tales, the sort he delighted in entertaining the locals with down at the pub. For a few moments, he remained silent, during which time he stared at us hard; a technique I'd often seen him use when he wanted to build tension.

"This isn't just a sea lion," he said finally. "This is a nightmare: a fully mature bull. And he's been sent to us for a reason." He drew a deep breath. "This sea lion was housed at City Zoo. It seems there was an incident… some woman made the mistake of leaning a little too far over his pen." He fell silent. He really had a knack for reeling you in.

"So… what happened?" Matt demanded. "Did he bite her?"

Rob answered quietly. "He tore her breast off."

"He did what?" The appalling image flashed through my mind.

For several seconds, no one spoke, then I asked the obvious question: "So, why are they sending him here?"

"They say he's a danger to the public and must be destroyed; but the Company won't do that because he's worth too much money. So,

20

some clever dick has come up with the bright idea of hiding him here and issuing a statement saying he's been put down. That way, the Company keeps its sea lion, and no one's any the wiser."

We sat in grim-faced silence, grappling with the implications. Eventually, Rob spoke again. "I had a friend who worked with sea lions in the States. He told me that the only way to train one of these things is with a bucket of fish and a club. It's the only thing they understand."

"Surely they don't expect us to train it?" I said.

Rob nodded. "That's exactly what they expect."

"Have you ever trained a sea lion, Rob?" Matt asked.

Rob shook his head.

"If *you've* never trained one, who's going to train this?" I blurted.

Dead silence. Then, "Oh, by the way, lads, more good news: the sea lion arrives this afternoon."

❦ 6 ❧

Rob and Matt had gone for lunch, which meant a pie and pint down at the local. I just hoped they'd stick to the planned menu and not embark on drowning their sorrows, because I didn't fancy handling the sea lion's arrival alone.

As I didn't like drinking in the afternoon, I hadn't joined them. Instead, I'd retreated to the office with a sandwich and a mug of tea. I hadn't even taken my first bite, when I heard a noise and looked up to find a grizzled face peering at me round the main door.

"I've got a delivery for you." The man gave a cynical laugh. "A sea lion!"

So, this is it, I thought... he's arrived.

It seems that the animal had been transported in a large wooden crate, which the deliveryman complained would barely make it through the tight corridor. But the swing doors opening into the pool room posed an even greater problem.

"There's no way we can get that crate through there," the deliveryman told me. "Those doors will have to go."

"Well, take them off, if you want. I don't care!"

By the time Rob and Matt arrived back, two deliverymen were already unscrewing hinges, with two more supporting the heavy doors. Rob immediately flew into a flurry of useless activity, offering advice and dancing around them distractingly. Matt stood well back, watching quietly as though mesmerised.

Since there was nothing I could do at this stage, I decided to sneak a peek at our new arrival. The delivery van had been left unlocked, so I tentatively opened the back doors and climbed inside. Greeted by a sonorous snort and a foul smell, I saw him for the first time: a bulky, ungainly sea lion, shuffling around inside a cramped crate.

The sea lion was enormous, weighing at least six hundred pounds. He had fluffy, tan-coloured fur, which surprised me as I'd always thought sea lions were sleek and black; but I quickly realised that this was only when wet. This fella actually looked cuddly; in fact, shrink him down, and he wouldn't look out of place in a cradle.

"Hello, lad, aren't you beautiful?" I said softly.

Sticking his nose in the air, he watched me warily from the corners of huge, strikingly green eyes.

"Right, give us room, lad!" Our quiet meeting ended abruptly as the four deliverymen returned to the van. From then on, it was literally *all hands on deck*, as we struggled to shift the heavy crate out of the van and into the pool building.

Since the corridor leading to the pool room was too narrow to accommodate us all, that part of the journey thankfully fell to the four deliverymen. Laboriously, they inched the crate along, huffing and puffing and cursing, whilst the sea lion sat inside, watching them and snorting his displeasure. By the time they'd managed to get the crate into position, all four were gasping for air.

"That's just about done me in," one of them blurted, rivulets of sweat trickling down his purple face.

"I'm knackered!" another agreed.

But, tired or not, they didn't hang around to rest. With impressive speed, they replaced the pool room doors, packed up the van and jumped inside. As the engine growled into life, the driver shouted, "Oh, by the way, his name is Bobby."

"Bobby?" I called after him.

No reply: the van was already disappearing over the crest of the hill. Like it or not, their problem had just become ours, and we couldn't do a thing about it.

❦ 7 ❧

That night, I didn't feel much like socialising, so sat alone in a corner of the pub. I knew no one would miss me, because Rob was again holding court, attended as always by an obedient Matt.

All I could think about was that poor sea lion, alone and stuck in a crate. I couldn't get him out of my head. What would we do with him?

My deliberations were interrupted by a couple of locals at the bar, loudly discussing a spate of house robberies in the area, and I couldn't help smiling as they described in blood-curdling detail what would happen to the culprit if caught. "Thievin' bastard! Hang 'im from the pit-head by his thumbs! He won't nick anything else in a hurry."

Still preoccupied with thoughts about the sea lion, I sank a couple more pints, then decided to call it a night. Bidding a bleary farewell to a slightly blurred Rob and Matt, I set off for home; but, on reaching my digs, instead of going inside, I stood wavering on the doorstep, staring across the croft at the dark silhouette of the pool. That poor lad, stuck all alone in a crate.

A few drunken minutes later, I found myself unlocking the pool's main entrance, unable to resist the temptation to take a closer look at the new terror that had been thrust upon us. Staggering uncertainly, I made my way down the dim corridor towards the pool room swing doors, then pushed my way inside to be greeted by yet another sonorous snort.

There he was, just as I'd left him, his huge bulk pressed hard against the side of his crate, nose pointing upwards, assessing me from the corner of his eye.

Squatting on the cold damp floor, I silently peered at him.

He silently peered back.

This mute watchfulness continued for a good few minutes then, suddenly and inexplicably, I became overwhelmed by a powerful urge to sing. Since we were pretty much alone – apart from Smelly and Worse, of course – I decided to treat him to a song from one of my favourite films, *River of No Return*, which, even if I say so myself, sounded pretty spectacular thanks to the acoustics of the pool room.

The sea lion lowered his head to listen intently; then, after a few minutes, he left the corner of his crate to shuffle nearer. He seemed to want a closer look at the drunken, serenading madman who'd disturbed his slumber. Pressing his face against the wooden slats, he scrutinised me until the very last note, then sighed. *Very nice. Now go home and sleep it off!*

He was right, of course, so, grabbing the slats of his crate, I hauled myself to my feet, not appreciating, in my alcohol-fuelled fug, what a risk I'd just taken. He could have had my hand off.

The sea lion never moved – just flashed his huge eyes.

"Goodnight, Bobby," I said, "see you tomorrow."

As I staggered away, I heard a resonant snort from behind me.

Goodnight, David. Look forward to it.

❦ 8 ❧

Arriving early next morning, I was surprised to find Rob already ensconced in the office. Normally, he'd still be in bed, nursing a headache courtesy of the previous evening's festivities. It seemed that Bobby's arrival had given him a sleepless night – probably the first of many.

"David, I've been thinking."

Rob thinking this early in the morning normally spelt trouble.

"When the dolphins arrive, I'll be pretty busy, so I've decided to put you in charge of the sea lion."

Thanks, Rob. He'd no doubt made this momentous decision at the end of last night's boozing session with Matt, and I wasn't happy about it. He knew as well as I did that the dolphin shipment wasn't due for weeks, so he wouldn't be 'busy' for ages. In other words, he'd worked a flanker on me. But he was the boss, and I was just the skivvy so, like it or not, I had to lump it.

After clearing up Smelly and Worse's usual night-time contribution, I returned to my digs for breakfast. There I found Ida, standing over the cooker, putting the final touches to my fry-up. A plate in the hands of Ida resembled an artist's canvas: everything beautifully yet strategically placed to maximise its appeal.

Her lord and master, Jim, sat buried behind his morning paper, every so often commenting on the particular story he happened to be reading: "I don't believe it!" or "Bloody fools!" Something like that.

He and Ida were so different from anyone I'd ever encountered at

26

home, yet I viewed them both with mounting affection. I just hoped that my new charge, Bobby, would start to feel the same way about me.

On arriving back at the pool, my first job was to feed the big fella, which I must admit gave me quite a buzz. He was very hungry and made short work of a bucket of herring. I noticed that both Rob and Matt kept their distances during the feed, despite the fact that Bobby was caged. Neither wanted any close encounters.

After Bobby had eaten, I unreeled the hosepipe and gave him a good showering. He thoroughly enjoyed it, chasing the water around his cramped surroundings, mouth open, seemingly eager to play. I repeated this routine every morning for just short of a week; but I never dared let him out.

Each night, I'd leave the pub, enter the pool then sit in the darkness by his crate, singing: always the same song, 'River of No Return'. And, each night, he'd move a little closer, until eventually he began pushing his head against the slats of his crate to allow me a sneaky tickle behind his tiny ears.

We were growing closer, yet Rob's story of his horrific attack continued to haunt me. I was afraid of him and, no matter how hard I tried, I couldn't shake my fear.

❧ 9 ❧

Another day's work had ended, and me, Rob and Matt were back in the pub, knocking down pints as if our lives depended on it: three grown men trying to drink away their fear.

Bobby was still locked in his crate and, no matter how drunk we got, that fact wouldn't change.

"Rob, you've got to let him out," I reasoned. "You can't keep him locked up: it's cruel. The dolphins aren't due for ages, so you've no excuse."

Rob looked up from his glass and nodded sagely. "You're right. Tomorrow, we let him out."

I breathed a sigh of relief: Bobby, free at last. I felt as though a huge weight had been lifted from my mind, and my spirits soared. In a celebratory mood, I drank a lot more than usual. I hardly remembered even leaving the pub – but I did remember visiting Bobby to break the good news.

Sitting by his crate as usual, I explained how things were going to change: how he'd get to swim and play and move freely about the pool room, exercise his cramped muscles and investigate his surroundings. Then, I sang his favourite song.

As always, Bobby moved closer to listen, head cocked to one side, eyes soft and sad in the dim light. "Poor lad," I whispered, after my song had ended, "it's no life, is it, big fella like you stuck in a small crate all this time?"

Bobby sighed in agreement.

"Anyway, never mind, 'cause tomorrow you get your freedom. Yes, tomorrow, everything will be put right." Another thought struck me. "Oh, by the way, Bobby, I hope you don't think it was me who kept you locked up, because it wasn't. No, it was Rob. He's the boss, so, any problems, see him!"

That's okay, David; I know it wasn't you.

The sympathy in his expression gave him a look of vulnerability, sweeping me away with compassion and regret. "Poor lad!" I repeated, then slid back the bolts of his crate and swung open the door. "Come on, my son, give me room."

Fleetingly, he looked taken aback; then he blinked and shuffled sideways to allow me in.

Still prattling, I clambered into his crate and made myself comfortable; the full implication of what I'd done only hitting me when I turned my head to find his nose just inches from mine.

Good God! I froze and fell silent.

Bobby stared at me bewilderedly; then, following a few tense moments, he heaved his huge bulk up against my body, sighed heavily and laid his head on my lap. I remained unmoving, the muscles in my shoulders, neck and jaw painfully taut. His sheer weight meant that I wouldn't be able to move now, even if I wanted to. Shifting his head around my belly, he found the most comfortable spot, then snorted contentedly and closed his eyes.

I was now firmly pinned against the slats of the crate.

Don't panic, David, don't panic! For pity's sake, stay calm! After a few moments' deep breathing, I tentatively reached out my hand to stroke his massive head, humming softly; and, within a short time, the side of his jaw was cradled in my palm. The minutes passed, and my rigid muscles gradually started to relax.

I must have drifted into an alcohol-induced sleep, because when I next opened my eyes, it was to find myself shivering in a considerably cooler pool room, my bottom numb, my back and neck stiff and sore. About two hours had passed, and Bobby, head still on my lap, was snoring contentedly.

I stared in disbelief: so, it hadn't been a dream.

Patting him gently, I whispered, "Come on, Bobby, I've got to go."

He opened his big green eyes, flashed me an understanding look then lifted his head, allowing me to slide from under him and out through the door of his crate.

Funny, when I'd first slid in beside him, I'd been as drunk as a mop. But now, leaving him, I was stone cold sober.

Bobby watched as I bolted the door to his crate, then gave a deep sigh and fell back into a slumber.

What I'd done tonight was stupid in the extreme, the potential consequences unimaginably horrible. But I'd got away with it; someone up there was certainly looking after me.

❦ 10 ❧

Next morning, Rob and Matt stayed well clear as I again slid back the bolts on Bobby's crate and swung open the door. At first, Bobby hesitated.

"Come on, Bobby, out you go!"

He snorted, then tentatively heaved his cumbersome body out onto the tiles and towards the water. He dived thankfully, ecstatically.

Once in the pool, this ugly duckling indeed became a beautiful swan. His form changed moment by moment as he twisted, weaved and glided through the water, rising now and then to take air and bellow a Tarzan-like roar of utter joy.

Free! Free! Free at last!

The water was where he belonged. He was now in his element and, in freeing him, I had made a friend. I'd also found peace of mind; perhaps tonight I'd enjoy a good sleep without the need to drink away my guilt.

Little did I realise, however, I'd also opened Pandora's Box.

❦ 11 ❧

A few days had passed, Bobby still enjoying the freedom of the pool room; but during feeding times, Rob and Matt were always conspicuous by their absence. They clearly had no intention of getting too close to him. They didn't like him. But, what was even more obvious, Bobby didn't like them. He could smell their fear. They were wise to keep out of his way.

One morning, I had to pick up a crate of herring from the fishmonger's and, as the pool was situated near the local colliery, I set out early to dodge the morning traffic.

Only one road led from the village to the pit: it ran up a steep hill, passing the pool about three quarters of the way up, and got very busy about twenty minutes before a shift change.

I didn't fancy lugging heavy slabs of fish any great distance, so instead of parking in my usual place round the side of the pool, I found a more convenient spot on the main road, a short way from the front entrance.

After dumping the fish in the sink to defrost, I began cleaning the usual overnight mess left by Smelly and Worse. Filling a bucket with hot water and bleach, I strode into the pool room, calling cheerfully to Bobby. "Hello, lad, how you doing, my son?"

It was important to greet the big fella properly: God knows, it must have been a bleak life for him locked up in that place twenty-four hours a day with nothing but two stinky penguins for company.

Bobby, messing in the water, responded to my shout by lifting his massive head, snorting a plume of droplets into the air and solemnly

32

regarding me with those big, green eyes. A blink of acknowledgment, then he dived to continue his subaqua meanderings.

I picked up the deck scrubber, walked to the far end of the pool room and started to scrub the floor. Smelly and Worse had been particularly productive overnight, leaving a fair number of stinky white pools for me to deal with.

Suddenly, the main doors to the pool room banged open, revealing a miner: early thirties and dressed in the usual drab garb of the village men.

"Hello? Can I help you?"

The doors hadn't even swung shut behind him before he started yelling abuse of the most remarkable colour. A potent shire accent delivered four-letter words with the efficiency of a machine gun and, as I stood there gaping, I managed to grasp something about... my car... HIS space... and get it shifted NOW!

It seemed the man was aggrieved because I'd parked in *his* spot: no small offence in North Liston, where the ownership of a *spot* was of paramount importance to the villagers. The village was so small and intimate that almost every square foot was deemed to belong to *someone*: be it a parking space, a lamppost to lean on, a wall to sit on or a stool in the pub. I'd transgressed seriously, and the man was determined to let me know it.

Like all the miners, he was short in stature, but wide and muscular in build, with a chest that looked solid enough to stop a small nuclear warhead. He rather put me in mind of a vertically-challenged Minotaur. His small, steely eyes flashed beneath his cap, the corners of his mouth twisting grimly downwards, then he pounded towards me across the tiled floor, fists clenched.

"Are yer listenin' to mi, or what? I said, are yer listenin'?"

He was very, very angry.

But he wasn't the only one: the training pool was supposed to be a high security facility, strictly out of bounds to the public. It galled me no end that this guy had had the nerve to even breach the main entrance, never mind intrude as far as the pool room.

Normally, he wouldn't have got past Rob and Matt; but, as usual, one too many at the pub meant that they were *still* sleeping it off.

"Ay, you – you *******! Get that ******* car out of my space!"

Before my eyes, the red mist started to form, and I struggled to steady myself and speak calmly. "You shouldn't be in here."

"Get that ******* car out of my space!" He was undeterred.

"Who do you think you're talking to?" I demanded, throwing the deck scrubber aside and stepping forward.

"I said get that ******* car out of my space!"

"Or what?" So enraged was I by his foul-mouthed assault, I could hardly breathe, never mind speak. Everything around me seemed to fade away as all my attention focussed on this nasty, bullish man, and my overwhelming desire to pound him into the ground. I launched myself at him, determined, dangerous and blinded by anger. He'd no intention of backing off either, and if we'd ever reached each other, I dread to think what might have happened. But we didn't reach each other, because a terrifying thought suddenly popped into my mind and all but paralysed me.

Bobby! Where's Bobby?

Distracted, I turned to see him: his massive, black head in the centre of the pool, immobile and watching. Then, ever so slowly, it swivelled round so that his big green eyes locked onto mine. For the oddest moment, it seemed as though I were looking in a mirror; then I felt all my aggression seeping away and saw it – actually saw it – filling up in those big green eyes.

Bobby's head snapped back round to look at the man; then he dived.

There was nothing left in me now but panic, blind panic. "Run!" I screamed. "The sea lion! Run!"

The man froze in bewilderment, sensing my terror. "What? What do you mean?"

"Just get out! The sea lion!" My voice had deteriorated into a shriek.

He stood there, jaw drooping foolishly, then whimpered, "Why, does it bite?"

By this time, the torpedo that was Bobby had almost reached the deck, a plume of water in its wake.

"Go, go!" I screamed; but the man was already gone, a pair of swinging doors the only evidence that he'd ever been there.

Bobby shot from the water like a ball launched in a pinball game, a loud, hoarse bark reverberating off the walls. He hit the tiles with a dull thwack, then slid headlong through the swing doors, sending them crashing off their hinges.

As he disappeared into the dark corridor, I grabbed the deck scrubber and chased after him.

"No, Bobby, no… come back!"

Down the narrow, winding corridor, he pursued his quarry, galloping clumsily and ineffectively like… well, like a sea lion out of water.

By this time, the man had made it out of the building, down the steps and onto the road, and might have believed – mistakenly – that he'd reached safety; but the avenging Bobby motored on.

"Stop, Bobby! You can't do this!"

Still bellowing his ear-shattering war cry, he burst through the main entrance, slid down the steps and galloped along the pavement, oblivious to the crawling traffic and gaping drivers. But he managed only five or six yards before his rampaging pursuit slowed to a half-hearted slither. His prey had escaped, and Bobby just wasn't built for manoeuvring along pavements. He flopped to a stop, then lifted his head to regard me apologetically. *Sorry, Dave. He got away.*

By this time, the traffic had come to a complete halt as the men intended for the early shift stopped to watch. How could this be happening in a tiny, unrecognised backwater like this? A sea lion? Most of them had never seen a sea lion, except in pictures. But this? A sea lion on a road in the middle of the shire?

Bobby ignored them. He was dejected, exhausted.

I blinked at him kindly, as he had so often blinked at me, then gently manoeuvred him round with the deck scrubber. "Come on, Bobby. We showed him. Now let's go home."

Bobby sighed heavily, then began the laborious journey back to the pool, hauling himself up the steps and through the entrance, still maintaining an audience of open-mouthed motorists.

As for the aggressive miner, we never saw him again.

❦ 12 ❧

Following the incident with the miner, Bobby spent another eight glorious days of freedom in the water, during which time he steadfastly refused to return to his crate – which gave us a problem. When the dolphins eventually arrived, we'd need a clear pool for training purposes, which meant we had to get Bobby out of the water and back into gaol, so to speak. And it was becoming increasingly obvious that this wasn't going to happen.

One morning, I arrived at the pool to find the main entrance doors open. Certain I'd locked them the night before, I immediately thought about the spate of break-ins in the area. Surely, no one would be so stupid as to try to get in the pool? After all, we'd got the best guard dog in the world: Bobby – no one would get past him. And, in the unlikely event that they did, there was always Smelly and Worse: no one was *that* lucky.

I crept furtively down the corridor, half expecting to stumble across the shredded remains of some unfortunate intruder, only to find fish thawing in the kitchen sink. Astonished, I made my way to the pool room and, lo and behold, there were Rob and Matt! They'd *both* arrived early. But they *never* arrived early. What could possibly have caused this welcome turn of events?

"Hello, what are you two doing here?"

"Me and Rob are gonna get the sea lion out of the pool!" Matt told me determinedly. "We've had enough of him."

I couldn't believe it; both Rob and Matt were terrified of Bobby and, what's more, Bobby knew it. I had a strong feeling that I was in for an entertaining morning. Whatever their half-baked plan, it would have been cooked up in a pub somewhere, probably after they'd downed seven or eight pints. This should be fun.

Rob stood beside me — a safe distance from Bobby — watching as Matt, fish bucket in hand, marched towards the pool, forcibly brushing aside the two penguins. Matt was indeed a man on a mission, determined to earn a few extra Brownie points. He positioned himself on the poolside, eyes narrowed, shoulders tense, squarely facing Bobby, who hung in the water, statuesque and unmoving. It reminded me of the *Gunfight at the OK Corral,* each antagonist waiting for the other to snap. Only question — who would snap first, Matt or Bobby? I could almost hear the sound of slapping leather.

Then, in one light speed movement, Matt drew his fish and dangled it directly in front of Bobby. The sea lion moved hesitantly, eyes flicking towards Rob and me, as if suspecting an ambush.

And he wasn't wrong: an ambush was indeed taking place.

Matt had another fish hidden behind his back (for what purpose I could only guess), and Smelly and Worse, who only a few moments ago he had so scathingly brushed aside, spied it. They were now stealthily creeping up behind him, determined to steal the prize. Like two bushwhackers, they moved within striking distance.

Rob leaned towards me and whispered, "Don't tell him!"

In a flash, Smelly grabbed the fish, and Worse launched a vicious attack on the back of Matt's legs. Matt, suddenly realising that he'd fallen victim to a sneak attack, spun around to face the two ornery critters.

Bobby seized his chance, leaping from the pool to snatch the now unguarded bait from Matt's flailing hand, at the same time knocking him off balance and propelling him along the tiles.

Stunned and prostrate on the floor, with only a thin tee shirt for protection, Matt was now ideally placed for a concerted penguin assault. The two birds, furious beyond reason, launched themselves at him, pecking at his arms and shoulders with a speed and ferocity that could only be described as impressive. They were having a ball.

Alas, the same couldn't be said for poor Matt: cut and bloodied, he clambered to his feet, cursing aggressively and jumping around in an effort to shake off the two little furies.

Rob watched thoughtfully.

"Well, that was entertaining," I said. "What was supposed to happen?"

He didn't reply, only shook his head before retreating to the sanctuary of his office, leaving a triumphant penguin duo and a laughing Bobby splashing about in the pool.

Bobby would enjoy another week of freedom before we received the all-important telephone call telling us that the dolphins were at last on their way; the telephone call that would herald the beginning of my journey into the magical world of the dolphin. I could hardly wait.

❧ 13 ❧

"Hello people! Big day today – dolphins are due, and I've got to have this place spick and span, so no time to talk."

Bobby greeted me with his usual loud snort as he heaved himself onto the poolside in anxious expectation of breakfast. He was hungry. We'd started to cut down his feeds over a week ago, hoping to lure him from the pool and back to his crate. But, up to now, we'd had no luck.

How about some breakfast, David? I'm starving here.

"Sorry, Bobby, no food till you're in your crate."

Aww, come on, just a bit of fish.

"No, not until you're in your crate."

Trying to ignore those pleading green eyes, I turned my attention to the tasks at hand. Firstly, defrost fish; secondly, clean up the pools of penguin dirt littering the tiles.

"How is it you two manage to deposit so much crap over such a large area in such a short space of time? It's not even as if you're very big."

Talk about Groundhog Day! Smelly and Worse squared up and issued challenges, as they did every morning. And I – gently but forcibly – shepherded them back into their cage with my trusty deck scrubber, as *I* did every morning. "Come on, you two, I haven't got time to mess around. Back to your cage." A deck scrubber wasn't just for scrubbing.

Eventually, Rob and Matt arrived – not bleary-eyed as normal, but buzzing with anticipation.

"I want everything in the pool to gleam today, because this is it!" Rob gleefully announced.

"All yours," I told Matt, thrusting the deck scrubber at him, "I'm off for breakfast."

Not ten minutes later, I was sitting at the table in Ida's kitchen. Between mouthfuls of her world-renowned sausages, I enthusiastically spoke of the dolphins' impending arrival – but not before securing an oath of *total secrecy* from both her and Jim.

"You mustn't say a word to anyone – not one single word – or you'll get me into trouble."

Their eyes bulged like organ stops.

"Don't worry, we won't say owt... not a bloody thing!" But Jim was already quite clearly having trouble containing his excitement. He shuffled in his chair, grizzled face twitching impatiently. "So, what time do yer think they'll arrive?"

"Not sure exactly, but certainly within the hour."

Without warning, he leapt to his feet. "Right, can't 'ang about – I'm late for mi shift, and I 'aven't got mi paper yet." And without another word, off he sped.

"What about yer tea? Yer've not finished yer tea!" Ida shouted, as Jim's bulky frame disappeared down the path and into his car. He never answered – a quick rev of the engine, and he was gone.

Jim was intent. He had no time to lose. In just under five minutes, everyone at the paper shop would know the dolphins were on their way. Within an hour, everyone who worked at the pit would know as well. So much for his vow of silence.

I sighed, took a final swig of tea, then prepared to leave. "Remember, Ida, not a word to anyone – it's a secret."

"I won't tell a soul," she replied, racing into the yard clutching her washing basket.

For the women of North Liston, there was no better way of spreading gossip than to hang out washing in the backyard. Whilst pegging laundry to lines, all the latest news could be speedily transmitted from household to household by simply shouting over walls. And, today, Ida couldn't wait to peg out. Secrets certainly didn't last long in this place. Me and my big mouth!

Just as I reached the pool building, the door burst open to reveal a breathless Rob.

"I was just coming to get you. They're on their way; they'll be here in thirty minutes."

This was it: in half an hour, I would see my first live dolphin.

❦ 14 ❦

By the time we'd finished, the pool room looked like the inside of a palace. Glass, tile and chrome gleamed. Sunshine flooded through the skylights onto the water, again creating the illusion of a mirror; but, this time, a mirror broken by the sleek, spiralling frame of Bobby as he weaved to the surface to steal oxygen.

Hearing the sound of a braking lorry, I dashed into the corridor, almost colliding with Rob and Matt.

"They're here! They're here!" Rob shouted.

Tell me about it, I thought, as we all raced to reach the main entrance, tripping over feet and bouncing off walls.

The lorry had shuddered to a halt in front of the pool steps, followed by a line of expensive cars carrying Philip Haynes and a dozen or so Company VIPs, eager to attend the launch of their dolphin project.

"Show time, lads!" Rob quipped.

We walked to the back of the lorry, then waited expectantly for the roller shutter doors to rise. I hung back as Rob jumped in to survey his precious cargo.

Inside the van was a young American boy who'd accompanied the dolphins during their long journey from the States. I stared at him curiously, trying to imagine the kind of life he lived. His sun-bleached hair and golden-brown tan gave me a pretty good idea. He shook Rob's hand. "They're all yours."

"Right, lads, let's get them in!" Rob ordered.

I heaved myself into the back of the lorry, and there they were: two long wooden boxes containing canvas slings, and in the slings, two dolphins, their bodies thickened with grease to protect them from air burns. I instinctively approached the right-hand box, peering inside to get my first close-up: a real, live dolphin, looking dejected, helpless and very vulnerable.

A label on the box read, 'Female Atlantic Bottlenose Dolphin (*Tursiops Truncatus*); Length Approx 6ft 2ins; Estimated Age – 3 years; Name – None Given.'

"Right, let's get him out, lads!"

First off the lorry was the male. He hung in his sling like a sack of potatoes, unmoving and silent as an entourage of handlers carried him into the pool.

I remained in the lorry with the female, bathing her with the water flooding the floor of her box. As I tended her, I noticed her eyes following my gold signet ring as it shone in the sunlight spilling through the lorry's open doors. Lifting my hand, I flashed the ring at her. "You like that, don't you?" I whispered.

It was then that I experienced the oddest thing: she lifted her gaze from the ring to my face, and I found myself looking into the most bewitching blue eyes I'd ever seen – not fish-like, but warm and inquisitive. Almost human.

Aren't you beautiful? I thought. I reached out and, as my hand made contact with this strangely different creature of the sea, my nervy excitement began to dissipate, leaving in its wake a sense of peace and calm. I felt *something*: a *connection* of some kind that made me feel light-headed. It was as if she were stealing my strength, leaving me weak and disorientated; yet I couldn't break free of her spell. I was totally and utterly captivated.

This animal was giving off some serious vibes.

Rob's excited voice boomed into the back of the lorry, shattering the moment. "We're ready for the female. Careful, boys, this is my life you're carrying!"

His words felt like an assault with a lethal weapon. I should have been happy that the dolphins had at last arrived; but I wasn't. Rob had claimed this female for his own, leaving me in an agony of jealousy. I wasn't a trainer or even a presenter yet, but just a kid who knew nothing about dolphins.

But one thing I did know, and know for certain: this female was *mine*, and nothing and no one would rob me of that prize.

❦ 15 ❧

As the handlers carried the female up the pool steps, I hung back nervously. Nothing I could do; time to watch and learn.

Once in the water, the dolphins began to school together sluggishly, working their cramped muscles back into action. The lubricant protecting their bodies couldn't hide their slate-grey colouring. Funny, I'd always thought dolphins were a light, silvery grey. These two looked almost dirty, and I said so to Rob.

"Don't worry about their colour," he told me. "A week in chlorinated water will soon clean them up. Chlorine acts like a bleach; it lightens the skin."

A stirring of anxiety. "If it does that on the outside, what does it do on the inside?" I asked.

"Chlorine's a necessary evil," Rob insisted. "Remember, dolphins are mammals, and their bodies operate in exactly the same way as ours. We literally have two sewage generators here and, without chlorine, the water would soon be a real mess."

What he didn't say, I later learned, was that chlorine is also a poison – a slow killer. The life spans of both these dolphins would be drastically reduced now they had entered captivity.

After much back-slapping and hand-shaking, the suited VIPs speedily vanished to the pub to enjoy an abundance of free food and drink. Only Philip remained.

"Look, Rob, I notice the sea lion's still in the pool. You'll need to remove him before training can begin."

Rob beamed confidently. "No worries; his feeds are well down, so we'll soon have him out."

As Philip made his way to the door, Rob winked. "That's your job, Dave. You're gonna have to figure out how to get your mate out of the pool."

I answered him with a pleading look, and he put an arm around my shoulder. "But not today, kid, not today, because today we're off to the pub for all those freebies. Today, we're gonna get smashed!"

❦ 16 ❧

The following morning felt like a hazy dream, and I drifted unenthusiastically through Ida's breakfast.

"What's wrong with yer?" Jim grunted

"Nothing. I'm just not hungry."

His stern expression softened with a rare smile. "That's what yer get for drinking too much. You city lads aren't used to good shire ale."

Ida immediately sprang to my defence. "Don't go on at the lad! He probably got a bad pint down at the pub."

"Aye, a bad pint my foot!" A shrug of the shoulders, a cramped laugh, and Jim disappeared behind his morning paper.

Jim was right, of course, and knew it. I hadn't even made my morning check on the pool yet, so I would have to get my skates on or I'd be in lumber. But, then again, I couldn't see Rob being in early either – not after the amount of beer he'd knocked back last night. And Matt still hadn't reared his ugly head, so there'd be no chance of him tale-telling. Nevertheless, I hurriedly drained my tea and headed for the pool.

There they were: two dolphins swimming in unison, closely followed by a curious sea lion.

"Hello, people!" I called.

Bobby lifted his massive head out of the water and looked at me with baffled eyes. *What* are *these things?*

Much of the lubricant had washed off the dolphins overnight, revealing their sumptuous flesh. I stood on the poolside, marvelling at

47

their sleek forms and incredible grace. I continued to watch them in an almost trance-like state for a good few minutes, then suddenly the pool door swung open, jolting me back to reality. To my surprise, the young American transporter walked in.

"Hi, everything okay?" He had a friendly, laid-back manner.

"Yeah, fine," I replied, turning my admiring gaze back to the dolphins.

Almost as if reading my mind, he said, "These *really* are two beautiful animals. I thought so during the catch."

During the catch? I was stunned – this young lad had actually been there when they were caught. Well, if he was fishing to tell a tale, I was eager to take the bait. Here was a chance to learn first-hand the true story of these dolphins.

"We got the female first," he continued. "Boy, did she put up a fight: took four catchers a long, hard struggle to subdue her and get her back to the boat. But the weird thing was the male: he could easily have swum away, made his escape. But he didn't. He refused to leave her, just followed her in. It took only one man to grab his dorsal fin and pull him into the second harness. No fight, just total surrender." He nodded his head thoughtfully. "They're a real *pair*."

A real pair! His words sent a thrill down my spine as I recalled Rob's story of *The Perfect Pair*: two dolphins who think and move as one. A trainer's dream. A trainer's fantasy. Rob's dream.

My dream.

❦ 17 ❧

Rob arrived at nine on the dot, subdued and clearly hung-over from the previous day's festivities.

"Okay, Rob?"

"No, not really. My head's splitting. Had a few too many last night."

"Don't suppose you've seen Matt, have you?"

"Why ask me? You're his roommate."

"Oh, so I'm chief cook and bottle washer again, am I?"

Rob dodged the question. "No more food for that sea lion," he snapped, "the only way he gets fed now is when he's out of the pool and back in his crate."

Bobby was becoming a serious problem. His reluctance to leave the water would delay the dolphins' basic training.

When Matt did eventually arrive, we both watched intently as Rob grabbed a bucketful of herring and tried to coax the two young dolphins to take food.

"You see, lads, these two have only ever eaten live fish. Getting them to accept it dead is the first step in their basic training – but it's gonna take time."

His steady coaxing continued for most of the day, but to no avail. Each time Rob threw a fish into the water, Bobby shot in and stole it.

"Damn sea lion! Can't do anything with him around. Can't you get him out, Dave – he's your mate?" Rob was becoming agitated.

"What can I do, Rob? If he doesn't want to go in his crate, I can't make him."

And that was the truth. Bobby might be my friend, but he was most definitely the boss, constantly barking guttural reminders that he was indeed the king of the castle.

And, despite all Rob's bravado, he was like a little boy lost, uncertain what to do next.

❧ 18 ❧

Next day, I found Rob lying on the poolside, trying to tempt the dolphins to take fish from his hand – a ploy intended to keep Bobby from stealing them. But neither dolphin showed any interest.

A few hours later, Philip arrived to check on the dolphins' progress. The vet had always been friendly whenever we'd met, but today he seemed strangely aloof.

He entered the office to retrieve the dolphin logbooks, which worked like personal diaries, listing medication and daily training progress. These books would remain with the dolphins throughout their lives, a written account of everything that happened to them – good or bad.

As Philip flicked through the virtually empty pages, his eyes repeatedly moved back to the sea lion. Rob had assured him that he'd have Bobby out of the pool; but this hadn't happened. Nor had the dolphins yet eaten and, although it was still early days, the sight of a struggling Rob dangling over the poolside clearly didn't fill him with confidence.

"Have you ordered platforms?" Philip asked.

Rob looked bewildered. "Platforms? What for?"

Philip answered sharply. "For accessing the dolphins. It's quite obvious they're afraid to come in to the side."

"I don't need platforms," Rob insisted nervously. "I'm all right working from the side. Don't worry, it'll be okay."

He had just given the wrong answer. Philip spun around in angry

51

silence, then marched out of the pool, his usual friendly farewell absent.

This brief meeting was the beginning of the end for Rob. This charming and likeable character was on his way out and, sadly, I could do nothing to save him.

Two more torturous days of failure had passed when Rob furtively called me into the office. "I need a favour. I've been sacked, and today is my last day. New trainers are due in tonight to bring the dolphin project back on schedule, and I can't be here when they arrive. I need a lift home."

Home was on the west coast, which meant I wouldn't be here to greet my new bosses. Yet how could I deny him this last request? All his dreams of being a dolphin trainer had been swept away. The awful truth had finally caught up with him: he wasn't the trainer he claimed to be. In fact, we later learned he'd never been a trainer at all; the closest he'd ever come to a dolphin was when working as an aqua clown in the States. Somehow, he'd managed to con his way into the position of Company head trainer.

Yet how could I refuse this likeable trickster?

"Okay, Rob. Matt can take care of the pool. We'll leave as soon as you're ready."

I purposely never told him about my talk with the young American catcher, as I didn't see any point in rubbing salt in his wounds. Poor Rob would never know how close he actually came to his dream of *The Perfect Pair*.

❧ 19 ❧

Next morning, I was up early. I had some explaining to do, and just hoped my new boss would understand.

Outside the pool, two men were unloading a large delivery van; and lying on the steps nearby were two large platforms and a host of materials to make props. Matt was scurrying around as if his life depended on it, and you didn't need to be a rocket scientist to know why. I walked past him, but he didn't speak, just glanced up from the corner of his eye.

Suddenly, the pool entrance looked forbidding.

As I made my way down the corridor, a fiery-looking redhead appeared at one of the doors. "Who are you?" she snapped.

"David," I replied nervously.

She regarded me for a second, then shouted, "Gerry, the wanderer has returned."

Within moments, I was faced by a well-built man in his mid-twenties. He had an air of unshakeable confidence, and the strength of his presence flooded the corridor. As I hesitantly approached him, he stretched out his hand.

"Name's Gerry Mansell. I'm the Company's new head trainer." He spoke with a soft southern accent. "This is Rachel. She's here to help me put this project back on track." He paused. "You ready to work?"

A smile and a nod sealed the deal, then I hurried into the pool room.

Gerry was a man of few words and hadn't asked me for an explanation. He was totally focussed and had only one goal: to meet the show deadlines. Training would start in earnest at last.

❦ 20 ❧

This morning, I am filled with nervous excitement: my training begins for real. I sense change in the air as I hurriedly dress and make my way to the pool. I am acutely aware that I won't be the only one in 'school' today; the Company is sending a host of presenters and trainers to polish up their skills, so competition will be hot and I must be on the ball.

Even the penguins' usual mess doesn't dampen my enthusiasm. Only the sight of a hungry sea lion can do that. Bobby has gone nine days on rations and three days with nothing at all, and I find it hard to ignore those pleading green eyes.

"You'll have all the fish you want when you leave the pool," I tell him.

He drops his head. Hungry or not, Bobby has no intention of leaving his watery playground.

Deck scrubber in hand, I begin to scour the floor tiles around the pool. I work for only a few minutes when I become strangely aware of the female dolphin's gaze.

She follows my every move, head cocked to one side. As I look back into those hypnotic blue orbs, an odd mix of calm and sickly excitement washes over me, just as it did when I first met her. It is as if she has made a telephone call, and I have picked up the receiver.

I place the deck scrubber on the tiles, take a step towards her and flash my ring. She swims closer, less than six feet away, eyes flicking first to the ring, then to meet mine. Closer… closer…

A door bangs, and she flies back to her mate.

"All right if I come in?" One of North Liston's men in blue stands by the pool room door. "I've come to warn you to be vigilant. There's been a spate of robberies around here in the last month."

"Thanks for the warning, I'll tell the boss."

I can't help but smile. His visit is a terrific excuse for him to see the dolphins and, over the next week or so, almost all of North Liston's finest will find some reason or other to pass through our doors.

A short time later, Gerry and Rachel arrive… but, again, no Matt… so, again, I am left to do all the cleaning. When Matt eventually rolls up, some thirty minutes later, I don't speak, but pointedly scowl at him before heading back to my digs for another late breakfast. He is pushing his luck, and I have the feeling that this new crew won't put up with it.

❮ 21 ❯

By the time I arrive back at the pool, two wooden platforms are overhanging the water by a good seven feet. Because the dolphins are loath to swim beneath them, this radically cuts down their space.

Gerry and Rachel each take a platform, lying full length, belly down, trying to tempt the dolphins to accept some herring. These confidence-building sessions last about twenty minutes each, punctuated by fifteen-minute intervals.

I notice that the female is growing bolder, edging ever closer. Then, during session number five, a short blast on the whistle signals that she has taken the bait.

The tense atmosphere suddenly lightens: the first dead fish has been gobbled down.

A fifteen-minute break, then both Gerry and Rachel are back in place. Within minutes, two more whistles mean that the female has taken two more feeds. Then, to everyone's relief, as she circles for her third foray, the male dashes from her shadow and snatches the prize.

Five whistles turn to ten! Ten turn to twenty! The excitement grows. A feeding bonanza erupts. For two glorious days, the hungry couple gorge themselves. The weight they have lost during the transport is quickly replenished, and, at the same time, a load tumbles from our shoulders.

Now stage two. Instead of whole fish, Gerry and Rachel offer half fish. Both accept, eagerly eating their fill.

But the same cannot be said for Bobby. Offered nothing at all, the hungry and disgruntled sea lion has no choice but to watch these newcomers steal his thunder – and his food.

❦ 22 ❦

Next day, Gerry and Rachel continued with the dolphins' confidence-building sessions, whilst Matt and I made props: to be exact, small rubber rings. These simple props would signal the start of trick training proper: basic retrieval. As I sat in deep concentration on the poolside, Stanley knife and sticky tape in hand, Gerry, who was working at the far side of the pool, shouted, "Hey, you've got an admirer."

Sure enough, only three feet from my side was the female. She was watching me, head cocked to one side as usual. I smiled at her, then twisted my hand to flash my ring.

"Typical female," I shouted, "she likes shiny things."

Gerry smiled kindly. "Would you like to do the next feed? I think it's about time you two got to know each other better."

My face flushed with excitement. At last, I was about to feed and, hopefully, work my first dolphin.

As I cut and prepared the fish, Gerry handed me a whistle.

"You'll need this. Remember, when she takes a fish, follow it with a soft whistle. Not too loud – you don't want to frighten her."

Minutes later, I was belly down, coaxing her to the side.

She drifted only inches away, but didn't take the fish. Instead, she bobbed just out of reach, seemingly bewitched by my ring as sunlight from the skylights reflected from its face. Then, very gently, she moved in and took the fish, pushing her head into my hand and allowing me to touch her cheek.

I gasped: she felt warm! I had always imagined that she would feel

59

cold, but this was almost like touching my own skin. Suddenly, there it was again: a feeling of calm, and sickly excitement that left me weak.

"What are you doing to me?"

She swam away, twisting her body so as not to break eye contact.

"She likes you," Gerry said.

"She's making eyes at you," Rachel added.

I smiled, but did not speak.

My message was personal, meant only for her, and consisted of a single thought.

As our eyes remained locked, I told her, *"I like you, too."*

❧ 23 ❧

"Do you want another cuppa, David?"

"No thanks, Ida, lot to do today."

There was a sound of rustling newspaper from across the table as broken-nailed, heavy fingers struggled to part pages. "I'll 'ave one," Jim grunted. Jim, a man of few words, continued to do battle with his morning tabloid in silence.

"That was lovely, Ida," I said, pushing away my empty plate and standing. "See you both later."

Ida gave me a sweet smile and Jim grunted again. No airs, no graces: two hard-working, genuine people whom you could trust with your life. I loved it here.

A few minutes later, I opened the pool room door to be greeted by a pair of beseeching green eyes. *When are you going to feed me?*

This couldn't go on for much longer, but I still had no idea how to get Bobby out of the pool. I looked away guiltily. Nothing to eat *again* today. He knew why.

"It's no good playing the hard-done-to card, Bobby," I told him, assiduously avoiding eye contact. "No food till you're out of the pool."

He snorted a nonchalant dismissal, then joined his new dolphin friends in a game of what could only be described as mammal water polo, where the balls took the shape of the unfortunate Smelly and Worse.

The rules of the game seemed simple enough: the female dolphin swam beneath a penguin, then flicked it with her nose to Bobby, who, in turn, flicked it to the male.

Seems like an entertaining game, I thought. It's good to see the children playing nicely.

The game came to an abrupt end with the arrival of Gerry and Rachel – but, again, no Matt. This gave the two harassed penguins their chance to escape. They quickly clambered out of the pool and wobbled unprompted back to their cage.

Well, there's a first, I thought. It's a shame Bobby won't do the same.

"David, when you're ready, I need to see you in the office," Gerry called.

My heart plummeted. What now?

After finishing my work, I hesitantly entered the office where both Gerry and Rachel were waiting, reminding me of judges about to pass sentence. Then, Rachel flashed a reassuring smile, calming the butterflies flapping around inside my stomach.

"I'm going to the States soon to bring back four more dolphins," Gerry explained. "Training mustn't stop while I'm away so, from now on, you're officially in charge of the female." He smiled widely. "I'll guide and tutor you from the poolside. Are you okay with that?"

As if he had to ask! I felt as if I'd just won the pools, and nodded vigorously.

My own dolphin, they'd given me my own dolphin. And it was the *female.*

Gerry continued. "Just one more thing. The dolphins need names. The male will be called Herb'e, and the female will be called…" He clicked his fingers. "What? Come on, David, give me a name!"

No hesitation. "Duchess, she's called Duchess."

"A beautiful name," Rachel commented.

Yes, a beautiful name… for a very special dolphin.

❦ 24 ❧

Later that morning, I found myself lying belly down on the wooden training platform. This was now my permanent position: me on the left, Gerry or Rachel on the right. All basic training would take place from here.

Once again, we began with confidence-building, feeding half fish. Both dolphins seemed eager and comfortable with this.

However, Bobby, who usually skulked at the corners of the pool, was circling closer and closer. He was very hungry, and the sight of free fish made him determined to get his share. He shadowed Duchess, swimming directly beneath her so they moved almost as one.

Although Duchess took the fish, she obviously wasn't hungry. She seemed to be craving attention – not only from me, but also from her new friend, Bobby.

"Gerry, I think we've got a problem," I muttered, as I dangled over the platform.

Now, not only was Duchess greeting me for fish, but so was Bobby. The dolphin and sea lion were almost cheek-to-cheek. I couldn't push Bobby away because it might spook Duchess, ruining all the confidence-building that had taken place. Besides, any sudden movements towards the hungry Bobby might result in a nasty bite.

We abandoned the training session.

"We'll try again in an hour's time," Gerry said. He paused, then added ominously, "We can't let the sea lion continue to interrupt training."

The next session was following pretty much the same pattern – Bobby pushing in and begging for fish, Duchess toying with hers – when, suddenly, Duchess cut away from the platform, swam slowly to Bobby and gave him her feed. As we watched bewilderedly, she quickly returned, snatched another fish and did it again. Duchess was actually feeding Bobby.

But that wasn't the only surprise. Herb'e suddenly began to copy her. Back and forth, to and fro: two dolphins working a rota system to provide the unfortunate Bobby with food. Amazing!

"Can you believe this?" Gerry grinned, shaking his head.

We continued to play along so we could observe this fascinating behaviour, while Bobby gloated as he gobbled down the offerings of his two new allies.

Finally, after losing four pounds of best herring, we both conceded that the plan to starve Bobby out of the pool had failed miserably.

"Looks like it's back to the drawing board," Gerry told me.

Our dolphin charges had officially laid down the gauntlet: feed us; feed him.

A day's training had been lost, a day we couldn't afford. We were at least seven weeks behind schedule and knew from this latest turn of events that things would only get worse.

"Can't put up with this any longer. We must get rid of this sea lion." Gerry picked up the phone and made an urgent call to City Zoo. "We need nets and men – preferably within the next forty-eight hours."

He followed this with a call to North Liston Police Station asking for off-duty volunteers. Mission: catch a sea lion.

In less than forty-eight hours, Bobby would be in for an unwelcome surprise: he would be forcibly removed from the pool.

❧ 25 ❧

Up earlier than usual, because we have to prepare for the arrival of Philip and the army of men from City Zoo. Today we will finally resolve the problem of Bobby. We've already lost ten days' training due to his antics, and starving him out of the pool clearly isn't working.

"Hello, people, big day today!"

Duchess looks on, head cocked, curiously watching my every move; and by her side is Herb'e, head down and showing little interest in anyone other than his beloved partner. And, of course, Bobby, flashing those mischievous green eyes.

I'm still here, Dave, and I'm not coming out. In fact, I'm never coming out.

I smile at him. That's what you think, sunshine, because, one way or another, today's the day.

As always, first job is thawing fish, closely followed by the big clean-up after Smelly and Worse's night on the town. I prepare a bucketful of hot water and disinfectant, grab my trusty deck scrubber then begin. An hour passes, then Gerry arrives, closely followed by Rachel, Matt and the rest of the handlers.

"It's bye-bye Bobby day," Gerry gleefully announces. "I want the pool spick and span because all the top people will be here to help with the catch."

"How are we going to get him?" I ask.

"Well, they're bringing a huge nylon net from City Zoo. The idea is to drop the net into the deep end of the pool, then slowly push

Bobby and the dolphins towards the shallows. It'll take a lot of manpower – probably ten or twelve men on either side."

"What about Duchess and Herb'e? What'll happen to them?"

"Well, that's the tricky part. We can't afford to get either of the dolphins caught up in the net, so you'll have to be in the water trying to herd them away."

I'm aghast. "Just me?"

"Yeah. I'm sorry, Dave, but they'll be spooked enough as it is. Two men in the water will just make the situation even worse."

I throw a wary glance at Bobby. The idea of being in the water with him when he starts to panic doesn't exactly fill me with confidence. His record already demonstrates his willingness to use those razor sharp fangs. The question is… would he use them on me?

"Right, I'm not going to die on an empty stomach, Gerry: I'm going for breakfast. Ida's expecting me."

Gerry raises a hand. "Forty minutes – no longer!"

❧ 26 ❧

Waiting for me back at Ida's is the usual glorious breakfast: two rashers of bacon, two eggs, baked beans and a potato cake, capped off with four sausages – two extra! Fantastic!

"I don't know whether I should eat all this, Ida – I just might sink."

"Gi' up wi' th'yammer, and get it down! Yer'll need all yer strength today if yer gonna catch that sea lion."

The one thing I could never be accused of is having a will of iron. I just couldn't resist.

"Yeah, you're right. I'll be in the water for a long time, so I do need to keep my strength up." That was my excuse, and I was sticking to it. "Right, Ida, I'm off into battle. See you tonight."

27

As I arrive back at the pool, Philip's beautiful top-of-the-range white Citroen pulls up, closely followed by a lorry transporting the manpower and net that will be so crucial in ending Bobby's reign. Even the local off-duty police have arrived early. After all, this sort of thing doesn't happen every day in a sleepy mining village.

As they haul the net through the tight corridors leading to the pool, Philip calls all the trainers and presenters into the office.

"Now, we have to get this animal out of the pool one way or another. If the netting fails, then I'll have to dart him. If that happens, there's every chance he'll drown, because he's too dangerous to hand-catch whilst fully conscious and, by the time the tranquiliser takes effect, there won't be enough time to get him out. This catch can only end in one of two ways, so it's up to you, lads. The dolphin programme can't be delayed any longer."

The top brass have decided on a dead or alive policy. There will be no second chance for Bobby this time; he has just been put on the expendable list.

Matt is given the unenviable task of catching Smelly and Worse, although even this proves to be much easier than usual. Clearly, the two penguins don't like so many people milling around.

There's nothing for me to do now but wait until everyone's in position – wait for the order to enter the water.

I stand at the poolside, removed from the to-ing and fro-ing of the men hauling the huge net along the tiles. Bobby is watching nervously and, every so often, those big eyes meet mine. *What's happening? What's going on?* He and the two dolphins are growing agitated, clearly aware of the looming threat.

I try to remain calm and focussed, but struggle to suppress the fear welling up inside me. If we fail to net Bobby, he will be darted. If I falter for even a few seconds in retrieving him, he will die. Yet I know that if I don't make it in time, no one will blame me. After all, what kind of a fool would attempt to wrestle a fully-grown sea lion? A man would have to be crazy – wouldn't he?

All these negative thoughts race through my head. Think positive, David! Think positive! We can't lose Bobby: he's too valuable and there are too many people around, too much bad publicity. Besides, he's your friend; how will you live with yourself if he dies because of you?

Gerry and Philip direct the placing of the net at the deep end of the pool. Bobby's cage has been moved to the shallow end. All is ready. Only a few last minute instructions, then the catch will begin.

Suddenly, the cackle of voices ceases, and the pool room falls deathly silent; you can literally hear a pin drop.

Then I hear the sound of footsteps as Gerry strides purposefully towards me.

"You know the drill. The most important thing is the dolphins. No harm must come to them. If they hit the net, they'll drown. Whatever happens, you can't allow them to get caught up. Leave Bobby to us. Understand?"

Words are pretty meaningless at a time like this, so I nod my head. Gerry flashes me a reassuring smile; then I go in.

As the water washes over me, it seems colder than usual, that feeling of exhilaration absent. I am actually shivering as I watch the men lowering the net into the water. It falls like a giant curtain, its sheer bulk anchoring it to the pool floor. Floaters hold the giant beast aloft, enabling the men to pull it slowly down the length of the pool. Even with twelve men at each side, it is ponderous, and its sheer weight makes it unmanageable. The net slowly draws to a halt as the men stop to catch their breath.

I quickly surface. "What's wrong?"

Gerry turns to the concerned vet. "We need more men." Then, glancing towards the exhausted pullers, he adds, "A lot more men."

As we already have off-duty policemen on the lines, a call to North Liston Police Station quickly secures us the promise of extra help. It will take at least another thirty minutes for the reinforcements to assemble and de-robe, so this gives me time to assess and adapt to this ever-changing situation.

Stay positive, David, you can't afford to make any mistakes. Stay focussed.

Herb'e and Bobby have already swum to the shallows, keeping well clear of the net. Only Duchess remains close, feeding her female curiosity. She surfaces six feet in front of me, head cocked as always, and assesses the situation.

She seems to generate a calmness that I sense immediately. It's as if we share a psychic link that I don't feel with any other animal. Only her. She is truly special. And, what's more, she's taking my fear away. She's beautiful.

My dreamy admiration for Duchess is broken by Gerry's voice echoing through the pool room.

"Okay, lads. Everyone ready?"

The extra manpower is assembled and a loud, collective groan signals that the net is again on the move. As it advances, Duchess' calm exterior suddenly disappears, and she repeatedly dives to the pool floor, searching for any weakness in the advancing colossus. She's panicking. I shadow her every move: I have to keep her away from the net.

Over three quarters of the pool is now cut off, and Herb'e and Bobby join her in darting around, probing the net for weaknesses. Bobby is swimming directly below Duchess, shadowing her closely, as he has so many times before. Duchess prods the bottom of the net with her nose. Herb'e, too. I chase them away, but their shrinking underwater world grows more and more chaotic as they frantically seek escape.

We're almost in the shallows when Duchess suddenly and unexpectedly rams the net. She hits it with such force that its huge form billows out... before surging back in a deadly embrace.

She's snared. I must reach her!

Her head has penetrated the net and is poking through the other side. Quickly, I dive to free her, only to be punched sideways by a concerned Herb'e, racing to join his partner. His momentum deposits me beside Duchess, and the three of us are snared like flies in a web. My right foot is fast in the mesh, my left arm pinned around Duchess. Panic, blind panic as I feel the net's tightening embrace. I'm stuck; can't move; can't get out.

Top side, Gerry has realised what's happening. Muscled arms bulge and straining hearts pump as thirty men pull at the heavy waterlogged net.

Thud! Something hits me in the back and, from the corner of my eye, I glance the snapping fangs of Bobby. With nowhere left to go, he's made directly for the spot where the three of us are trapped.

As the net continues to tighten, Bobby's body is drawn fast against mine. The four of us are strangled into immobility by the mesh.

Can't get air... none of us can... Duchess and Herb'e have gone limp... they are drowning... I am drowning. Only Bobby fights his fate, glinting fangs slashing at the nylon web.

Top side, the muffled sound of chaos. Voices screaming. Pull! Pull! Get them out! For God's sake, get them out!

We are dragged into the shallows. I push Duchess' and Herb'e's heads towards the light. My snorkel pops through the net. Air at last; air for all three of us.

Blinded by panic and drowning, I have acted instinctively to save us all; but now a new and equally grim reality hits me. Bobby has somehow ended up facing me, his massive bulk sticking to my body, his big head only inches from mine. And, as his powerful jaws slash relentlessly at the net, I realise that, in his panic, in his frenzy, he could easily turn and take my face off.

I don't move. I cannot move. And I dare not let go of my dolphins; no matter what happens, I must keep their heads above water.

Suddenly, Bobby is gone: he has succeeded in shredding a hole and freeing himself from the net's deadly embrace... only to encounter a hail of blows as the City Zoo handlers descend on him with clubs and deck scrubbers. He is beaten out of the water and onto the poolside. Confused and terrified, he flees aimlessly from the horde of men who pursue him, screaming and waving sticks, until only one route of escape remains: the wooden crate that had been his home for so long in those early days at the pool.

Before he realises it, the heavy wooden door slams shut, and his days of freedom have come to a violent end.

By now, I am able to stand. Duchess, Herb'e and I are still enmeshed; but the danger of drowning is past. We remain motionless as we are painstakingly unravelled from our nylon snare.

Ten minutes later, both Duchess and Herb'e are powering their way back to deeper water, seemingly none the worse for their ordeal. It is over, and we have an excellent result. Fortune has smiled on us; the day could so easily have ended in disaster.

"Are you getting out or what?" Gerry quips. I see the relief in his smile.

"Good job, Dave," Philip tells me. "Good job."

I sit on the poolside for several minutes in an almost hypnotic trance. All the fear and agitation is seeping away, leaving me sleepily calm. I am oblivious to the activity of the helpers as they begin the onerous task of removing the giant shredded net. Bobby has certainly done a number on that.

Bobby! I have almost forgotten the reason for this mêlée. In the corner is his crate; and, inside, a totally dejected sea lion.

"Hello, Bobby, are you okay?" I speak gently; but he turns his head to avoid eye contact, totally refusing to acknowledge me. He heaves his bulky frame to the corner of his cell and snorts. He feels disappointed, betrayed and defeated. But at least he is alive and fit enough to fight another day.

I have a feeling there will be many more adventures in store for Bobby; but not with me… definitely not with me. Thank God.

❦ 28 ❧

Talk about the morning after the night before. The next day literally felt like a new dawn, as we could at last do some serious training without the interference of the sea lion; though I must admit, when I saw the empty space where Bobby's crate had been, I got a lump in my throat. But Bobby had a new life now, and hopefully the debacle that had resulted from him being here would teach Management a much-needed lesson.

Gerry called us into the office, where he passed out papers listing the basic tricks. They read: rings, sunglasses, hats, handshake, football, hurdle, highball, toothbrush, big hoop and tail walk. Only when the dolphins had mastered these would further tricks be added.

The first and most simple tricks involved the retrieval of an object, such as a rubber ring. In this instance, you'd show the ring to your dolphin, then throw it about eight feet into the water. The dolphin would then hook the ring over her nose and bring it back.

This simple retrieval trick was deceptively important. Firstly, your dolphin learned confidence around props and, secondly, in returning the ring, she learned that she'd receive a reward: one short blast of the whistle and one chunk of fish. Once she had learned the trick using one ring, she could add to it. Two rings over the nose earned two whistles and two fish; three rings, three whistles and three fish, and so on.

Similarly with the sunglasses and hats: you'd throw them into the water, and your dolphin would bring them back, sunglasses on nose, hat on head.

Although these tricks were not complicated, they helped you to bond with your dolphin, shaping an understanding that would hopefully grow throughout training, helping you to progress to bigger and better things.

Handshake training began by reaching down to touch your dolphin's flipper. Over time, this progressed until, instead of you reaching down, your dolphin actually rose out of the water to meet your hand – a result achieved painstakingly, step-by-step and over many sessions.

The handshake also had hidden benefits. One, it taught your dolphin to lift her head out of the water to look at you. Two, the skills she learned could be developed into the spectacular *tail walk* – always a big favourite with the public.

But what about the dolphin's favourite? Well, once your dolphin had learned to look directly at you, the toothbrush trick quickly followed. This involved 'cleaning' her teeth with a toothbrush – actually, a back scrubber. With her head out of water, your confident dolphin would allow you to put other things into her mouth besides fish – and the toothbrush was always a treat. What could be easier than opening your mouth to get an enjoyable tickle with a firm brush? Great sport. Then, to top it all, you get a chunk of fish as well.

Almost every trick on this basic list formed the foundation for teaching a more complex trick. Training was like building a wall – brick by brick. And Gerry had given me a chance in a million: the chance to build a wall of my own.

Early days, but even then, I was ambitious, committed and determined that my wall should be bigger and better than anyone else's.

In the coming weeks, Gerry was true to his word. I performed almost all the training with Duchess, while Gerry took the lion's share of the training with Herb'e. Rachel had contractual agreements elsewhere.

For hours on end, the two of us would lie belly down on the training platforms, wringing every hour out of every day, and every minute out of every hour as the training of Duchess and Herb'e moved relentlessly on.

The cleaning of the pool and preparation of the fish now fell to a reluctant Matt. His constant late arrivals had been duly noted. Gerry Mansell and company were nothing like Rob. Those boozy late-night sessions at the pub were truly a thing of the past. From now on, we followed a new code: live, eat, drink and sleep dolphins, and, gradually, we began to claw back lost time.

Duchess had made good progress through most of the trick list, but was finding the large hoops challenging. Training was meant to begin by getting her to swim through a hoop under water. Gradually, and over time, the hoop would be raised until finally she would have to leap out of the water to get through it. But Duchess resented the hoop's touch and was reluctant to even make a start. We needed more time.

"Gerry, can I come in at night to train? I need more time on certain tricks."

"Well, you won't get paid any more if you do," Gerry replied.
This meant *yes*. It meant that I would be allowed to train alone and unsupervised. The original plan to teach me to be a presenter had already been abandoned, and I had been promoted. I was being taught to train, and being treated as a trainer.

Night training would give me that precious extra time to work on Duchess' trick list. My social life, which had been dwindling steadily since the dolphins' arrival, was now non-existent. I had unknowingly stepped out of the world of people and into the strangely different world of dolphins. Or, should I say, dolphin, because I found it harder and harder to leave Duchess' side. She had totally and utterly bewitched me.

Later that evening, I excitedly informed Jim and Ida about my night-time training sessions.

"I 'ope they're paying yer more money, 'cause yer work 'ard enough as it is," Ida said.

My silence gave me away.

Jim's paper rustled. "Nobody works for nowt! Yer need paying!"

They didn't realise that being able to work alone was payment enough for me. Now I would experience things that money just couldn't buy.

A concerned Jim peered over his paper. "Anyway, if yer gonna be late, remember to lock and check the doors when yer come in. Another three 'ouses were burgled this week, and it's only Friday."

After demolishing an enormous roast beef dinner, I sluggishly waddled back to the pool. The fish I'd left earlier was now thawed and ready for cutting. I decided that, instead of feeding quarter-cut herring, I would now feed eighth-cut herring, allowing me more training time before the dolphins felt full up.

The pool had an eerie feel to it at night. Sound reverberated off the walls, and a hazy mist hung low as cooling air met heated water. As the two dolphins excitedly approached the training platform, the atmosphere was charged with an energy I could actually feel. And I do mean *feel*. It was strange. In my short time working with Duchess, I had changed; I was suddenly becoming very aware of my surroundings. My senses somehow seemed keener, feelings sharper. Things were no longer presenting themselves in just black and white.

I'd already caged Smelly and Worse, so they wouldn't be able to interrupt us. Within minutes, I was lying belly down on the platform, fish bucket to my side and whistle around my neck.

First, a little petting to put us all at ease; then on to the training.

I always worked through the trick list in the same order, so as not to confuse the dolphins. We began with the retrieval tricks, eventually working our way to the hoop – the trick that Duchess didn't like. This session was very different from any I'd done before because, for the first time, I was actually working both dolphins together.

Herb'e was a lot more confident with the hoops than Duchess, so I somehow had to get *him* to help *me* train *her*. We worked steadily, during which time I never spoke a word. Instead, I mentally painted pictures, which I tried to communicate to the dolphins. We'd worked this way for almost an hour, when suddenly I began to experience *that feeling*, the one of overwhelming calm and deep nausea.

The *connection*.

It was there again. I hadn't felt it for some time.

Duchess was hanging motionless under the water, no more than three feet away, those twinkling eyes fixed on me, unblinking and drawing me in. I felt myself being pulled slowly away. There was no verbal sound, no mental banter, just a gentle drifting to who-knows-where, leaving me almost comatose. The vision of me lying prostrate on the training platform became distant and grey. I was aware; but time had stopped.

It was if she had taken me by the hand, guiding me, leading me to a place I'd never known, a different reality. Somewhere where *she* could make *me* understand. A place where we could talk freely without verbal distraction. Somewhere very special.

Suddenly, the clock started ticking: she'd deposited me back onto that cold, damp platform.

The audience was over.

It was like crashing out of a dream. Had this really happened, or had I imagined it?

❦ 29 ❧

A ten-minute break in the office to compose myself, then straight into the second session to work solely on the hoops.

I assume my position on the platform and hold the hoop six to eight inches above the water line.

"Come on, Duchess, come on! You can do it!"

No sooner is it in position than Duchess shoots from the water and propels herself through it. No hesitation, no fear – only certainty.

"Yes, that's it! Yes!"

A prolonged, excited whistle breaks the pool's eerie silence, and I bombard her with food. Whistle – fish! Whistle – fish! Whistle – fish! Whistle – fish! Whistle – fish! Five times as an excited Duchess milks the moment.

"Good girl, Duch, good girl!"

Next through the hoop is Herb'e, quickly followed once again by Duchess. The hoodoo is broken, and three euphoric souls celebrate the night's achievement.

My empty fish bucket signals the end of the session.

"What a great night's training, people – absolutely fantastic!"

Just one more job left: release Smelly and Worse from their enclosure, giving them the freedom of the pool for the night. Matt will have the pleasure of seeing them next, when – or should I say *if* – he makes an early morning appearance.

Tonight, I feel very privileged, very special, because Duchess has taken me on a journey, not physically, but mentally. She has transported

78

me to her special place — somewhere *in between*, and although I still don't fully understand what's happened, I have learned a lot.

But a question has also been raised: just who is training whom?

Just maybe I should give Duchess the whistle. Maybe it should be Duchess administering the reward — though I must admit, fish is *not* one of my favourite dishes.

❧ 30 ❧

Over the next few weeks, I worked the night shift religiously and, as a result, Duchess and Herb'e raced through their trick list.

Gone were the days of those early morning clean-ups with Smelly and Worse. This job now fell to a disgruntled Matt: he was the one who issued the *good mornings*, deck scrubber in hand.

He was still struggling to get up in the mornings because of the late hours he kept. He rarely got to bed before three o'clock, and I often wondered where he'd been and what he'd been doing, although I never asked. Even though we shared a room, we didn't share a friendship. In fact, we barely spoke. Besides, I wasn't really interested in anyone or anything: all I cared about was my dolphins.

After each night's training session, I meticulously recorded their progress in the logbooks, and it soon became obvious that night training was more productive than day training. The dolphins were definitely more receptive when darkness fell and, consequently, training was soon back on schedule.

One morning, Gerry called us into the office to break some important news. "As you all know, I will very shortly be travelling to the States to collect four more dolphins. To accommodate them, we will need two extra training pens, so I've ordered materials for building two new booms. This means we're gonna have workmen traipsing all over the place, so you'll all have to be patient."

Just what I needed: Duchess and Herb'e had been making excellent progress in their training, and now it would be disrupted.

"I don't yet know when I'm leaving," Gerry continued, "but it will be sooner rather than later, because the Company has just confirmed the locations of the new dolphinariums."

I listened eagerly: perhaps I'd get some idea of where my future home would be.

"The first – and most prestigious – is Hendle Safari Park."

Hendle Safari Park! That wasn't far from home – it would be great if they sent me there.

"The second is the seaside venue, West Coast. Unfortunately, it's behind schedule, so won't be up and running for some time." He paused. "But, more exciting still, a third venue has been added: Welby Park."

Murmurs from the staff.

"The Company is already advertising for more presenters, but these will be sent directly to their designated dolphinariums.

"For Hendle – as premier pool – the Company has acquired an established trainer by the name of Sally Summers, who will open her shows with Duchess and Herb'e."

I cringed: it wasn't as if I hadn't known right at the start that Duchess and Herb'e would eventually go to someone else; but neither had I reckoned on the strength of my feelings for Duchess. I'd just been dealt a body blow.

But the bad news didn't end there.

"New orders for today," Gerry continued, "from now on, Matt will take all Duchess' training sessions. David, you're getting too involved."

I felt numb, my mind in turmoil. Was this to be my reward for all my hard work? What had I done wrong? Was Gerry trying to protect me from the upset of losing Duchess and Herb'e? Or did it go deeper?

Maybe, just maybe, he thought I'd got too big for my boots.

I wanted to sob: I felt used, angry and betrayed. Rightly or wrongly, I believed that the Company had taken advantage of my naivety. Young, foolish and eager, I'd given heart and soul. But no more. I'd just learned my first corporate lesson: trust no one and be loyal only to yourself.

❧ 31 ❧

All morning, I busied myself about the pool room. I fed Smelly and Worse and bottomed their living quarters, then set about cleaning the poolsides. I didn't speak to anyone, but scrubbed silently and aggressively in an effort to work off my anger.

As always, Duchess trailed me, head cocked to one side. Her calming presence soon began to soothe me, drawing the sting of betrayal – and my first smile of the morning.

"Hello, gorgeous."

Matt was receiving last minute instructions from Gerry as he prepared to take my place on the left-hand training platform – the platform I'd made my own. Now, I could do nothing but watch from a distance as Gerry and Matt took their positions.

Herb'e immediately swam towards the right-hand platform.

Duchess, however, didn't move. Instead, she hung back and regarded Matt thoughtfully.

I held my breath. Something was happening: it was as if the atmosphere had become charged. Then, it hit me, that feeling of nausea: the *connection* had kicked in.

"That's right, Duchess, don't go to him!" I gazed at her, gazed *into* her, focussing every bit of energy into transmitting my message. *"Don't go to him! Give him NOTHING! It's you and me, only you and me!"*

Whistles shrieked, fish buckets rattled, but my concentration never wavered. *"Remember, Duchess: NOTHING!"*

The link held firm: Duchess steadfastly refused his advances.

After a few minutes, a frustrated Gerry switched platforms, putting Matt with Herb'e. This immediately paid dividends for Matt as Herb'e again showed his willingness to please; but Duchess remained aloof, treating Gerry with the same contempt as she'd treated Matt.

"That's right, Duchess, ignore him!"

Gerry glanced across the pool and, as our eyes met, I found it hard to conceal a smile. I didn't speak, but repeated my message to Duchess, over and over: *"Give him NOTHING!"*

A furious Gerry hauled himself off the platform and snatched the fish bucket. "She's fat, lazy and full of fish! Starve her for an hour or so, and she'll work."

"That's what he thinks! You won't work, will you, gorgeous?"

He stormed out of the pool room and into the kitchen.

Duchess' eyes followed him as he left, then turned to meet mine. The expression in them was smug, almost sly. She knew exactly what she was doing.

I laughed softly. *"Thanks, beautiful! Keep it up."*

Two hours later, Gerry returned to the platform, only to receive the same dismissive treatment as before. Irritated, and sorely aware of my self-satisfied gaze, he snapped, "You think you can do better?"

"I know I can."

Within minutes, I replaced him on the platform and flashed my ring. I'd barely had time to lie down before a jubilant Duchess came to my hand. She gazed up at me, eyes shining, and rolled onto her back for a tickle under her left flipper.

"Thanks, girl – that showed 'em."

I glanced up at Gerry: there was a semblance of a smile, then he marched out of the pool room.

What Gerry had sought to avoid had already happened. Whether he liked it or not, Duchess had chosen her handler, and nothing would change her mind.

❧ 32 ❧

19th March 1972… My 19ᵗʰ Birthday

My future is uncertain. Yesterday, Gerry's authority was severely tested. The big question now is, how will he react today?

Once again, Matt arrives late, so the morning meeting is delayed. Gerry seems impatient, and his customary talk is terse and hurried.

"No training today, I'm calling a rest day," he announces. "Training is back on schedule, and the dolphins need worming, so let's seize the moment. I'll be off to the States soon, and everything here needs to be right for when I get back." He takes a breath, then pointedly looks at me. "Oh, and for the next few weeks, we'll give night training a rest."

Well, there's a surprise! As I suspected, he's still smarting about yesterday; but I don't let it worry me. Gerry isn't stupid; he's being paid a lot of money to produce shows on time, and he won't risk further delays. He might be digging in his heels now, but it won't last forever. He needs me.

The worming tablets, along with the usual array of vitamin pills, are hidden inside a herring. We achieve this by pushing the tablets, one by one, through the fish's gills, loading it as you would a ball-bearing gun. This way, we can administer eight or nine pills per fish.

Duchess and Herb'e greedily gobble down the vit-fish. Now, we wait.

Matt and I repair props in silence. Our relationship has suffered yet more damage as he realises he's lost out again. Duchess will only work for me. He resents me; but, in truth, he has caused most of his own problems.

Duchess isn't her usual inquisitive self either, and I wonder if the medication could be making her nauseous. Gerry still says very little, and even Rachel is quiet, which is unusual for this normally bubbly redhead. All is not well. It's a strange morning.

Then Herb'e starts to pass a tapeworm, and everything wakes up.

At first, we see about three feet of tape, then six, then more. Herb'e suddenly becomes aware that something is trailing him. He begins to panic. His speed picks up. He races blindly around the pool, hoping to shake off his unwanted pursuer; but even as he swims, the worm grows longer.

I can't believe it. We all gasp in amazement. It billows from Herb'e's rear like a streamer, now at least forty feet in length and still growing. Poor Herb'e is frantic.

"Whatever happens, don't touch the worm!" Gerry yells. "It's so contagious, a mere touch will infect you."

Duchess, perplexed, dashes for the corner of the pool so as not to collide with the distraught Herb'e, who continues to speed through the water like a missile. He generates so much power that the normally calm pool becomes a maelstrom, crashing waves onto the sides. He is a blur: a grey bomber speeding in vain to outrace the tape that streams behind him. Danger levels are critical; at this speed, he risks smashing into the pool walls.

And, still, the worm grows.

We stand on the poolside, gaping in disbelief, powerless to help.

The anxiety is intolerable: I can hardly breathe, hardly bare to watch – yet I cannot turn aside. Then, suddenly, thankfully, the panic-stricken dolphin begins to slow, and the tapeworm comes away.

Bewildered and relieved, Herb'e deposits the worm in the shallows, then flees to deep water to seek solace from Duchess. There, both dolphins hover, nervously eyeing the monster tape.

Gerry begins to bark orders. "Get it out, quick! We can't let the dolphins come into contact with it."

We all don rubber gloves, then use long poles to painstakingly lift the horrific giant from the water. We carry it to wasteland at the rear of the pool building, then arrange it in straight lines. Gerry and I take measurements. Matt builds a fire.

Thirty minutes later, we log that Herb'e has passed a staggering eighty-two-foot six-inch tapeworm. It's so incredible that we know no one will believe us. We need proof, so Gerry returns to the pool building to fetch a camera.

A couple of hours later, Herb'e's monster worm is joined by a wimpy twelve-foot contribution, courtesy of Duchess.

We burn both worms, and excited conversation flows for the remainder of the day, banishing the cold and difficult atmosphere between Gerry and me; although how long this fragile peace will last, I cannot tell.

Tomorrow, both Duchess and Herb'e – particularly Herb'e – will be unusually hungry; but, until then, I must wait anxiously to find out if Gerry will allow me back on the training platform. It will be difficult to sleep tonight.

Oh, and by the way, Happy Birthday, David!

❮ 33 ❯

A new day and I expected to be greeted by two very hungry dolphins. I was still reeling from the size of Herb'e's tapeworm, and didn't doubt that everyone else was feeling the same way. No wonder he'd had such a good appetite; he'd literally been eating for two.

And it was also decision time. Following a night's deliberations, Gerry would have decided who would be handling Duchess from now on, and I just prayed that he'd chosen in my favour. It must be me; please let it be me!

As I approached the pool building, a long, flatback lorry, loaded with scaffolding and plastic-coated wire mesh, shuddered to a halt in front of the main entrance: materials for constructing the booms.

Once built, the booms would effectively divide the pool into four training pens, ready for the second dolphin shipment. They would also signal the arrival of Sally Summers, come to claim her prize: the Hendle show, and all that went with it. My time with Duchess was growing short. What would I do without her?

Gerry and Rachel had already arrived in expectation of the delivery. "No training today – just feeds. Too much to do!" Gerry ordered brusquely.

Rachel followed me into the fish store, her manner altogether gentler. "David, today Matt will feed Herb'e and you will feed Duchess."

A reprieve: Duchess was still mine. But for how long?

Throughout the remainder of the day, the clang of metal poles slotting together echoed throughout the pool room, yet when we left in the evening, the booms were still nowhere near completion. That would take another three days at least – three more days with Duchess.

To construct a boom, the workers first had to build a metal skeleton consisting of a frame and two vertical strengtheners, which they then covered with plastic-coated wire mesh. This meant that, despite being apart, the dolphin couples would still be able to communicate, so wouldn't feel lonely. They would also be able to watch one another being trained, learning a thing or two about what would be expected of them.

Only two dolphins would occupy each small pen. They would feel cramped, but Gerry believed that this would force them into being more attentive during training.

Only Company dolphins would be here for the next few months, and a roll-on, roll-off system had been devised where, as one pair left, another would immediately replace it.

But the owners of the pool had big plans for the future: after our Company had departed, they would let the pool to other, rival companies, who would break and train raw dolphins of their own.

This pool was destined to become the UK's key training centre, deliberately concealed within the sleepy mining community of North Liston, where the compassionate or concerned would never think to look for it.

❧ 34 ❧

As I lay in bed, the irresistible aroma of sizzling crispy bacon lapped at my taste buds, lifting me from slumber, causing my nose to twitch in anticipation. I rose in slow motion, like a bewitched cobra to a snake charmer, following the smell as I floated downstairs and into the kitchen. There was Ida, lovingly arranging one of her magnificent fry-ups.

"Morning all!"

She greeted me with a smile.

"They've still not caught anyone," Jim mumbled, rearranging his newspaper.

"Caught anyone for what?" I asked.

"The robberies!" he snapped. "Three 'ouses have been done this week."

"My, someone's been busy," I quipped.

A stony silence, broken only by Elton John singing 'Your Song' on the radio.

"I like this song."

"Bloody police are useless," Jim grunted, "utterly useless. It's got so bad, they're organising a special team to catch the robbin' bastard. Organising a special team? That lot couldn't organise a piss-up in a brewery!"

His colourful concerns reflected those of almost all the North Liston residents. This sort of thing was rare in such a close-knit community, and the local rag was having a field day feeding the escalating atmosphere of suspicion and resentment. If you couldn't trust your neighbours, who could you trust? Anyway, it wasn't my problem – I had enough on my plate.

Thirty minutes later, after demolishing yet another of Ida's breakfast specials, I walked into the pool room.

"Hello, people!"

A couple of snorted greetings echoed across the water, then Duchess and Herb'e returned to the important business of tormenting the penguins. Same old game: 'flick the penguin'. As always, within ten to fifteen minutes, the game ended, allowing a harassed Smelly and Worse to leave the pool and wobble grumpily back to their enclosure.

There was then just enough time for a quick poolside clean before the workmen arrived to lower the booms. After today, Duchess and Herb'e would no longer have the freedom of the full pool; the next open water they'd see would be at Hendle Safari Park.

Within an hour, the workmen and handlers had assembled, ready to join forces in positioning the heavy structures. Grunts and groans accompanied the lowering of the partitions.

Duchess and Herb'e watched uneasily from the far corner of the pool as new boundaries fell into place. For them, loss of swimming space was only the first blow; training was about to intensify and, from now on, it would be all work and very little play.

❦ 35 ❧

Next morning, I was greeted by a relieved Smelly and Worse splashing around in one of the three empty holding pens. Poor Duchess and Herb'e watched dejectedly as their former playthings cheekily paraded themselves behind the safety of a boom. Strange, I could swear I sensed penguin laughter as they taunted the two dolphins. *"Nah, nah, nah-nah, nah — you can't get us!"*

It was a strange turn of events. Smelly and Worse now had the freedom of the pool — at least until the arrival of the second dolphin shipment — whilst poor Duchess and Herb'e were effectively caged. How life can change. Freedom gained; freedom lost.

As I thawed and cut fish, I waited anxiously for Gerry and company to show up. I still wasn't sure if Duchess was mine again, but knew that the start of serious training would force Gerry into a final decision. He'd probably make his announcement during the morning talk.

He did.

"David, until further notice, you will be Duchess' sole handler. Matt, you will be given one of the new dolphins when they arrive."

Matt's face dropped; it would be at least a month before the second shipment arrived, so it was back to cleaning and cutting fish for him.

I, on the other hand, had been given more time to cement my claim on Duchess before the arrival of Sally Summers and, with everything to play for, I didn't waste it. Within minutes of leaving the office, I was lying on the platform, flashing my ring, whistle round my neck and fish bucket by my side.

"Hello, Duch, it's just you and me again." Just time for a cuddle and tickle before starting the session.

This was the day I'd start training the hurdle, a six-foot high jump destined to become another crowd-pleaser. In time, the dolphins would learn to make three consecutive jumps, allowing camera buffs to get spectacular shots.

The jumps led seamlessly to another trick: remove the pole and you had the opening and closing bows.

I was ecstatic yet determined as, once again, I slipped out of the world of people and into the world of dolphins. My future would be moulded from this very platform as I set out to carve myself a place in training history.

A week passed. Gerry and I were getting on well again, and Duchess and Herb'e's feeds had steadily increased as they flew through their trick list. In fact, we were so far ahead of schedule, we actually threw in an extra trick or two.

My only disappointment was that I hadn't shared that powerful *connection* with Duchess for some time. Had I imagined it, or was it intended only for me? Since my reinstatement, I'd never trained alone, Gerry always working by my side. Perhaps *his* presence interfered with the link. Other than that, everything was running smoothly and I should have been happy. But I wasn't; I felt deeply apprehensive. Why?

Later that afternoon, Gerry unexpectedly summoned us to the office: our new colleague had arrived and he wanted to introduce us. Suddenly, I stood face-to-face with the girl pencilled-in to steal my dream. My nemesis had finally arrived. No wonder I'd been so anxious.

Sally Summers was a tall, pretty girl with flowing blonde hair. She seemed quietly confident, yet had a charming vulnerability that would virtually make slaves of all the male staff at the pool. Already, the men clustered about her like bees around a honey pot. Only I didn't succumb: she sent a cold shiver down my spine.

I hung back, watching her warily. This girl was a threat, and I was determined to give her minimal co-operation.

As I prepared the feed for the final session of the day, I pondered how much longer I would keep my beloved Duchess. I surely had only a couple of days at most before Sally Summers would stake her claim.

❖ 37 ❖

A week passed, and Gerry allowed me to work Duchess without interference from my beautiful adversary, although this may have had something to do with the steady decline of the training sessions. Both dolphins were becoming sloppy. Maybe they were tired, maybe they were bored, but both Duchess and Herb'e fell into a couldn't-care-less mood.

"I've seen this sort of thing before," Gerry said. "They're trying their hand. We'll give them a couple of days, but if they carry on like this, we'll have to take action. We can't fall behind schedule again."

Two days passed quickly and, despite all our efforts, the disinterested duo continued to just play around their pen.

"Okay, that's it!" Gerry barked. "Everyone clear the pool! Lock the doors as you leave, and don't come back for an hour."

As I lifted myself from the platform, he turned to me. "Not you – you're staying!" He handed me a long pole.

"What's this for?" I asked.

Gerry's expression was dark. "There can only be one boss, and it's time these two learned just who that is."

He directed me to the far side of the pen, then started to shout instructions. "We're going to beat the water with the poles, scream and shout and generally frighten these two to death. Understand?"

I nodded numbly.

"Now, let's wake them up!"

We both began to shout and beat the water with all our might.

Duchess and Herb'e fled around the pen in blind terror, desperately seeking an escape; but, of course, there wasn't any. Their only solace was to take refuge in the middle of the pen, where they cringed like two frightened children until the discipline was over.

Gerry's expression remained grim. "Give them half an hour to think about it, then we'll go straight back into training."

When we returned thirty minutes later, both dolphins swam to the platforms, pitifully eager to please. The discipline had worked.

I never questioned what I'd done, but felt deeply ashamed and upset. Later, I learned that this was known as a 'shake session' – something almost every trainer resorted to when the situation became desperate.

Within an hour, the others returned, none the wiser as to what had happened. Gerry and I continued to train in virtual silence; but when I looked into Duchess' eyes, I saw not love, but fear. How would I ever put this right?

After the final feed, Gerry called me into the office, obviously aware of how bad I was feeling.

"Look, David, only *you* were allowed to participate in the shake session because, out of all these so-called trainers, you're the only one who's got what it takes." When I didn't reply, he added, "Don't forget, I'm not just Britain's top trainer, I'm Europe's top trainer. You don't get that far unless you have something really special. I have it, and I recognise it when I see it. I see it in you. You're the same as me, and I've known it for some time."

I still didn't speak, but hung my head, staring at the floor.

"The head trainer of Hendle Safari Park has to be strong," he persisted. Then, he added emphatically, "*You've* got to be strong."

I've got to be strong? Why?

I raised my eyes to meet his as I suddenly realised what he was saying. He was giving *me* Hendle dolphinarium. He was giving me Duchess and Herb'e.

I should have been ecstatic, but the news just washed over me. I'd got what I wanted; I'd achieved what I'd set out to achieve. But at what cost?

After everyone had left, I stood by the pool and watched Duchess and Herb'e swimming around their cramped pen. The gleaming water that I'd so often compared to a mirror had suddenly lost its sparkle and clarity. In that one day, it had become muddied, and no matter how hard I tried, it would never look the same again.

❧ 38 ❧

Next morning, Gerry called Sally Summers into the office to break the news about Duchess and Herb'e. I took no pleasure in seeing the devastated look etched across her face. She'd long since been promised the Hendle show, and now that promise had not been honoured. Gerry had effectively shuffled the pack in my favour. My long working hours and close association with Duchess had paid dividends.

During the team talk, Gerry informed us that he would be travelling to the States within the next twenty-four hours, leaving Rachel and *me* in charge. My advancement through the ranks was continuing at pace.

Encouraged by this latest news, I told him, "Gerry, I want to bring back night training. I need to get closer to my dolphins."

Gerry nodded. "Okay, you're the boss. Rachel's still tied to outside contracts, so I'm sure she won't object, and the dolphins are yours now anyway. Just keep them up to scratch."

The dolphins are yours now. Boy, that sounded good.

Gerry told us that he would be gone for two weeks, and I planned to use his absence to try to make up with Duchess and Herb'e, to search for what I had lost. That night, I slept fitfully and awoke with a dull headache, the shake session still vivid in my mind. Even Ida's jumbo breakfast didn't seem important. I needed to get back onto the training platform. I needed to recover the trust I'd strived so hard to win, yet had so surely lost during that five minutes of madness.

The discipline might have worked, but I firmly believed there must be a better way to achieve my goals. I needed what I craved most: the key to that special door leading to Duchess. I needed the *connection*.

Gerry had only been away for a few days and the training pool had already undergone a quiet transformation, his strict disciplinarian outlook giving way to Rachel's altogether softer approach.

I'd just finished my morning training session, so headed into the office to write up the logbooks. Minutes later, Rachel joined me.

"It must be wonderful to travel the world as a top trainer," I remarked. "All that excitement."

She gave me a warm smile. "It's not all it's built up to be: the inside of a dolphinarium is pretty much the same the world over." She poured a mug of tea before continuing. "Gerry has a lot to do once he hits Florida."

"Florida! I've never been to America, but I've heard of the Florida Keys," I said.

"You will have. That's where most of the catching organisations operate from." She smiled mischievously. "You know, one of the US transporters recently told me a real funny story about Gerry's first open water catch." She sat down with her tea. "I don't know if you're aware, but the catchers pursue the dolphins in high-powered boats, dropping nets to encircle the schools. Once they've got them trapped, they go in and actually wrestle their chosen dolphin."

"You mean they catch by hand?"

"Yes, it's the only way." She became serious. "But it's also very dangerous: the dolphins literally fight for their lives. And an added worry is sharks: the Gulf of Mexico is infested with them and, what's more, you can't see them because of the milk water."

"Milk water?"

"Well, the water off Florida teems with life, billions of microscopic organisms making it cloudy. You can't see anything, so if there's a shark around, you don't know about it until it's too late. You have to rely on the spotter back at the boat. If he sees anything dodgy, he sounds a hooter, which means you get out of the water fast." Rachel's eyes twinkled impishly. "It was during one of these catches that it happened."

I could hardly contain myself. "*What* happened?"

"Gerry was wrestling a large dolphin, when one of the spotters saw the dorsal fin of a hammerhead — a good twelve-footer. It had surfaced from deep water, probably to investigate all the commotion. Only trouble, it came up between Gerry and the boat."

"What did he do when he saw it?"

"That was the problem: he didn't see it. Nor did the spotter sound the horn to vacate the water."

"Why ever not?"

"Because if he had done, Gerry would have released the dolphin and swum right into the shark."

My blood ran cold, just imagining what the monster fish might have done.

Rachel eased back in her chair. "The catchers only told Gerry about the shark *after* they'd returned to port." She laughed, throwing back her long red hair. "When they met up for a drink later that night, they told everyone that, when the Englishman spied the shark, his entire body rose out of the water and he performed the most spectacular backward tail walk they'd ever seen, generating a wake of white foam all the way back to the boat."

I had to laugh. Obviously, Gerry hadn't *actually* performed a tail walk, but it wasn't hard to imagine the scene.

Having finished her tea and her story, Rachel lifted herself from her chair. "Well, tea break over — the dolphins won't train themselves."

As I resumed cutting the fish, I couldn't help but marvel at my strange new career. I wondered how many adventures the world of dolphins would hold for me.

❦ 39 ❧

With Gerry in the States, Rachel took over the team talk. She purposely had me stand by her side, so the other handlers would be left in no doubt as to my new position in the pecking order.

"Gerry has taken charge of four dolphins: three males and one female. That means four of you will have new charges. Two of these are destined for West Coast dolphinarium, which is now back on schedule, so training will be intensive." She turned to Sally Summers with a smile. "*You* will be head trainer at West Coast."

A relieved Sally beamed. She'd got her pool, just not the one she'd been promised. I was happy for her.

"In the meantime, I have other obligations," Rachel continued, "and will be away for the remainder of the week. This means David will be in charge until my return."

I couldn't believe it: I had been elevated to head of pool, even though by default. With this new power, not only could I reinstate night training, I could also implement my own training ideas. My shackles had been removed. At last, I had the freedom to go my own way – and I didn't waste a second.

My first change was to add five minutes' petting to the end of every training session. This applied to day and night sessions alike, and finally culminated in a well-deserved evening swim. Up to now, nothing like this had been allowed so as not to distract the dolphins from their rigorous training schedule, but – as we were now ahead of schedule – I felt we could afford some quality bonding time. Duchess and Herb'e needed to know that it wasn't all just work, work, work.

My two stars immediately seemed happier, so much so that I was even able to introduce some new tricks. They worked willingly, relishing their rewards of affection and play – although there was still no *connection*.

For me, life rolled by as a delicious mixture of contentment and anticipation: working, playing and eagerly awaiting that all-important telephone call from the States. Eight days passed before it came, but when it did, the news was exciting: Gerry was about to start the transport and would be back in less than twenty-four hours. The second dolphin shipment was on its way.

❧ 40 ❧

All next morning, excited trainers and presenters busied themselves around the pool, some scrubbing floors, others cleaning the kitchen. The pungent smell of disinfectant filled the air and, if it could be cleaned, we cleaned it. Even the normally neglected office windows gleamed.

The huge, previously empty freezers were now fully stocked with slabs of frozen mackerel and herring in anticipation of the arrival of four hungry dolphins. By lunchtime, everything was ready and all we had to do was wait. The clock ticked, the hours crawled by, then suddenly we heard the hiss of air brakes from outside the pool. They were here.

The lorry had pulled up in front of the main steps; behind it, Philip's white Citroen and, behind that, Rogers' black limousine.

As the lorry's shutter door rolled back, the first thing I saw was a wet and weary Gerry. He hadn't slept for well over twenty-four hours, and there was no mistaking the exhaustion and disorientation etched across his unshaven face.

"Good to have you back," I told him cheerfully. "How did the transport go?"

Gerry heaved himself unsteadily from the back of the lorry. "I've had a nightmare, an absolute nightmare. One of the dolphins fought and thrashed all the way from America, and the transport boxes were packed too tightly for me to reach him."

I was shocked. "Surely you didn't transport alone?"

"Yes I did; the Company refused to pay for an assistant."

I stared at him numbly. I couldn't believe it — only one man to transport four dolphins?

By now, a concerned Philip was barking orders, his voice urgent. "We need to get these animals into the water ASAP!"

We could hear the dolphin that had been such a problem still thrashing around inside the lorry, and the male staff wasted no time in trying to reach him.

"Get that one out first, but don't put him in the water," Philip shouted, running up the pool steps. "I need to check him out."

It took six men to carry the distressed dolphin up the steps and into the pool room. They gripped the harness tightly as he continued to twist and jerk, then lowered him as gently as possible onto a large foam mattress on the poolside.

I lay beside him and tried to hold him still, my arms locked around his body, my hands gripping his flippers. Matt held him on the right, and a third man anchored his tail. We held him in a vice-like grip whilst Philip examined him for injury.

"Oh, no," he groaned. "This animal's lost an eye!"

It seemed that, as the dolphin had been thrashing about, his canvas harness had torn, lashing his face and slashing his eye. Thanks to the Company trying to save money by dodging the cost of an assistant transporter, he had sustained a serious injury — one that could have been avoided.

And the news got worse.

To everyone's horror, Philip announced that the left eye was also injured. There was now every chance this dolphin would be blind.

Philip abandoned further checks after only three minutes, as the distraught dolphin continued to fight. "Let's just get him in," he groaned.

As four men carried the struggling dolphin towards Pen Number Three, I jumped into the water, preparing to disentangle him from the damaged harness. I couldn't afford to let him panic and ram the wall. But, once free, his cramped muscles barely allowed him to float, let alone swim.

With the first dolphin now safely in the pool, we wasted no time in bringing in the other three.

The girls had stayed in the lorry, bathing the remaining dolphins with water, totally unaware of the first dolphin's injuries.

As I boarded the lorry to help remove the second dolphin, my eyes were suddenly drawn to a box at the rear. It was a horrible feeling: not the calm I'd felt with Duchess, or the nonchalance I'd felt with Herb'e, but a cold dread. The best way to describe it is as if the colour black could radiate an emotion: cold, empty, soulless.

I checked the label on the dolphin's box. 'Female Atlantic Bottlenose Dolphin (*Tursiops Truncatus*); Length Approx 6ft 2ins; Estimated Age – 4-4^1/2 years; Name – Bubbles.'

For a bewildering moment, I felt as if I was peering into a grave; then someone called out, and I was back. No time to ponder; the dolphins needed to be in the water fast.

To everyone's relief, the remaining dolphins stayed calm and, within an hour, Philip had checked them all and released them into their pens.

Duchess and Herb'e bobbed at the water's surface, eyes locked on the new arrivals. After a few minutes, they pushed their noses through the mesh and began waving their heads, as if in conversation. I wondered what they were saying.

"Hello, beautiful, see all the company you've got?"

Duchess didn't look at me, but drifted, watching.

On the far side of the pool stood an exhausted Gerry. He looked shell-shocked, and as I watched him gazing into the water – looking, yet not looking – I realised that this transport had taken its toll on both dolphins and man alike.

The usual congratulations followed, as they always did after events like this, everyone laughing and joking as if all was well.

But all was not well. As always, the men in suits had eyes that chose not to see.

Not only did I feel sick and disgusted about the possibility of a blind dolphin, but I also felt unnaturally drawn to the pen that housed the dolphin called Bubbles. I felt as if we'd just accepted the Wooden Horse of Troy.

This animal was not giving off bad vibes – she was giving off no vibes at all. Nothing.

She was void.

❦ 41 ❧

After the commotion had died down and the dignitaries had left, I collected the labels from the empty transport boxes. This information was important, as it would form the first entry in the dolphins' official logbooks. I noticed that all the dolphins were named – which was unusual – and realised that Gerry had probably done this whilst in the States.

The first label read, 'Male Atlantic Bottlenose Dolphin (*Tursiops Truncatus*); Length Approx 5ft 7ins; Estimated Age – not determined; Name – Scouse.' This was the dolphin who had fought so hard during transport, the dolphin who had lost an eye. I wondered if his chosen trainer would indeed record the truth about his injuries. I noted that the vet hadn't been able to determine his age: even though he was relatively small, it didn't necessarily mean that he was young.

The second label read, 'Male Atlantic Bottlenose Dolphin (*Tursiops Truncatus*); Length Approx 5ft 3ins; Estimated Age – 2-2½ years; Name – Stumpy.' I had noticed that this dolphin only had half a flipper, probably due to a shark attack early in his life. More disturbing, however, was the sweet, flowery smell on his breath. From what I'd read, this was never a good sign.

The third label read, 'Male Atlantic Bottlenose Dolphin (*Tursiops Truncatus*); Length Approx 4ft 8ins; Estimated Age – 2½ years; Name – Baby Dai.' Without doubt, someone had deliberately falsified this information: the dolphin was no more than 4ft 2ins long and clearly too young to have been taken from the sea. I was no expert, but it wasn't rocket science to figure out how old he was by using the other labels as a guide. In my opinion, Baby Dai was under two years of age, and had therefore been illegally imported.

The final label read, 'Female Atlantic Bottlenose Dolphin (*Tursiops Truncatus*); Length Approx 6ft 7ins; Estimated Age – 4-4½ years; Name – Bubbles.' This was the dolphin who had disturbed me. Going on looks, she appeared to be healthy, but she filled me with an awful sense of foreboding. Perhaps it was just my imagination, but I believed not. I seemed to be acquiring a sixth sense around dolphins, courtesy of Duchess.

The inventory was now complete; the respective trainers would log all relevant information. And so ended a stressful day.

But, for me, there was one light shining at the end of the tunnel: Ida's culinary delight. I wondered what she was cooking tonight.

❧ 42 ❧

Next day, Rachel again took command of the morning meeting, giving Gerry the chance to catch up on much-needed sleep following the transport. She was to allocate the dolphins, so the office was buzzing with excited and expectant trainers.

"Sally," Rachel began, "you will take Baby Dai. I think you're the best choice because he's an infant and will need mothering."

Sally smiled kindly. "No worries, Rachel, I'll look after him."

"Matt, you will be part of the team in charge of Bubbles and Stumpy. Gerry and I will work Scouse, because he'll need a lot of help coping with his blindness. David, Duchess and Herb'e are now your sole responsibility."

"Fantastic!" Everything was falling into place: I now had both Duchess *and* Herb'e, which would give me the opportunity to chase my dream: *The Perfect Pair.*

Training started immediately for the new dolphins. As always, the first task was to persuade them to take dead fish, and it wasn't long before Baby Dai, Scouse and Stumpy took the bait. This was made all the easier thanks to the guidance of Duchess and Herb'e, the elder statesmen of the pool.

The only dolphin who refused the fish was Bubbles, the dolphin who had given me so many misgivings on her arrival. She showed no interest in anybody or anything. She didn't even check out her new neighbours in their adjoining pen. All she did was swim around in circles, totally and utterly oblivious to her surroundings.

Very worrying, but these were still early days, with plenty of time for things to change.

The arrival of the new dolphins certainly boosted the training of Duchess and Herb'e, who seemed eager to show off in front of their fresh audience. In fact, despite the horrors of the transport, things seemed to be going incredibly well. Nevertheless, I couldn't shake the feeling that this was the calm before the storm – although nothing could have prepared me for the chaos to come… chaos only days away.

❦ 43 ❧

Four days had passed and all the dolphins seemed to be progressing nicely, except Bubbles. I'd already expressed concerns about her, and these were beginning to look well-founded.

Gerry called Philip at City Zoo, who immediately set off for North Liston. He needed to examine Bubbles urgently, which would mean catching her and removing her from the water. A catch was a two-man job, so Gerry would need a partner, and, since I was the pool's strongest swimmer, I was his obvious choice.

I'd had limited experience of catching dolphins when we'd removed Bobby from the pool, but Bubbles would be my first proper catch, the first time I'd actually have to wrestle and subdue a dolphin in the water.

Gerry explained the technique, which was always the same, be it in a pool or in the wild. The main (or head) catch was the first manoeuvre, the idea being to grab the dolphin's pectoral flippers, roll behind its neck and take the strain as it fought to escape. During this short time – approximately eight seconds – the dolphin would thrash its head about and, more likely than not, try to bite its way free.

Eight or so seconds locked behind the head of a panicking dolphin would seem like an eternity, which is why it was so important for the secondary (or tail) catch to be quick and decisive. Anchoring the tail fluke would dead weight the dolphin's momentum, stopping it from using its flank, the strongest part of its body.

If the dolphin succeeded in throwing off the lead catcher, the unfortunate tail catcher would get a good hammering, so it was important that both catchers were in sync. A mistake by either one would directly impact on the wellbeing of the other.

"When you do something like this, you need to be fast. You mustn't give the dolphin time to think," Gerry told me. "The mantra is *Don't think; just do*."

Don't think; just do. His very words filled me with an eager excitement. I could feel my heart racing like a rodeo star waiting in the chute – I was ready for it.

But, judging from the strained look on his face, Gerry was not. It had taken him over two days to recover physically from the transport, but it would take him a good deal longer to recover mentally – and having Scouse there as a daily reminder didn't help. There had been no respite for him, yet now he was to be thrown into another physically and mentally exhausting battle.

It was several hours later when Philip finally arrived. One look at Bubbles and he roared into action. "Right, we'll have her out," he barked, "I need to look at her."

A harness – the same harness that had transported her during her journey from the States – was laid on the tiles beside her pen, along with the foam mattress.

"I'll take the head, and you take the tail," Gerry told me, then quietly slipped into the water.

I remained on the poolside, giving him as much space as possible to herd Bubbles into a spot where she would be vulnerable. I watched closely as he dissected the catch area, my senses at a high. Choosing the right moment was vital. I couldn't afford to get it wrong.

Suddenly, Gerry's body arched and the water exploded into a frothing cauldron: he'd made the catch and Bubbles had started to fight.

Instantly, I was in the pool and anchored around her tail. This should have slowed her, but she fought with incredible strength and determination, head flailing and jaws snapping. Then, with one energetic jerk of her powerful neck, she catapulted Gerry into the air like a rag doll.

I held on fast, my arms locked behind her tail, my head reeling and the breath whipping from my lungs as she beat me from side to side.

Can't let go… got to hold on!

The strength began seeping from my body, my arms turning numb – then, suddenly, the assault ceased, and I knew that Gerry had retaken her head.

Slowly, we swam her into the side and wrapped the harness around her exhausted body. The poolside trainers hauled her from the water and onto the foam mattress, pinning her down as she resumed the battle. Seconds later, Gerry and I joined them, helping to restrain her.

As Philip checked her over, he commented that she appeared to be perfectly healthy. She was certainly strong, as both Gerry and I could testify, so why wouldn't she eat? Philip injected her with a hypodermic of multivitamins and took a blood sample from her tail fluke – normal procedure following any examination – then, after another brief check, told us to release her.

Once back in the water, Bubbles gave a single snort from her blowhole, then fell back to the old routine of swimming mindlessly round and round.

Philip hastily packed his bags, eager to deliver the blood sample to the testing facility. "We'll see what the blood reveals," he told us. "But whatever the result, if she's still not eating in two days' time, we force-feed."

Gerry nodded resignedly. We were both battered and bruised, and the prospect of another catch was something he didn't need. We retreated to the office to recover, leaving Matt and the others to put away the mattress and disinfect the poolside. Gerry looked pensive.

"What's a force-feed?" I quietly asked.

He slowly lifted his head to look at me. "A trainer's worst nightmare, that's what."

I tried to reassure him that we hadn't reached that stage yet; but as the excitement of my first manual catch quickly dissipated, my reassurances were as much for my benefit as they were for his. All the foreboding I had felt around Bubbles was justified. Deep down, I knew it was just a matter of time: and when the time came, I'd be on the front line.

I'd never actually seen a force-feed, but I had a vivid imagination – and I imagined it would be horrific.

❦ 44 ❧

Next day, every inch of my body ached; I felt like I'd done five rounds with Sonny Liston. But, more worryingly, my right arm had swelled like a balloon and turned blue.

I telephoned my local GP and, after explaining to the receptionist what had happened, was able to get an appointment within the hour. The fact that the injury had been caused by a dolphin undoubtedly catapulted me to the head of the queue. It also gave the excited receptionist a chance to relate my tale to everyone passing through the surgery doors, glorifying my injuries and casting doubt on my chances of survival as she did so. So much for patient confidentiality. Soon, everyone in the village would know how I'd almost died (and still might) due to being attacked by a vicious dolphin. Now, North Liston residents had something else to talk about other than the house robberies still plaguing their village.

The doctor's verdict was somewhat less dramatic, but equally interesting. "Nothing to worry about, Mr Capello – no apparent damage. You appear to have an ability to lock your arm: in all probability, you couldn't have released the dolphin even if you'd wanted to. However, the arm lock has put great stress on your muscles, and this has caused them to swell. Everything should be back to normal within the next four to five hours."

It seemed I had a secret weapon – an almost bionic arm – something I feared I'd have to use on an increasingly regular basis.

By the time I arrived back at the pool, it was mid-morning. I'd expected to find Gerry lying on a training platform as usual, but instead he was standing on the poolside, shouting instructions to the other handlers. He moved stiffly, obviously in great discomfort, and lifted his tee shirt to reveal a black and blue torso. "I think I've bruised my ribs," he groaned.

"Has she eaten anything yet?" I asked.

Gerry shook his head gloomily. "No – and if she doesn't eat within the next two days, we're gonna have to do this all over again."

❦ 45 ❧

Due to all the problems, Duchess and Herb'e's progress had slowed considerably. In fact, it was only thanks to my reinstatement of night training that it hadn't taken a giant leap backwards. But a clever Management, clocking the advantages of night training, had decided that from now on all trainers should work nights as well as days – for no extra pay, of course.

A dark cloud had descended over the pool with the arrival of the second shipment, and spirits were as damp as the atmosphere. Then, next morning, Gerry made an announcement that gave everyone a much-needed lift.

"Exciting news, folks! Tomorrow, we're holding an official press conference. All the Company bigwigs will be here, along with reporters and photographers from all the national and daily newspapers. It'll be a huge event."

He went on to explain that Duchess and Herb'e would star, with me presenting and him supplying the show commentary. I was over the moon – my dream of fame was about to come true.

We scrubbed the pool until it gleamed, fuelled by the prospect of national coverage – and, what's more, this new development meant we had two extra days before having to face the unenviable task of a Bubbles force-feed.

Later that day, Rachel led two deliverymen into the pool room. They were carrying a large metal bathtub, which they placed beside Duchess and Herb'e's pen.

"What's that for?" I asked.

"I'm not sure," she replied. "They'll probably fill it with ice and stack it with drinks for the dignitaries."

"It's a bit close to the pen, isn't it? Won't it spook the dolphins?"

"No, they'll be all right." She flashed me a knowing smile, then made her way back to the kitchen.

I resumed work, never giving it a second thought, instead concentrating all my efforts on Duchess and Herb'e. Tomorrow was their big day, and they had to be at their best.

Later that evening, we tried to coax Bubbles to eat, but she still showed no interest. Eventually, we decided to shut up shop for the night and try again next morning. But, before leaving, we made sure to cage Smelly and Worse – the last thing we needed was them messing up the place.

Next day, we dressed to impress, turning out in our finest gear. The girls lined the corridors, meeting and greeting our guests, and Gerry escorted a proud Rogers, whose job it was to outline the Company's aims to the press. The pool room was heaving with beautiful and influential people, when I suddenly noticed that the most glamorous of all was conspicuous by her absence. Where was Rachel?

I didn't ruminate on the mystery for long: my big chance was only minutes away, and my excitement was building. I could almost visualise the newspaper story – *David and his Dolphins!* – along with a large photograph of me directing Duchess and Herb'e as they performed something sensational. This was it: my first step on the ladder to fame and fortune.

Gerry gave me the nod, then took the microphone, made the customary introductions and signalled the start of the show.

"Come on, you two, don't let me down! Let's show them!"

Both dolphins performed beautifully, seemingly sensing the crowd's anticipation. Together, we gave our best performance to date, wooing photographers and bosses alike.

"This will be the first of many shows, people – our first taste of stardom."

At the end of the performance, we invited questions – but not before shepherding everyone to the far side of the pool away from

Duchess and Herb'e's pen: this was their first experience of a large audience, and we didn't want to overexcite them.

Gerry and I were standing shoulder to shoulder, proudly courting the attentions of the press and relishing our moment in the spotlight, when, suddenly, a stunning redhead strolled nonchalantly into the crowded pool room. She stood by the door… wearing nothing but a short, white towel.

"Hello, boys, everything okay?"

The room fell silent as everyone stared, open-mouthed.

Rachel drifted past without uttering another word, heading towards the bathtub by Duchess and Herb'e's pen – a bathtub now miraculously filled with fluffy white bubbles. She turned her head towards the stunned crowd, tossed back her flame-red hair and gave the photographers a come-on wink. Then, slowly, she let the towel slip.

What happened next could only be likened to a stampede: photographers charged headlong in the direction of the bathtub, knocking one another aside in the rush to snap that all-important photo before she disappeared into the sea of bubbles.

Gerry and I stood alone and dazed, reporters, photographers and bosses alike gone, leaving us to watch bewilderedly as they clamoured around the bathtub like a pack of hungry lions.

Rachel had stolen our thunder, and we had no chance of stealing it back. I looked woefully at Gerry. "Now we know what happened to Rachel."

He chuckled softly, shaking his head. "Never trust a woman, David – especially not a beautiful one."

For just how long Rachel had planned this caper, I could only guess; but I had to admire her style as she expertly manipulated a frenzied press.

"Well, I guess that's the end of our interview, because I can't see that lot coming back." Gerry was right, of course; we had both been quickly despatched into the second division.

Next day, the press reports on the training pool had suddenly been elevated to page three status, with a huge photograph of a naked girl in a bubble bath, alongside a small photo insert of a dolphin's head – Duchess' head, to be precise.

As for Herb'e, Gerry and me, we were nowhere to be seen.

❦ 46 ❧

Next morning, Rachel behaved as if nothing had happened, and no one mentioned her publicity stunt. In fact, the only reference to the previous day's media circus was during the morning team talk when Gerry read out a message from Management congratulating the staff.

Rachel did, however, inform us that her temporary contract with the Company was almost at an end, and that she would be gone within the week. This glamorous and clever redhead had not only gone out with a bang, but had timed it perfectly, because if Bubbles refused to eat today, the force-feeds would begin, and life would get very unpleasant.

Throughout the morning, the trainers worked their dolphins half-heartedly, repeatedly glancing at Pen Number Four: Bubbles' pen. Their apprehension was justified: Bubbles continued to ignore the fish, and we abandoned our final attempt to feed her after little more than fifteen minutes.

A concerned Gerry disappeared into the office. Everyone knew why. He was arranging for Philip to attend the pool and lead the first force-feed.

Training drifted into the afternoon as we all nervously awaited the vet's arrival. We removed extra fish from the freezers in preparation – then Gerry called me into the office.

"Okay, David, this is what will happen."

I listened intently as Gerry explained the catch and force-feed procedure. As before, Gerry would make the main head catch and I would take the tail. We would place Bubbles on the foam mattress, where Matt and the others would hold her down. Two gags would be employed. These would take the shape of two torn and disinfected towels, one wrapped tightly around the bottom jaw and held by Gerry, and the second wrapped around the upper jaw and held by me.

Gerry would then perform the force-feed, his task being to push the fish so far down Bubbles' throat that she would have no choice but to swallow. Not until she had swallowed four fish would we allow her to close her mouth and take a minute's rest; then we would begin again, repeating the entire procedure until Philip deemed that she had consumed sufficient food. Of course, if future feeds were required, Philip wouldn't be here, so the weighty responsibility of deciding when and how much would fall to Gerry.

After he had finished telling me this, we remained in the office, awaiting Philip in silence. The procedure sounded horrific, and neither of us had recovered physically from our last encounter with Bubbles. Gerry, in particular, was still moving gingerly due to his bruised torso. This would indeed be a traumatic test of character for everyone working at the pool; a test we hoped we wouldn't have to repeat.

❦ 47 ❧

We are still sitting in the darkened office, silently preparing ourselves for the approaching ordeal, when a hurried Philip bursts into the lobby. "Okay, lads… you ready?"

Gerry nods and we follow the vet into the pool room.

The harness and foam mattress are already in place, alongside a bucketful of fish. Gerry, still bruised and aching from his last encounter, hobbles to his position on the other side of the pool.

As I clear my face mask, I notice that Bubbles, as if sensing the imminent threat, has suddenly ceased her laboured swimming to bob like a float in the water.

Gerry, preparing to submerge, lowers himself onto the tiles and dangles his legs into the pool.

Big mistake. Realising his intention, Bubbles suddenly goes rigid. Then, she curves her body, raising her tail to hold it ominously above the water line, and launches into an aggressive bout of head nodding. This is her final warning: get in, and I attack.

Gerry's eyes flick to mine, filled with apprehension.

Don't think; just do! The words flash into my mind. Feed her anger, Gerry, feed her anger!

He slides into the water hesitantly but, instead of dissecting the catch area, begins to swim nervously around the edges of the pen. I sense his fear. And if I can sense it… so can she.

His anxiety boosts Bubbles' confidence. Like a hunter stalking her prey, she turns her head to follow him; then, without warning, she smashes her powerful tail into the water and propels herself towards him.

Instead of trying to dodge her, Gerry remains motionless, watching her as if mesmerised. She rams him in the groin, smashing him into the pool wall. Panicking handlers scramble to drag him out of the water before she has time to make a second sortie.

Thankfully, Gerry has managed to avoid serious injury by using his hands to shield himself, but he is nonetheless bruised, confused and in no fit state to make a second attempt at the catch.

Worse still, his defeat has left a more confident and dangerous dolphin in the pool. Bubbles was always going to fight, but now that she has a victory under her belt, she will fight even harder.

Philip assesses the situation anxiously. "This animal must be fed. David, do you think you can make this catch?"

I know I can. My entire body is crying out to make this catch, but I still need a secondary catcher. "Matt, are you up for this?"

Matt nods, so I quickly don my mask and snorkel.

I grow high, drinking in Bubbles' anger and focussing it back at her. I am determined. Bubbles won't be calling the shots. I will.

Don't think; just do!

Within seconds, I have entered the water and dissected the catch area, and Bubbles is preparing *not* to attack, but to defend. She senses my power, my commitment. She is no longer the cocky champion, but a frightened dolphin seeking an escape.

With nowhere to go, she poises to ram; but I channel my aggression towards her, and suddenly she turns in panic.

I see my chance: my arms are around her head and I am rolling my body onto the back of her neck. The struggle is soon over as Matt quickly anchors her tail; and within minutes she is on the poolside, attended by Philip and a battered Gerry. A few minutes to calm her down before the awful task of force-feeding begins.

We can only hope that this horrendous experience will shock Bubbles into eating normally, otherwise this nightmare scenario could become a daily routine.

❦ 48 ❧

Later that evening, I proudly replayed the catch in my mind, trying to identify what I'd learned. For the foreseeable future, Gerry wouldn't be fit enough to attempt any more catches, so it would be down to me, and I had to make sure that I didn't get hurt. This was my chance to cement my position at the top of the tree.

The most important lesson I'd learned was that you couldn't afford to hesitate or give the dolphin time to think. If you saw an opening, then you took it. Speed and decisiveness were vital to avoid risk of serious injury.

Gerry had left the pool directly after the force-feed, physically unable to cope with the night training session. Of more concern, however, was his mental state: it was his own fault that he'd been injured, and he knew it. He'd paid the price for hesitating, and next time he might not be so lucky. Over the coming days, he'd have a lot of soul-searching to do.

I respected Gerry more than anyone else I knew, but I now realised that even he was human. There were chinks in his armour, and his air of invulnerability was now gone forever.

He was just a man – a special man – but, nonetheless, a man.

<h1 style="text-align: center;">❦ 49 ❧</h1>

Next morning, Bubbles again dashed all our hopes by refusing her feed. This meant we'd have to carry out another force-feed under Philip's supervision. As expected, I took on the mantle of main catcher, assisted by Matt and a number of other handlers. To add to our problems, Rachel leaving meant we were one man down at a time when we could least afford it.

Gerry commented that all dolphin feeds were dropping noticeably. When they'd first arrived, the new batch were eating nine to ten pounds of herring a day; this had now dropped to five. Duchess and Herb'e's feeds had also fallen, but only slightly. Obviously, Bubbles was disturbing both humans and non-humans alike. Only Scouse, the blind dolphin, remained unaffected.

Another worry, I still hadn't experienced that special *connection* with Duchess again, but this may have been because the situation around Bubbles was leaving me anxious and exhausted.

There were also fresh worries about Stumpy, the dolphin with the flowery breath. He was in the pen directly next to Bubbles, and she seemed to be affecting him worst of all.

The pressure was intense: force-feed followed force-feed, and the days began to blur together.

❦ 50 ❧

Ten horrendous days into the force-feeding, Philip announced that he wanted to take us out to show his appreciation for all our hard work. It was Friday night and he'd booked each of us a three-course meal and a room at the Palace Hotel, a top-notch establishment standing by the side of the main motorway. Only Matt was not invited – somebody had to stay behind to babysit Bubbles, and he had drawn the short straw.

That evening, a still sore Gerry gingerly eased himself into Philip's luxury car, whilst I climbed into the pool's clapped-out old Mini. On arrival at the hotel, we put the cars to bed and prepared for our well-deserved treat – the first night in ages when we could all just relax and forget about work.

The festivities continued into the small hours, Philip's guests one-by-one drifting off to their rooms until only the die-hards remained – Gerry, Philip and me.

Oh, this is the life, I thought, as I melted into a plush leather armchair, three sheets to the wind and puffing on a big cigar with not a care in the world. Fantastic – I'd almost forgotten how much I enjoyed times like these. For the first time in weeks, my body didn't ache, no doubt due to all the beer I'd consumed – and I wasn't finished yet, no sir!

Then, vaguely, I became aware of a telephone ringing in the distance, followed by the concerned voice of the hotel receptionist. I felt my arm being briskly shaken and opened my eyes to see the three faces of Gerry. I tried to readjust my vision, but there was little improvement.

"God, you look rough, Gerry."

"Never mind me, we've got to go."

"Go where?" I muttered stupidly, hoping and praying that this was just a bad dream.

"There's a problem at the pool – it's Bubbles."

"Oh no, please tell me you're joking."

"No joke. I don't like this any more than you do, but we have to leave; we have to leave now."

As I heaved myself from the blissful comfort of the chair, all my aches and pains came flooding back with a vengeance. The three of us staggered across the deserted restaurant and into the lobby in search of the exit. With one short telephone call, Matt had succeeded in ruining the night.

"What's wrong with Bubbles?" I asked.

"She's floating funny," Gerry replied.

"Floating funny? What's that supposed to mean?"

Gerry shrugged his shoulders.

This smelled like the work of a disgruntled Matt exacting revenge for having been left behind. Nevertheless, we had to respond.

For the second time that night, Gerry and Philip climbed into the white Citroen. Moments later, it sped from the car park, straight across the motorway's central reservation and off towards North Liston.

I clambered into the battered Mini, then struggled to follow the same route. Unbeknown to me, lurking in the shadows of the motorway bridge was a police car, its occupants watching us in total disbelief. I bumped the Mini unceremoniously across the central reservation, then chugged it along the carriageway, concentrating hard on the road ahead, completely oblivious to the pursuing traffic cops.

I could hear the wail of a police siren, but didn't know where it was coming from. Then, to my horror, I saw the cascading blue and red lights clashing and merging in my rear view mirror.

"Oh, no... nooo, I don't believe it!"

For one insane moment, I actually considered taking flight; then, remembering that the Mini couldn't do more than fifty miles per hour, I begrudgingly pulled onto the emergency hard shoulder instead.

As the Mini shuddered to a halt, I frantically tried to concoct an excuse. Think, David, think! Then, a flash of inspiration – if I got out of my car and walked calmly towards their vehicle, the officers might not realise how drunk I was… Some hope, I could hardly stand, let alone walk! Still, anything was worth a try.

My plan immediately went awry as I fell out of the open door and bounced like a pinball against the rear wing of the Mini. This didn't look good – I knew that instinctively – besides, the two officers looked furious, scowling at me with narrowed eyes and tight lips. I decided that my only course of action was to plead with them instead, but, as I opened my mouth to speak, I suddenly and without warning got a violent attack of the hiccoughs.

The situation was growing worse by the minute.

"You've just driven over the central reservation," one officer growled, "and, what's more, you're pissed."

"Yes, I know, and I'm sorry, I'm really sorry." Pointless trying to deny it. "I've had a few, I admit it, but it's not my fault. I'm from North Liston dolphin training pool, and I've just received an emergency call. It's vital that I get back quickly. Look, if you don't believe me, please get in touch with North Liston police and ask them to verify my story. Then, if you're going to arrest me, could you please do it later, because I must get to the pool? It may be a matter of life or death."

Their faces grew sterner. "What do you take us for – a couple of morons?"

"Please just talk to North Liston police, that's all I ask."

Whilst one of the officers radioed back to the station, I struggled to convince the other of my predicament. My only hope now rested with the police at North Liston. Would they corroborate my story? And, if they did, would these two officers show mercy?

"We've checked your story," the officer told me, "and, amazingly, it holds up. So, for now, we're happy to escort you off the motorway and back to the pool. However, this isn't the end of the matter."

I couldn't believe it: the two officers who would shortly be booking me for being drunk in charge were now actually going to escort me back to the pool, demonstrating once again the amazing effect the word *dolphin* had on the people in this area.

The police car duly shepherded me off the motorway and along the dark, winding roads back to North Liston. By the time we arrived, two panda cars were already parked in front of the pool's main steps.

"God, now everyone's involved!"

The two officers followed me through the corridors into the pool room, where I approached Gerry, leaving them to make conversation with the local police. Gerry was still in an alcoholic daze; but Philip immediately recognised my problem. Clearly, so did a sheepish Matt, as he did his best to sink into the background.

"Is Bubbles okay?" I asked.

Philip gave Matt an angry glare and spoke just loudly enough for him to hear. "No change in her condition." Then, he ushered me into the office. "David, losing your licence would be a disaster; we have to get the boys in blue off your back, so we need to make them think that this is a real emergency. We need to make a big show of catching Bubbles and giving her an injection – only multivitamins, but it should fool them. Is that okay by you?"

"I don't see that I have any other option – if something doesn't happen, I'm going to be banged up."

Philip nodded. "Right, let's get it done."

Turning angrily to Matt, I growled, "Get your trunks on – we've a catch to make!" It was the last thing we needed, the last thing poor Bubbles needed, but we literally had no choice.

Thankfully, the catch went well, the high alcohol levels in my blood merely hardening my resolve. Once Bubbles was on the poolside, Philip injected her with multivitamins, then told us to release her.

Our police audience watched with consternation. "Will she be okay?"

"Only time will tell – but, thanks to you, she at least stands a chance. I know I was out of order, but now you'll understand why I acted as I did."

Apparently satisfied, they gave me a verbal warning, wished us luck, then left.

I breathed a sigh of relief: I'd got away with it – no thanks to Matt. His malicious act had backfired: all he'd done was elevate himself to the top of the expendable list.

From now on, everything he did would be scrutinised and, no matter how carefully he trod, he was on his way out – and, in my book, the sooner the better.

❦ 51 ❧

Time went on and there was still no end to the force-feeds. Bubbles' weight loss was now showing markedly, that deep, tell-tale dip behind her head plain for all to see. Even more worryingly, all trainers reported that feeds were still dropping. Only Scouse remained immune.

Duchess and Herb'e's training was barely progressing as they became more and more preoccupied with events around Bubbles. But more disturbing was the feeling I was getting from Duchess: she was drifting away from me, and I was powerless to stop her.

On a lighter note, the local police invited us for a tour of North Liston Police Station as a thank you for allowing their families to visit the dolphins. We felt obliged to accept, especially after the way they'd supported us during my drunk-driving adventure. So, after setting up the night training sessions, four of us headed down to the local nick for our PR special: me, Gerry, Sally and – surprise, surprise – Matt. Gerry had obviously decided to give him the benefit of the doubt.

The police station housed many smiling faces, which I recognised either as having helped with Bobby's catch or having simply dropped by with their families. Sally being in our company was an added bonus, as she attracted a lovesick band of police officers, all eager to help. Everything seemed to be going nicely, when – for some reason that only he would understand – Matt suddenly grabbed a fire extinguisher from the wall and activated it.

"Let's liven things up a bit! Yeah, let's have a bit of fun!"

We stared in horror as Matt leapt about, spraying water in all directions and shrieking with laughter. "Come on, who wants a good dousing?"

The sergeant giving the tour wrestled the extinguisher from him and ran outside with it, leaving the rest of us stunned and standing in a vast pool of water.

"What's wrong with you? It's only a bit of fun."

Gerry, face scarlet, began apologising profusely for 'the boy's high spirits', but struggled to make himself heard above Matt's persistent, noisy braying. "Come on, you miserable lot, it's a laugh, for God's sake – just a laugh!"

His behaviour brought our tour to an abrupt end, and embarrassment turned to silent anger as we were escorted from the premises.

Matt had tarnished our reputation and irreparably damaged our relationship with the local police; yet, even then, he seemed wholly unaware of the thin red line he was walking.

It wouldn't be long before he realised that he'd just stepped over it.

❧ 52 ❧

As usual, the day started with the morning team talk. Trainers reported on the progress of their dolphins, and the all-important logbooks were reviewed. They didn't make good reading. Feeds were still well down in all pens, and the training of the new dolphins was well behind schedule. Even basic retrieval tricks were causing problems. Bottom of the class was Stumpy, one of Matt's dolphins: his other, Bubbles, still hadn't eaten of her own free will.

I was concerned about Duchess: she wasn't sick, but something was wrong, something I couldn't put my finger on. The bright light she used to radiate seemed to have gone out, and she was beginning to affect Herb'e.

The problems were endemic. Even the night training sessions weren't bearing fruit, and you didn't have to be a brain surgeon to know why: Bubbles. This was all down to her, and things wouldn't improve until she ate.

Besides all this, Sally and the other girls were expressing unease about working at night, reporting strange noises coming from the old girls' changing rooms up in the bell tower. They also complained of a feeling of being watched. Understandable – the pool did take on an eerie quality after nightfall.

Three days had passed and no mention made about Matt's behaviour. However, I knew Philip would be due in later to supervise Bubbles' daily force-feed, and if Gerry had reported Matt to Head Office, Philip would no doubt have something to say.

After the team talk, we all began training as usual. Once again, Duchess and Herb'e showed little interest in work, but both wanted petting – which was unusual because, whereas Duchess had always enjoyed a cuddle, this was the first time I'd experienced such behaviour from Herb'e. He demanded affection, forcibly pushing Duchess out of the way. Had he finally accepted me, or was he just taking advantage of an off-colour Duchess? Whatever, I was grateful for the chance to bond with him at last. Perhaps this would be a new start for us both.

"Come on, Herb'e, give Duch a chance – she can't get near!"

Duchess soon tired of Herb'e's boisterous behaviour and swam to the corner of the pen, sulking. This wasn't like her, and only reinforced my belief that all was not well. I decided to speak to Philip about it.

Once the morning sessions were over, the dreaded task of preparing for yet another force-feed began. Philip arrived later than usual, but instead of coming straight into the pool room, he disappeared into the office. A few minutes later, he summoned Matt.

When Philip eventually joined us in the pool room, Matt was conspicuous by his absence. Neither Gerry nor I asked where he was, but just got on with our work.

The force-feed took longer than usual because Bubbles kept vomiting. Finally, we had no choice but to return her to the water. If this carried on, it wouldn't be long before the unthinkable happened: two force-feeds in one day.

The worried faces of Gerry and Philip starkly mirrored the deteriorating situation – and I was about to add to their anxieties. "Philip, I have a bad feeling about Duchess. She's not eating properly and I fear she's going the same way as the others."

Philip gave a deep sigh and shook his head. "Okay, David, keep me informed." He grabbed his case and hurriedly headed for the door. "Oh, almost forgot, you'll be getting a new trainee presenter within the next few days, because Matt has been dismissed with immediate effect. So, look after the new boy."

I was gobsmacked: it seemed that Gerry had reported him after all. So, Matt was gone – just like that – his dismissal announced with no explanation, no hint of regret, but just a few clinically uncaring words.

Yet another reflection of the harsh world I'd entered into, where everyone and everything was expendable.

I glanced questioningly at Gerry, who snapped, "It's been coming for a while. If anyone deserved it, he did!"

So, I accepted the news and never gave Matt another thought. I was too preoccupied with other things – particularly the horrible prospect of a second force-feed.

By the end of the day, Gerry and I were again sitting in the office, silent and exhausted. Suddenly, Gerry lifted his head from his hands and said, "Do you fancy a drink later?"

I raised my eyebrows in surprise, then nodded. In all the time I'd known him, Gerry and I had never had a drink together, except, of course, on that ill-fated Company night out. His sudden urge for an alcohol comforter reflected his feelings of desperation – feelings that I shared.

An air of hopelessness hung over the pool, and my dream job was fast deteriorating into a nightmare. This couldn't go on much longer.

Something had to give.

❧ 53 ❧

As I walked to my digs, I agonised over what to say to Matt. He'd be feeling pretty low and, even though I didn't like him, I couldn't help feeling sorry for him.

I opened the back door to find Ida preparing food and Jim sitting at the dining table, head hidden behind a wall of newspaper.

"Matt got sacked," he grunted.

"Yeah, I know. Where is he?"

"Gone."

"Gone? That was quick."

Jim lowered his newspaper, his expression steely. "Aye, the police took him and put him on the next train back to the city."

"The police? What have they got to do with it?" I asked, open-mouthed. Yes, Matt had been sacked, but what could he have possibly done to warrant a police escort from the village? I waited for an explanation, but Jim, seeking sanctuary behind his ruffled tabloid, said nothing more. Ida, too, remained silent, her gaze fixed firmly on her pans.

The suspense was torturous. "Why did the police come?"

"The thievin'! The house robberies!" Jim growled. "Something to do with them, although no one's saying owt."

I gasped. I couldn't believe it: could Matt somehow be connected to the spate of robberies plaguing the village?

"So, what's happened – have they charged him?" I asked.

Jim shrugged his shoulders, then repeated his last statement. "No one's saying owt."

I could guess why. If Matt had been involved with the robberies, then it would not be safe for him to remain in North Liston. This close-knit community — a place where people called a spade a shovel — would not accept trouble from outsiders, and any transgressors could expect particularly harsh treatment.

"I still can't believe it — if what you say is true, he's been stealing since day one."

"Aye, it looks that way."

As I laboured to prise more information out of Jim, I couldn't help but wonder how much damage this one person had done to local goodwill. Only time would tell.

But, suddenly, it all made sense: Matt's late-night disappearances, his problem getting to work on time. The pieces fell into place like some kind of giant jigsaw puzzle.

But now he was gone — and good riddance!

❦ 54 ❧

That evening, fine rain was falling, creating a damp mist that clung to faces and blurred streetlights. As I headed to the pub, Ida's latest masterpiece rumbled around my tummy. But it was the bizarre happenings of the day that I found hard to digest. I'd been so wrapped up in my dolphins that it had never occurred to me that Matt could be responsible for the robberies. How could I have been so blind?

The rainfall suddenly became heavier, and I hurried through the doors of the working men's club. Entering the vault, I immediately saw Gerry sitting alone in a corner. He was fidgeting uneasily with a beer mat, and I couldn't help but compare him to Rob: the extrovert who had leaned confidently on the bar, recounting tales and wallowing in the admiration of the locals. How different these two men were.

Within minutes, I had joined him, pint in hand. As always, we talked only about the dolphins and the problems we faced at work. Bubbles was the number one topic, and I couldn't resist asking a question that had niggled at me for some time.

"Why did you bring Bubbles back, Gerry?"

He thought for a while before answering. "I don't know; it seemed the right thing to do." He took a sip of beer. "Of all the dolphins I'd ever transported, Bubbles was the toughest to catch. It took six men to subdue her in the water and another four to get her into the harness. She was still fighting on the boat, and she didn't stop fighting until they put her in the pen. She was magnificent, and I was convinced I'd found a real prize." He shook his head. "But then she wouldn't eat, and it

136

was too late to do anything about it."

"Why?"

"Because I'd already made a commitment to buy her." He sighed. "I hoped she'd get over it." A cynical laugh. "How wrong can you be?"

He looked as if he was about to burst into tears. "My entire trip to the States was a disaster. The transport was a nightmare from the start, what with Scouse thrashing around and me not being able to reach him. But, even worse, when the plane took off and the pressure in the cargo hold changed, all the dolphins began to give off a high-pitched whistle, as if they were screaming. It was horrible." His face was etched with anguish.

"And Bubbles – how did she transport?"

Gerry answered quietly. "She never made a sound, never moved. Not once. Just hung in the harness like something dead."

"It sounds to me like she went into shock and never recovered," I commented. "Her mind must have snapped… completely closed down. Poor Bubbles, now I know why she wasn't giving off any vibes when I first saw her."

Gerry didn't reply, but just stared into a half-empty glass. Then, abruptly, he said, "And now, to add to our troubles, we've got the 'things that go bump in the night' routine with the girls. They're freaked out and refusing point blank to work the night shift."

"Well I haven't seen or heard anything," I replied.

"No, neither have I, but they're insistent, and I can't talk them round. They're frightened, really frightened, so it looks like it's down to you and me. We're gonna have to start work later in the mornings and continue later into the evenings. There's no other way to get back on schedule."

I listened in depressed silence. If I started arriving later, someone else would begin working Duchess and Herb'e. I couldn't allow that so, like it or not, my working day had just been extended – the last thing I needed.

Dejectedly, I hauled myself to my feet. "I think you and me need another couple of pints."

❦ 55 ❧

The morning team talk began with the introduction of Matt's replacement, Vance Martin. Vance was strikingly tall, at least six-foot three, with a leanness that emphasised his height. With his long, black, wavy hair, bushy sideburns and thick moustache, he looked like he'd just flown in from Woodstock.

Next on the agenda was the girls' refusal to work nights because of the so-called weird goings-on. This led to much debate, but eventually we reached a compromise where they agreed to start work a couple of hours earlier each morning, allowing them to be out of the pool by nightfall. However, they'd unknowingly inherited the delightful task of cleaning up after Smelly and Worse. Ha – that would wake them up!

Finally, we discussed the continuing decline in training, a situation that wouldn't improve unless Bubbles rallied, which – in view of what Gerry had told me the previous night – was highly unlikely.

After the meeting, I hurried back to the platform, eager to see if Duchess seemed any brighter. But even though both dolphins appeared to enjoy the training session, Herb'e ate heartily whilst Duchess ate nothing.

"What is it, Duch, what's wrong? If you don't eat, you're gonna get sick."

Duchess toyed with her fish, holding it between her teeth for a few moments before letting it fall to the pool floor. This worry was not going away. Still, I was in a better position than the other workers were in, especially the new boy, Vance, who faced the daunting prospect of taking over Stumpy and Bubbles. Talk about baptism by fire – rather him than me.

❧ 56 ❧

Poor Stumpy's progress was virtually non-existent. This likeable but weak little dolphin found it hard to cope with the rigours of training.

Baby Dai, on the other hand, was a keen student and no doubt top of the class. But, even more surprisingly, he was generous and caring, and took great pains to help his disadvantaged partner. Blind and unable to see hand signals and props, Scouse should have been impossible to train, but the big-hearted infant coached him through the trick list. Baby Dai was the one jewel in a nightmare second shipment.

The day progressed, and I spent much of it in my usual belly-down position on the platform, relentlessly pushing on with Duchess and Herb'e's training. It was strange but, the more I worked them, the less I seemed to need verbal communication. Virtually all our sessions were conducted in silence, yet our mind conversations rivalled those of three pals in a bar – animated and noisy.

My psyche had almost nonchalantly moved up a gear. I was now training on a new level – a different plane – yet that special, overwhelming *connection*, the one that left me feeling sick and weak, was still missing. What I was experiencing now was totally different: it was as if Duchess had scanned my mind, drawing me not only closer to her, but closer to Herb'e as well.

Scholars believe that the human brain has many rooms, the vast majority hidden behind closed doors and unused; yet I fully believed that Duchess held the keys to mine.

Despite the problems, our psychic link was getting stronger.

❦ 57 ❧

Last session of the day and, as I hung over the pool, I felt a sudden give in the training platform. The mind conversations stopped abruptly as I lay frozen, staring at Duchess and Herb'e – then, the sound of splintering wood, and both dolphins were gone.

They watched wide-eyed from the corner of the pen as I helplessly awaited my fate. A final crack, then the platform broke, depositing me head first into the water, fish bucket following closely behind.

I floundered like an injured duck, struggling to swim against the weight of my water-filled wellies. As I hauled myself dripping onto the tiles, I met a barrage of laughter. In the meantime, my two concerned charges busily gobbled up the spoils floating from the fish bucket.

"Well, that's one way of getting Duchess to eat!"

"You couple of turncoats! Talk about I'm all right, Jack!"

Grinning faces everywhere – so good to see. It had been a long time since we'd had something to smile about. Of course, this was all Ida's fault, and I decided there and then to ask for smaller portions.

Then I remembered last night's banquet and thought again.

Maybe not.

❦ 58 ❧

That evening, I waddled from my digs to the pool, my discussion with
Ida about the size of my meals put on permanent hold.

Tonight would be a new challenge: I no longer had a training
platform, so would have to conduct the session from the poolside,
Duchess to my right, Herb'e to my left. If successful, all future training
would be done this way.

By the time I arrived, Gerry was already hard at work.

I dropped the steel fish bucket onto the poolside with a noisy clunk.
The response was immediate: both Duchess and Herb'e swam towards
me.

"Hello, people, ready for something new?"

Moments later, they were working from the side for the very first
time.

Gerry took a break from training to view this milestone occasion.
"You're on your way," he shouted, relief clear in his voice. "At last,
we have a team of dolphins capable of opening a show."

Yes – and I was now in a position to shape my charges into my
dream team, *The Perfect Pair.*

After a gratifying training session, Gerry and I sat by the pool, our
banter light-hearted, almost relaxed. Then, from the corner of my eye,
I suddenly spied a small rubber training ring hovering about three feet
in the air.

What the...? I had to be imagining things!

I watched in disbelief, struggling to maintain a normal conversation.

Then, without warning, the ring shot across the pool and into the water as if someone had physically thrown it.

I didn't react. This couldn't be happening... could it? I'd been saying something to Gerry... what was it... ah yes!

"Hold on a minute!" Gerry suddenly leaned forward and placed a hand on my arm. "Did you just see that?"

We both stared at the ring, which by now had become the object of a game for Duchess and Herb'e.

"I saw it," I said quietly.

Gerry turned his puzzled gaze to mine. "Thank God, I thought I was going mad."

With those words, he confirmed what I had sought to dismiss.

We retired to the office, still baffled about what we'd just seen, still not quite believing.

"Better not tell the girls, or they'll resign," I warned.

"Look, we both saw it, and we can't *both* be crazy," Gerry reasoned.

"So, what do you suggest?"

"A ghost trap."

"Okay," I laughed, "so, what's the plan?"

"Before we leave tonight, we put a beach ball in Bubbles' pen. If it's not there in the morning, then we know that someone – or something – has moved it, because it certainly won't be down to her."

And since the only keys to the pool were held by Gerry, Sally and me, neither would it be due to any human activity.

We each agreed not to enter the pool building until morning, and to keep our experiment secret. We also had to arrive before Sally, so it would mean an early start.

My digs were only fifty yards away, so I had a good view of the pool from my bedroom window – a view I meant to exploit just in case Gerry planned on doing any midnight creeping. I literally slept with one ear cocked, and next morning ate my breakfast by the window to make sure he didn't arrive early. It wasn't that I didn't trust him – it was just that... well, I guess I didn't trust him.

When he did arrive, I raced out to meet him. Before going inside, we stood on the front steps, eyeing each other suspiciously, each swearing to the other that neither had entered the pool building overnight.

The doors to the pool room swung back to reveal Bubbles' pen – the pen where we'd left the beach ball. It was gone. A quick search and we found it floating with Duchess and Herb'e.

"How did it get there?" I asked. "That ball has jumped three pens."

We stared at each other. "Well, don't look at me!" Gerry complained.

"Well, it didn't get there on its own."

"Well, it wasn't down to me."

But there was more.

When we had left the pool room that previous night, all props had been neatly stowed against the walls. Now they were littered along the walkways as if someone had purposely hurled them about. A couple were actually floating in the water.

We viewed each other with suspicion.

If we hadn't moved them... who had?

❧ 59 ❧

Two weeks passed and no other strange occurrences took place. Both Gerry and I kept true to our vow of secrecy; nevertheless, we were acutely aware of the eerie atmosphere when training at night.

None of the dolphins seemed to be affected by the so-called hauntings, which made us wonder if our imaginations might not be getting the better of us. After all, we had been under tremendous pressure over the last month or so, especially with Bubbles. However, we had a job to do, so any further ghost hunting would have to be put on the back burner.

Haunting aside, I decided to give Vance a hand with Stumpy. It seemed like a good way to get to know him; after all, in the not too distant future, he would be accompanying me to Hendle, so the sooner we established a good working relationship, the better.

Stumpy had a beautiful temperament and was a great favourite with everybody; but his training was slow and ponderous. It wasn't that he didn't try – he did – but this little dolphin wasn't strong and obviously had serious health issues. Stumpy was ideal for Vance who, until a few weeks ago, had never even seen a dolphin, let alone worked with one. Poor Vance had been with us for only a few short weeks, yet all he'd experienced were the horrors of the force-feeds. What a way to start a new job.

We continued training until six o'clock, then it was back to Ida's for dinner, once again to be greeted by Jim's newspaper wall.

"Robberies seem to 'ave stopped," he grunted.

"Have they?" I answered furtively.

"Yeah, they 'ave. After *light-fingers* disappeared, everything went back to normal." Jim emitted a low growl, then continued battling with his broadsheet.

As I tucked into yet another of Ida's specials, I realised just how much I'd miss these two lovely people. My time at North Liston was drawing to a close: Duchess and Herb'e were successfully working from the sides, and Hendle dolphinarium was nearing completion. I reckoned I had two months at the most before I'd have to say goodbye.

Later, I returned to the pool for the night shift. After only a few minutes, I suddenly experienced an overpowering feeling of being watched. I gazed around nervously until my attention settled on the large hole that peered across the pool from high in the far wall. The hole had once held a huge clock – now long gone – and opened into the girls' old changing rooms up in the bell tower.

I struggled to focus on my work, acutely aware of its gaze and growing more and more unnerved. I'd never set foot in the bell tower before, and didn't particularly want to now, but this couldn't go on.

I made my way up the stone steps into the darkness. The changing room lights had long since blown, so the only illumination came from the pool room itself. Shining through the hole where the clock had once been, the broad but scant beam probed the darkness like a searchlight, yet failed to penetrate the deep shadows of the cubicles. The damp air here was noticeably colder than anywhere else in the building, forming a tenuous layer-mist as it met the warm air rising from below. The result looked horribly eerie, giving me second thoughts. I stood in the doorway, loath to enter. Do I or don't I?

Then, a door banged downstairs, shattering the uneasy silence. "What you doing up there?"

Gerry – thank God!

"Nothing, just looking," I called, running downstairs, perhaps a little too quickly.

Gerry laughed loudly. "Looking for ghosts, are we?"

I didn't reply but gave him a sheepish smile and returned to the pool room.

❧ 60 ❧

We were about an hour into training when doors suddenly started banging throughout the building.

"What the hell's that?"

Gerry didn't answer, but just stood there, looking perplexed. He knew full well that we'd secured the building before starting work, so were totally alone.

Then… the banging stopped.

We stood on the poolside, staring at each other, rigid and silent… then, without warning, a fish bucket fell over.

This was immediately followed by a grating noise beside me, and I turned to see another bucket sliding along the tiles – slowly at first, but gradually picking up speed before tipping up and spilling its contents onto the floor.

This wasn't the work of overwrought imaginations; this was really happening.

"That's it, I've seen enough – let's get out of here!" Gerry bellowed.

In a matter of minutes, we were locking the doors behind us, leaving the dolphins swimming in their pens, unperturbed and seemingly unaware of anything out of the ordinary.

We needed time to take in what had happened; we needed time to think.

Maybe this pool had a past.

HELLO

HENDLE

Duchess – the love of my life!

Herb'e - my lovable bundle of mischief!

The opening bows… in perfect unison!

My beautiful, beautiful Duchess

Duchess and Herb'e's double fish-hand

Hold – hold – go!

I'll be in later, Duch

A tickle under the flipper for Herb'e!

Come on, Herb'e, give Duchess a chance!

Duchess – chattering away!

Now, be a good boy, Herb'e!

A rough 'n' tumble with Herb'e

Give us a kiss, gorgeous!

What's wrong with the water, David?

❧ 61 ❧

Mind racing and unable to sleep, I stared from my bedroom window at the pool building, its dark form accentuated by a crisp night and full moon. The early evening's events were still jingling in my head. Just what had Gerry and I seen? Was it some kind of supernatural happening tied to the pool's history, or was it something completely unrelated? On a personal note, I knew that since beginning work with my dolphins, I had changed. Subconsciously, things had never been the same since that first encounter with Duchess, begging the question... could these strange occurrences have something to do with her and the other dolphins?

I already knew that these intelligent mammals had no vocal cords with which to verbalise their thoughts. However, that didn't mean they couldn't talk; they just did it in another way – mind talk, or *telepathy*, as we humans liked to call it. Scientists already knew that the dolphin brain was larger than man's. Why was that? There had to be a reason: that extra capacity must be used for something. Might dolphins have telekinetic ability? I didn't know the answer, but it was certainly food for thought. I did know, however, that the dolphins hadn't been spooked by what had happened. For them, it had been business as usual. Maybe our *bumps in the night* theory was merely an excuse for the fact that we didn't understand. Anyway, who was I to say? I was just a highly-privileged grunt lucky enough to be working with the people from Atlantis.

Long may it continue.

❦ 62 ❧

One week merged into the next without any further spooky occurrences. The force-feeds continued, progress with the dolphins slowed even further and Duchess' feeds became minimal. Duchess was now on the verge of refusing food altogether, but nonetheless seemed to enjoy performing her routine without claiming her reward. This was now a serious worry.

But it wasn't all doom and gloom: Herb'e's pleasant disposition continued, and as he did his best to make himself amicable, I couldn't help but wonder if perhaps *I* had been the cause of our problems during those early days.

I remembered the young American telling his story about Duchess and Herb'e's capture. I recalled how Herb'e had refused to desert Duchess, even as she had fought and lost her battle for freedom. He had chosen Duchess as his mate a long time ago and was determined to stick by her, come what may.

Then, I had rampaged into their lives, and my immediate *connection* with the love of his life had clearly got him rattled. I could see where he was coming from: Herb'e had been jealous because his pride and joy was giving me the wink!

Only now, after all these months, had he finally decided to accept me – at least for the time being. Maybe he was biding his time until he could devise a plan to discredit me. Who could tell?

But I'd learned a lot about these two dolphins during my short time with them, and their characters were developing in a way that only I seemed able to understand.

Their generous, smiling faces might appear fixed, but they were not. They had expressions. The eyes were the give-away. They say that the eyes are the windows to the soul and, certainly in this case, I found it hard to disagree.

Looking into the waters of their pen was like looking into an enchanted mirror. In Duchess' and Herb'e's eyes, I actually recognised myself – my mannerisms, my frailties. It was as if they were ever so slowly stealing bits of my personality, then reflecting it back, so *they* could make *me* understand *them*.

My dolphins had become my drug. Duchess and Herb'e were my fix. I was an addict who couldn't get enough of them, and no matter what the rights or wrongs of this exploitive business, I believed deep down that I'd never really escape it.

I'd heard the dolphins' song, and it would haunt me for the rest of my life.

❧ 63 ❧

Chewing on one of Ida's sumptuous sausages, I decided to ask Jim about the pool's history. It had been weeks since Gerry and I had seen anything unusual, but I was still curious.

"History? What do you mean?" Jim frowned.

"Well, has anything strange ever happened there?"

He chewed thoughtfully on a piece of crispy bacon before answering with a knowing smile. "Why, you havin' trouble?"

I nodded, then began to tell him about the strange things that Gerry and I had witnessed.

His eyes lit up like twin stars. "Well, after the accident, people started hearin' things."

"Accident? What accident?"

"Little girl. Drowned. Tragic. Upset the whole village. Lot of people stopped swimmin' after that." He put down his fork and leaned toward me. "But them that did go said they 'eard strange noises – whispering, like."

"So, what happened then?"

"Pool attendant packed it in, and the place closed." He flashed a delightedly evil smile. "Then you lot showed up."

This clearly pleased him no end and, emitting a grunt of satisfaction, he resumed attacking his breakfast with renewed vigour.

As for me, I had my answer: the pool did indeed have a history.

❧ 64 ❧

The morning brought even more anxiety. Duchess was now refusing to eat anything at all and her weight loss was showing markedly. Moreover, she didn't want to work.

I'd been recording my concerns in her logbook for the last few weeks, and had even discussed them with Philip; but I hadn't pushed the issue because the last thing I wanted was to see her force-fed.

"You've got to eat, Duchess. Don't listen to Bubbles!"

However, later that afternoon, Gerry delivered the ultimatum I had been dreading. "Look, David, if Duchess continues to refuse food, we're gonna have to force-feed."

I had no grounds to argue – Duchess was looking very thin – but, despite this, I didn't sense illness or death and believed that a force-feed was unwarranted. I desperately needed Duchess' *connection* to guide me.

"Talk to me, Duchess, talk to me."

But she remained silent.

All I could do was pray that she'd have a change of heart, otherwise Gerry would have to follow procedure.

And I would have to witness the unbearable sight of a Duchess force-feed.

❧ 65 ❧

Two days have gone by and Duchess is still refusing to eat. Her weight loss is showing patently, the dip at the base of her neck pronounced. This can't go on for much longer. To add to my concerns, Herb'e has joined her in refusing food.

Additionally, the handlers of Baby and Stumpy are reporting the same problems: it's only a matter of time before all the dolphins follow Bubbles' lead.

I glance at Bubbles' pen as she swims aimlessly round and round. She reminds me of a siren calling passing sailors onto the rocks. Her song spreads to the other dolphins like a cancer, calling... calling... She is the catalyst for disaster.

Gerry watches from the far side of the pool, strain etched across his face – what to do, what to do? Not only are the show deadlines well behind but, if this gets any worse, we'll have no dolphins left to train.

"David, we start force-feeding Duchess this afternoon. If we don't, we could lose her."

I look into Duchess' eyes as she swims, head cocked to one side. As grave as the situation is, I still don't sense death – just an indifference to life.

The unthinkable is now going to happen: three force-feeds today – two for Bubbles and one for Duchess.

Although I am weary, my strength is growing daily. My arms are pumped up and every muscle and sinew in my body ripples. The constant force-feeds have honed me into the perfect catching machine:

they have made me super fit and brought forth a controlled aggression that I never knew I had. As strong a catcher as Gerry was, I am in a different league. I have become the champion of this watery arena.

Likewise, Duchess has emerged as leader of this chaotic band of dolphins, as they struggle to find order within the tragic world of disorder in which they now find themselves.

Her eyes draw me in. As I mentally prepare for the catch, she senses my adrenaline rush.

"You won't do to me what you do to Bubbles!"

She breaks eye contact and swims away. Her cocky dismissal draws a rare smile.

"We'll try her again in a couple of hours; but if she doesn't eat then, we'll have her out," Gerry tells me.

Easier said than done, I think. All I can do is hope that we are able to avoid this impending confrontation; but my gut instinct tells me that both Duchess and I are already preparing for the battle to come.

Handlers wander aimlessly, banging on fish buckets in an attempt to entice their charges to eat. But, as feared, all dolphins are now refusing food. Even blind Scouse is falling under Bubbles' spell.

Time for the first force-feed of the day. "Okay, Vance, are you ready?"

We strip off to catch Bubbles. Again, I make for a head catch. A short struggle. I lock my arm, and it's all over. Vance easily anchors her tail. She doesn't even put up a fight, but just accepts being manhandled onto the poolside, gagged and loaded with fish. She knows that she's not strong enough to stop me; but she still defies the force-feed by regurgitating every fish forced on her.

"It's no good, Gerry: she's just closing her throat and throwing up."

Gerry checks Bubbles' continuing weight loss, then we unceremoniously dump her back into the water.

The force-feed has failed. I don't give Bubbles a second thought. I'm already preparing mentally for the second catch – the one I've been dreading – Duchess, my beautiful Duchess.

She's the only bright light I've encountered since training started, and now all that hard-won trust is about to be seriously tested.

The other handlers are instructed to bring the foam mattress to Pen Number One.

As I move towards her, I feel her: she's invoked a silent *connection*, an open wavelength with no sound. Her eyes never leave me. Totally oblivious to Gerry and the others, she weighs me up. I am now the impending threat and, as the leader of the pack, she cannot afford to lose. I feel her adrenaline building.

I hear Gerry's voice. "Do you want me to do the main catch, David? I know how you feel about her."

"No – the quicker we catch her, the quicker we put her back." I can't bear the thought of anyone else touching her.

"It's me and you, Duch – it's only ever been me and you."

As I sit on the poolside donning mask and fins, Duchess circles nervously. I note how she jinks to the left when picking up speed. This is an important observation – I can't afford to get this wrong.

God, I'm not even in the water, and her head is jerking from side to side. She's giving me a final warning.

"I told you before: get in, and I'll have you!"

My adrenaline pump is working overtime. All my senses are at a high, yet I feel calm and focussed. Determined. I slide into the water, making hardly a ripple. I dive to the bottom of the pool, eyes fixed on her every movement.

Herb'e swims between us, shadowing her, guarding her. He knows what's coming.

"I know what you're doing, Herb'e. Get out of the way."

He's not listening: he's trying to draw me away; but I don't take the bait. I point at my target and flash my ring. Duchess searches frantically for a way out: Herb'e's zigzagging in front of me.

"Move, Herb'e – it's her I want!"

Still, he shields her. If I'm going to succeed, I must get the timing right.

Herb'e's only six feet away; six feet to my left. Now's my chance...

A sudden thrust towards him leads me to her. In blind panic, he cuts left. I glance off the side of his body and take Duchess side-on, left hand to left flipper.

Got it!

A final surge as my right arm pulls over her neck. As my body hits her, I roll around, right hand frantically fumbling for right flipper.

Got you!

She's fighting now. I am holding on like a bull rider in a rodeo. She's going so fast that I can't lock my arm... got to lock my arm! Where's Vance? I don't see him! I don't see anything!

Suddenly, her speed drops. Vance has made the secondary catch and locked onto her tail, anchoring her. This gives me a chance to roll fully up her neck and apply the arm lock.

She's thrashing her head from side to side, snapping, trying to bite her way free; but I'm fast behind her, and she can't turn on her tail. A few seconds more and it's all over.

Vance drags her towards the poolside, tail first. I'm locked on like a limpet mine, arms knotted, totally exhausted. The canvas sling is waiting, and the handlers haul her from the water and onto the foam mattress.

Normally, I'd try to catch my breath before leaving the water, but I hear her cries of panic.

The *connection* – it's there again. It's like turning on a radio, and I am the receiver.

"I'm sorry Duchess, I'm so sorry! I had to do it! There isn't any other way!"

She doesn't believe me. I've betrayed her trust. She's afraid and confused and, as I look into her eyes, I realise that she's crying – she's actually physically crying as the handlers hold her down so she can't move during the force-feed.

I flash my ring. *"I'm here, Duchess! Everything's okay – I'll not leave you; I'll never leave you!"*

But she doesn't understand what's happening.

"David, hold the bottom gag and keep flashing your ring and talking to her." Gerry is aware of the *connection*! How long has he known? My head spins with the intensity of it all; what's happening to me?

The force-feed is quickly and efficiently dealt with; but Duchess' eyes are dulled. I can't feel her anymore. I feel totally empty.

We put her back in the water, and she slowly swims away, only a snort breaking the silence.

"I can't leave it like this; I can't lose her!" I turn to Gerry. "I'm going back in."

Gerry smiles sympathetically. "I know. Keep alert – she's not pleased, and there's nothing any of us can do if she turns."

I don't speak. I just nod my head, grab my mask and fins and silently slide back into the water.

❧ 66 ❧

I dive in search of the main sump: its heavy cover will act as an anchor while I work out what to do next.

"Please forgive me, Duchess, I had to do it, there was no other way."

She's not listening and in no mood for conversation. Duchess circles me, about seven feet between us. Those beautiful blue eyes are swollen with rage and hate, and her generous smile has become a snarl.

Beneath the water, angry clicks reverberate from every direction, a dolphin mob literally baying for my blood. What's more, they're all moving to the edges of their dividing booms, searching for the best vantage point, eager to witness the upcoming event. This is what they've been waiting for: fight night. And guess who's top of the bill? This is where I get my come-uppance.

The aggression channelled at me is so strong, it's overpowering. I can physically feel it, probing, squeezing... I'm drowning in a sea of rage.

Only Bubbles remains aloof – unseeing, unhearing – trapped in her own nightmare world.

Duchess' challenge echoes through the water: a deep ratcheting sound, not unlike that of a football rattle. This time round, Herb'e does not shield her, but instead makes his way to the corner of the pen – best seat in the house.

I swim up for air, but my eyes never leave Duchess. I dare not let her out of my sight. My clumsy attempt at making up has merely given her an opportunity for revenge.

157

The sound of her rattle continues to build until it's almost deafening. Meanwhile, the dolphin audience wills her on.

Gripping the sump grill, I try to clear my head.

Stay sharp, David – too late to get out now!

Duchess is picking up speed, head thrashing from side to side. She's going to attack. Daren't let her out of my sight – but she's moving fast, darting in and out of the corners of my vision. She jinks left, then right – then she disappears... she's gone.

Where's she gone?

She's behind me!

It's like listening to sound through headphones, clicks and rattles sweeping from ear to ear at full volume. She means to ram me in the back.

I dare not trust my eyes; I must stay focussed.

Where's she coming from? Left or right? If I choose wrongly, I'm in a wheelchair – or worse. I wait and wait; the threat decibels are now deafening. I need to know exactly where she is.

Left... or right? Can't be sure. She's continually changing sides. Must feel her; must try to embrace her rage.

God, where is she?

My right... she's on my right!

Sound decibels have just gone critical. She's attacking, and there's no time for me to get out of the way. Got to hold... wait... wait... MOVE!

She glances off my side, knocking me off balance, but I keep hold of the grill. This grey torpedo has missed her target – and she's only getting one chance. Now it's my turn. Adrenaline courses through my body, and I focus my anger.

"How dare you attack me? How dare you...?"

I release the grill and push with all my might, slicing through the water like an arrow from a bow. *"Payback time..."*

Duchess turns too late. Fists clenched, I ram the side of her head. Physically, I can't hurt her; but, emotionally, my raw aggression can. I'm giving her what she gave me: rage, pure unadulterated rage.

My surprise attack has her confused. Time enough for me to roll around the back of her neck and lock my arm. Now we wrestle under water. The strain on my arms is unbearable, but anger sustains me. Rolling rapidly around, she tries to shake me loose. I can't hold on much longer. But I daren't let go… I won't lose… I can't lose… I can't…

Then, suddenly, she's limp. Aggression gone. Total submission. It's over. I've won.

I feel her again – the *connection*! She hasn't just turned off *her* rage, she's turned off *mine*. I release my grip and gently allow her to glide past my body, my left hand slowly sliding along her underbelly as she swims to the right.

All my aggression is washed away. I am again at peace.

I turn and swim from her.

When I first entered the pool, I came to *her* for forgiveness. Now it is Duchess who must come to me. I open a *connection*.

"It's up to you now, girl."

Ignoring her, I swim triumphantly along the sides of the pens, flashing my ring at our dolphin audience. They are disappointed: this isn't the result they hoped for.

Suddenly, I spy Duchess swimming alongside me. I remain silent, refusing to look at her, but instead offer her my right hand, which she gently grips in her mouth. Over one hundred razor sharp teeth; but such is her gentleness, my skin isn't even punctured.

"Hello, beautiful, are we friends again?"

I surface to take in air, then dive back down to deep water. The strangest thing happens: Duchess silently swims directly beneath me, belly up, and slowly connects with my body. Her flippers hold me in embrace, and we glide as one through liquid sky. In dolphin terms, this is a sexual act of love and submission – total surrender. I milk her attentions – not just for me, or her, but for the onlookers, both dolphin and human alike.

Herb'e has left the corner of the pool and is shadowing my left-hand side, so that the three of us are moving as one. This is the forging of a team, the cementing of a bond that will stay with the three of us forever. Only this time there's a difference: the *connection* isn't just with Duchess, it's with Herb'e, too.

"Hello, my son, nice to see you."

The dolphins that only minutes before were howling for my demise now turn their heads aside, carefully avoiding eye contact, acknowledging me respectfully from the corners of their eyes.

I am a gladiator indulging the crowd; Duchess has handed me her crown. The chaotic life of the dolphins has a new structure; the pecking order has changed, and I am now their leader.

As I haul myself from the water, the first to congratulate me is Gerry. "God, I thought you'd had it then – it doesn't come any closer than that!"

He's right – it doesn't. The love of my life has just tried to kill me; but that was in another reality. This is a new dawn.

I now have three teachers: Gerry, who will guide me in the practicalities of becoming a good trainer; and Duchess and Herb'e, who will shape my psyche, forging me into a *great* trainer. I am now part of two cultures, constantly learning, constantly pushing back boundaries.

But having a foot in both camps means that, one day, I will have to choose between them.

A couple of hours later, Gerry tries Duchess and Herb'e with food and, to everyone's relief, they gobble down three and a half pounds of best herring. There is equally good news from the other pens – all dolphins are eating and eager to work.

The day's events have broken Bubbles' spell; she no longer has any hold over the dolphins at North Liston. This poor creature is now totally and utterly alone. There is nothing more anyone can do for her.

Later that evening, Gerry calls everyone into the office. His message is stark and simple: extra vigilance for Pen Number Four.

Bubbles has officially been put on suicide watch.

❦ 67 ❧

As much as I care for Duchess, she's really done a number on me today. I'm aching from head to foot, and my arm is blue and swollen. To make matters worse, the pain in my elbow is excruciating and I can't straighten it. It's too late to visit the doctor, so if the swelling doesn't go down within the next three to four hours, it will mean a trip to hospital.

As always, Jim is stuck behind his newspaper, bulbous head venturing out every so often to pass editorial comment. "Can you believe it? Beggars bloody belief!"

"What does?"

A few rants later, he moves to the comfort of his parlour, paper still in hand. I must catch him before that grizzled face disappears for the rest of the evening: once settled in his easy chair, he's on hallowed ground and strictly out of bounds.

I peek furtively into his inner sanctum. "Jim, please could you look at my arm?"

He sighs deeply. "Why, what's wrong with it?"

"I don't know – that's why I'm asking you to look at it."

Planting his newspaper firmly on his armrest, he hauls his body from the sumptuous embrace of chintz upholstery, and examines my ever-bloating arm. His lined face squints before delivering his diagnosis. "Don't like the look of that – could be broke." Another thoughtful squint. "You need to go to 'ospital."

My brief audience is over and, without another word, Jim allows the armchair to suck him back into position.

A short time later, I'm sitting in the local hospital's A&E department. After what seems like an age, I'm sent into a consulting room, where I find a middle-aged Indian doctor who, though pleasant in manner, is clearly struggling to master the English language.

As I remove my shirt for examination, the concerned doctor views my bruised torso. "How did this happen?" he gasps, appalled.

I reply without thinking. "I've been catching dolphins every day for the last month, and I'm black and blue. Today I got a particularly good hammering."

The bewildered doctor doesn't speak, but smiles condescendingly. He doesn't believe me; he thinks I'm having a joke at his expense — and who can blame him? I wouldn't believe me either.

I show him my locked arm, which is now swollen down to the wrist. The doctor points to the lacerations on my hands and, with narrowed eyes, asks, "What are these?"

"Penguin bites," I reply.

His eyes flick to mine. Again, he makes no comment, but smiles and nods reassuringly. He thinks he's dealing with a crackpot.

He tentatively examines my arm before asking the question that I've been dreading. "How did this happen?"

I cringe and hesitate before answering. "You're not going to believe this, but a dolphin rolled on me." I look into his disbelieving eyes. "It's true – I swear it!"

He passes no comment, but continues his checks. Eventually, he assures me that my arm isn't broken, just bruised, and will return to normal over the next twenty-four hours.

Now that I've been given the all-clear, I try to dress and get out before he has chance to ask any more embarrassing questions.

As I hurry to the door, he breaks his silence. "You're a very funny man... a very funny man," he tells me, shaking his head and smiling broadly. "Always making jokes. Yes, you are a very funny man."

I nod embarrassedly and return his smile. "I'm glad you think so – but you don't know the half of it, you really don't!"

❦ 68 ❧

Next morning, the dolphins were all eating up. Better still, the early training sessions showed marked progress. Even though it was undoubtedly too early to celebrate, the atmosphere at the pool *felt* different, as if a cloud had lifted, albeit not fully – the sight of Bubbles swimming blindly around her pen was a stark reminder of troubles yet to come.

The most important things for me were Duchess and Herb'e, and as long as they were happy and well, I could learn to live with whatever came next.

Since the 'big fight', the three of us had become permanently linked. It was no longer only Duchess scurrying around inside my head; it was Herb'e, too. This extra *connection* would mentally take its toll. Nevertheless, I'd got what I'd craved most: Duchess and Herb'e were mine, and woe betide anyone who tried to steal them away.

I stood on the poolside, watching with pride as my two beautiful charges spun and weaved through the water. I marvelled at their precision, both dolphins breaking the pool's surface at exactly the same time. My job now was to make these two *perform* as one – to create a shadow ballet. I now had the ammunition to birth *The Perfect Pair*.

Gerry decided that night training should continue, as this would enable us to keep a close eye on Bubbles. Even the girls agreed to resume working nights, though no doubt they wouldn't have been so accommodating had they known about the banging doors and moving fish buckets. Luckily, Gerry and I had kept quiet on that score, so they were none the wiser.

The afternoon came all too quickly, bringing with it the first of Bubbles' daily force-feeds. Since his last encounter with Bubbles, Gerry had left the catches to me and my new partner, Vance, who was proving to be a more than able substitute for Matt.

Once everything was in place, I entered the water and dissected the catch area as usual. By now, Bubbles was a shadow of her former self, and her catches were becoming easier and easier. In truth, she seemed to have given up her fight for life: trance-like, she accepted the inevitable.

After completing Bubbles' feed, we returned her to the water. She had taken no more than two and a half pounds of herring. This was not sufficient to sustain her, which meant that the two force-feeds a day threatened to become a permanent fixture. Bubbles' torment was about to get even worse.

My euphoria of that morning collapsed, and I prepared for yet another sleepless night. It seemed as if I spent half my life in the water, catching. Not only did I feel physically tired, I felt mentally exhausted, and the prospect of any further force-feeds made me feel like screaming. There seemed to be no end to the horror of it all. I was coming to the end of my tether.

❧ 69 ❧

I awake next morning, still aching from the catches, and struggle to prepare mentally for another nightmare day. I can't remember ever feeling so low and, although I know that everyone else feels the same way, I am resentful and bitter. They aren't the ones having to make the catches. They aren't the ones having to assist with the force-feeds.

I need to rest. I feel as though I'm going mad. I need to escape the pool; but I cannot. I have responsibilities: to Duchess, Herb'e, poor Bubbles and, of course, Gerry – this is no picnic for him either. I can't let them down; I must carry on as normal.

Later that morning, as I work Duchess and Herb'e, Vance suddenly shouts me from the far side of the pool. "David, something's wrong with Bubbles."

I have a feeling of dread. "What do you mean?"

"She's picking up speed – swimming fast."

I can't see her from where I'm standing, but I can see the churning waves spilling over the poolsides. I know instinctively what she's doing.

"My God, she's going to ram the wall! She's going to kill herself!"

I break into a run that feels more like a slow-motion sprint: my legs don't seem to be functioning properly, and it takes an age to reach her pen.

She's into her final approach, and I leap fully-clothed into the water, causing her to jink laterally before she hits the wall.

Vance and the others stand rooted to their spots.

"Where is she? Where's she gone?"

I see her!

Bubbles has gone limp, and I embrace her, lifting her, pushing her head skywards. "Come on, Bubbles, breathe, breathe!"

She floats, unmoving, and I hold my breath – then a short, sharp snort erupts from her blowhole. "Thank God!"

She is alive – stunned and disorientated – but alive. Her attempt to avoid me as I entered the water has robbed her charge of its power.

"Take it easy, Bubbles – I've got you." I remain with her, holding her, gliding her through the water until she is capable of continuing unaided.

I have heard stories about suicide dolphins, yet never believed them – until now. I am in no doubt that Bubbles has just tried to kill herself. Thank goodness, I stopped her. My instinctive action has saved her life.

I did the right thing.

Or did I?

The gaunt faces of my worn-down colleagues tell me a different story.

❧ 70 ❧

The scheduled force-feeds were abandoned for the day because Bubbles was not fit to cope. And no wonder, her psyche was shot, totally shot. When would this nightmare end?

The atmosphere at the pool had become surreal. Handlers moved like automatons, struggling to come to terms with what they'd just witnessed. Training had become impossible.

Shortly before the close of the afternoon sessions, I asked Gerry if I could skip that evening's training. "I've had enough, Gerry – I need to get out of here."

Wearily, Gerry lifted himself from his platform. "You're not the only one; everyone's nerves are shredded. I think I'll cancel all sessions for the next three nights."

I'd never been more pleased to finish what felt like the longest workday ever. Tonight it would be early to bed, to try – if possible – to put this horrible day behind me and catch up on some much-needed sleep.

I fell into bed just before nine o'clock, where I tossed and turned for at least another hour and a half. But it was no good: my neck and shoulders felt rigid, my pillows like rocks, and I just couldn't sleep. Finally, I decided to go downstairs for a drink.

I knew that Jim and Ida were still up, because I could hear the television thundering away. Jim was a little deaf to say the least.

As I pulled on my jeans, I routinely glanced through my bedroom window towards the pool building and noticed what appeared to be smoke belching from the bell tower. Almost luminous, it was clearly visible through the darkness, and I realised with horror that the building must be on fire. I stumbled downstairs, wrestling with my tee shirt, then galloped out of the house and across the croft towards the main entrance.

Moments later, I was haring up the stone stairway leading to the girls' changing room. Flinging open the door, I steeled myself to meet the expected inferno – but found nothing.

Everything looked normal, and the only sounds were the snorts of the dolphins echoing through the hole where the clock had once been.

I pondered, shivering in the cold air. Then, I checked the cubicles. Nothing.

I returned downstairs and began to check the rest of the building – office, kitchen, fish room, main pool.

Nothing.

Tired and under pressure, I must have imagined it. "Get a grip, Capello!"

Feeling foolish, I locked the main entrance, then walked slowly back across the croft... and, of course, I couldn't resist giving the pool a second look.

There it was again: blue-tinged smoke coming from the bell tower.

Surely, I couldn't have missed something!

Anguished, I raced back – main entrance, lobby, corridor, stairs, bell tower...

Again, nothing...

Not a single flame, not a trace of smoke, not even the faintest whiff of burning. "God, David, are you losing it or what?"

Locking the door for a second time, I ran down the steps and onto the croft. There, I watched the smoke as it continued to whirl around the tower. What struck me as strange was that it didn't disperse, nor move haphazardly. Instead, it swirled and weaved as if it had intention, crocheting itself into a specific shape.

I watched for a good ten minutes, during which time the blue-tinged phenomenon continued to twist and dance, maintaining its tenuous structure – a structure that looked almost like a doorframe.

And, within the doorframe, a darkness that resembled a doorway.

What was I seeing?

I stood, transfixed, for at least another five minutes, during which time all my apprehension melted away, leaving me with an overwhelming feeling of peace. Whatever I was witnessing radiated purity or, for want of a better word, spirituality; it was truly special and I knew that I was privileged to see it.

Much later, tucked up in bed and free of all agitation, I sank into a blissfully deep sleep.

Next morning, I felt like a new man, renewed and eager to return to work. But, as I entered the pool room, I immediately knew that something was wrong: Gerry and Vance were standing silently on the poolside, staring into Pen Number Four.

Bubbles was dead.

My actions the previous day had merely postponed the inevitable: it seemed that she had deliberately stuck her nose into the mesh of the boom and drowned herself.

This poor, broken creature was now at peace. Sometime during last night, Bubbles had at long last won her fight for freedom.

❧ 71 ❧

Bubbles' body was removed that same day, along with her logbook: the written record of her miserable time in captivity. It wouldn't make good reading, but was a crucial testament to her short life and would help the vet to ascertain the cause of death.

A post-mortem would be carried out – routine practice on the loss of a dolphin – and her death certificate would no doubt read *drowning*. Nothing more. No mention of yesterday's events. After all, everyone knows there is no such thing as a 'suicide dolphin'.

Once Bubbles' body had been removed, relief elevated the atmosphere. Cruel as it might seem, we didn't mourn her. We wanted only to forget and move on.

I never spoke about the apparition I'd seen on the night she died, as I strongly believed it had been meant only for me. Equally, I believed it to be unrelated to the earlier hauntings involving the rubber rings and steel fish buckets. Besides, sceptics would say that what I'd seen was merely a result of warm air meeting cool.

But I knew differently.

Would there be any other unexplained events at the pool? I would never know, for the death of Bubbles heralded my departure from North Liston. On 19th June 1972, I would bid goodbye to Jim and Ida and all the other good people of this small shire village.

In two weeks' time, Duchess, Herb'e, Vance and me would embark on a new adventure – an adventure that would take us to Hendle Safari Park.

MAKING OF A TEAM

❦ 72 ❧

Monday, not only the start of a new week, but a new life. Today I would bid farewell to North Liston.

My belongings – suitcased and standing at the foot of the stairs – swamped the kitchen with a fishy odour. It was so bad that even I could smell it. Nevertheless, no one commented. Ida simply carried on toiling over the range, whilst Jim remained buried behind his newspaper, both living their lives in peaceful conformity. Gosh, life without them was going to be hard; I was missing them already.

Minutes later, a breakfast fit for a king lay before me; my last one here. And there they were: two extra homemade sausages – my favourites. The last time I'd been given extras was on the day of Bobby's catch. Funny, that seemed like a lifetime ago, yet I'd been here for only eight months.

I couldn't help smiling as Ida's eyes met mine. "Thanks, Ida."

"Have you got everything?" Jim blurted out, peeking over his newspaper.

I nodded. "Everything there, Jim."

Leaning towards me, he gave me a concerned, fatherly stare. "You listen 'ere. Look after yourself, lad, because me and Ida's gonna miss you." His grizzled face broke into a rare smile.

"Miss you both, too, Jim."

Ida silently turned back to her pans, but not in time to hide the tear trickling down her cheek. The stiff upper lips of these loveable shire folk standing firm to the end.

Breakfast finished, I drained my last mug and prepared to leave. All my goodbyes had to be said now, because once the transport had started, there would be no time – speed would be of the essence.

As I walked across the croft, I looked back at the old terraced house for one last time. The waving Ida and Jim were now moving into my past, and my quest to become a leading trainer was entering a new era.

Inside the pool, excited staff hurried around in preparation for the forthcoming catches.

"Everything ready, Vance?" I called, heading towards Duchess and Herb'e's pen.

"Ready as it ever will be."

Vance would not only carry out the secondary catch today, he would also accompany me on the transport; one man for each dolphin. This was my first transport, and I was taking no chances.

Philip was also in attendance: he and Gerry were to follow by car, just in case anything went wrong.

A large box van had been hired for our short journey to Hendle, its sides plastered with two huge posters heralding the coming of *Flippa…* yes, *Flippa…* Herb'e had at last been given his stage name. Now it was up to Vance and me to make sure that he and Duchess got to Hendle in one piece.

I had no idea how my dolphins would transport, and just hoped that neither would fight too hard. Recalling Herb'e's docility following his journey from the States, I decided to make him my first catch.

As I sat on the poolside, donning mask and fins, Duchess and Herb'e swam around their pen excitedly, as if they could sense that something big was happening.

I slid into the water and both swam up to me, eager to play, Duchess pushing into my right side and Herb'e burying his head under my left arm. *"No time for games, you two. We've got to go."*

Poor Herb'e – before he knew it, I was wrapped around the back of his neck. *"Got you! Sorry, Herb'e, but we're off to see the wizard."*

Vance and I guided him into the waiting harness.

"That wasn't so bad," Vance commented. He was right: it had been one of the easiest catches ever. Perhaps Herb'e was aware of the forthcoming adventure after all.

Once we had him harnessed, I flashed my ring to reassure him, then helped carry him through the narrow corridors leading outside to the van.

Duchess next, drifting close to the poolside. *"Hello, beautiful, we're leaving."* Again, I flashed my ring. *"No fighting, please, Duch – just a nice, simple catch."*

Obediently, Duchess complied and, minutes later, she was lying in the van next to her partner.

"Hey, you two, isn't this exciting?"

A few last minute checks, then we were off. Bye-bye North Liston and good riddance Smelly and Worse – we were Hendle-bound at last.

During the journey, Vance tended Herb'e, whilst I tended Duchess. Both dolphins remained calm, listening attentively as we chatted and doused them with water. *"Not long to go now, people; you'll soon be in your new home."*

As the van sped down the motorway, excited drivers honked horns and waved in response to the huge posters.

"That sign's doing a good job, Vance," I said, peering through the open roller shutter doors. "Talk about instant stardom!"

By the time we'd turned off the motorway and onto the dual carriageway leading to the safari park, we were spearheading a convoy of motorists, all eager to get a closer look at our precious cargo. Unfortunately for them, however, their journeys came to an abrupt end with the security men at the park gates, leaving us to navigate the winding roads leading to the dolphinarium alone.

Our adventure was about to begin: in just three days, Duchess and Herb'e would perform publicly for the first time.

Roll on!

❦ 73 ❧

I couldn't help but be impressed by the sight of the new dolphinarium: the huge structure dominated the entertainment area, overshadowing the nearby restaurant and souvenir shops.

"Would you look at that, Vance? Just look at the size of the place!" I gasped.

We pulled up at the rear of the building, there to be greeted by journalists, photographers, Company bigwigs and a horde of excited park workers, all eager to glimpse our dolphins.

Philip and Gerry addressed an expectant press, whilst Vance and I remained in the van, awaiting the go-ahead for the transfer.

First out was Duchess. Gerry and I, attended by several helpers, manoeuvred her through the side doors leading to the pool and auditorium. "Careful with my girl, lads – she's special," I told them proudly.

It was then that I got my first view of Duchess and Herb'e's new home: a huge, oval pool, flanked by seven-foot holding pens and overlooked by a sprawling auditorium of blue upholstered seats, sufficient to house over two thousand people. The blue-tinged water twinkled like a billion diamonds in the sunlight.

"It's magnificent, Duch – absolutely magnificent," I enthused, as we laid her on the poolside. *"You're gonna love this!"*

Philip took the mandatory blood test from her tail, then gave her a final body check. "Right, lads, get her in."

"In you go, girl – enjoy!"

Clearly unaffected by her short journey, she immediately began to speed around, excitedly investigating her new home. After a few lightning circuits, she bobbed back to the stage and lifted her head to flash the biggest dolphin smile I'd ever seen. *"David, it's beautiful!"*

There it was again – the *connection*. I could feel her euphoria washing over me... or was it *my* euphoria washing over *her*? Either way, I was suddenly experiencing that light-headed serenity which always accompanied her psychic bond.

I stood at the water's edge, soaking her up, basking in her sheer radiance, when suddenly I felt a hand on my shoulder. It was Gerry, rebuking me gently. "Let's not forget Herb'e."

As they were still ensconced in the van, neither Herb'e nor Vance had yet seen the dolphinarium's interior. So, Gerry and I hurried out to fetch them, leaving Duchess joyfully showboating for the crowd of press photographers dangling over the pool security railings. Shortly afterwards, she was joined by an equally enthusiastic Herb'e, who raced flamboyantly around in an effort to steal her thunder.

Cameras flashed and the auditorium echoed with 'oohs' and 'ahs' as the delighted dolphins leapt from the water, purposely showering their admirers. Their joy was palpable, infectious.

"This is only the beginning, people," I assured them. *"We've just become instant celebrities."*

After at least another hour of showing off, Duchess and Herb'e finally settled down, leaving the crowd to make its way to the park restaurant for refreshments. The huge dolphinarium, which only minutes earlier had rattled with staccato chit-chat, was now silent and still.

"I guess that's the end of the show," Vance remarked, gazing at the empty auditorium.

"No, not the end, Vance," I smiled. "Just the beginning."

❧ 74 ❧

A couple of hours later, a rather tipsy Gerry arrived back from the restaurant.

"I've come to tell you that Head Office has arranged temporary digs for you, not far from the park. Your landladies are Mrs and Miss Crouch, and they've been paid three days' keep in advance. After that, you're on your own."

"Wow, that's really pushing the boat out – three days is all we get?" I moaned.

"Yes, that's your lot," Gerry replied, grinning crookedly. Then, he grew serious. "Right, before I leave, I need to explain how things are gonna work from now on. David, you are now the trainer in charge of Hendle. I will remain at North Liston to supervise the training of Baby, Scouse and Stumpy. But, as you already know, Baby and Scouse are well behind schedule, and Stumpy is just too sick to cope. This means we're going to have to buy in a third shipment."

Gerry went on to explain how from now on he would be commuting to Hendle regularly to offer guidance and support. This was not welcome news: although Gerry was both my teacher and mentor, I bitterly resented the thought of him interfering in the training of Duchess and Herb'e. They were my dolphins now – not his. Besides, I had ideas of my own and desperately wanted to break free of Gerry's shackles. I bid him goodbye with a smile and a wave – and a secret determination to assert my independence.

After he'd gone, I joined my two stars in the pool to play. Both keenly competed for my attention and, before long, we were joined by Vance, eager to earn acceptance into our little club.

"You two will be seeing a lot of this funny-looking fella," I told Duchess and Herb'e with a smile, *"so be gentle with him."*

When playtime was over, Vance and I bid Duchess and Herb'e goodnight, then headed off to the prosperous, lush green belt of Hendle in search of our new digs. Parking on the deserted rural road, we pushed our way through rusting iron gates and began the journey down a pathway overgrown with weeds and feral shrubbery.

Standing before us was a three-storey mansion, magnificent in structure, but in urgent need of renovation. Splintering window frames, flaking plaster and crumbling pointing gave it a weary look, and somehow it managed to give the impression that it was sagging beneath the weight of its huge roof.

"If a guy with fangs and a black cape answers the door, I'm off," Vance quipped.

He was right: the house was a dead ringer for 'Munster Mansion'. We peered uncertainly at the worn oak door, then I gave Vance a nudge. "Well, what you waiting for?"

Grimacing, he grasped the knocker and banged hard. The sound resonated hollowly throughout the house. After a minute or so, we heard shuffling footsteps approaching the door... then stopping just behind it... The seconds ticked by.

"Do you think they're going to let us in?" I whispered.

"Don't know," Vance replied. "They seem to be having second thoughts."

Taking a deep breath, I called, "Hello, anyone home?"

Heavy bolts scraped back, then the door opened a crack, revealing a pair of faded, elderly eyes. "Who are you?"

I glanced uneasily at Vance. "David Capello and Vance Martin from the safari park... your new lodgers."

"New what?"

"New lodgers."

"Stop mumbling – can't hear you."

"Your new lodgers... we're your NEW LODGERS."

The door opened a little wider whilst the woman scrutinised us, then, reluctantly, she said, "You'd better come in."

The hallway we entered was spacious but old-fashioned, its highly polished wooden floor scattered with worn rugs. Faded walls reached up towards a high bas-relief ceiling, adorned by a magnificent chandelier – a reminder of a house that had seen better days. Against one wall stood the biggest grandfather clock I'd ever seen, and the entire room reeked of lavender and beeswax.

"Nice place," I remarked.

"Nice what?"

"I said it's a very nice place."

Now I could see the woman clearly, I realised that she wasn't as old as I'd first imagined – maybe mid to late sixties. But her drab, outmoded clothes and tightly scraped back hair gave her an air of time and disappointment – a life not lived.

We had no idea whether this was Miss or Mrs Crouch, and she didn't seem in any hurry to enlighten us. Instead, she assessed us suspiciously, then said, "Follow me – and don't forget your suitcases."

Leading us up the winding staircase to the first floor, she took us to our rooms, both of which were clean and unexpectedly bright. As she led us, she maintained an uneasy silence, speaking only to give instructions or to answer questions.

"I'll call when dinner is served," she said, as she left us to unpack. Then, as an afterthought, she added, "Oh… just one more thing – the second floor is *strictly* out of bounds." And, with that final cryptic comment, she made her way downstairs.

Vance and I hadn't even opened our cases, yet we were already feeling distinctly uncomfortable. After unpacking our belongings, we loitered in our rooms, waiting like two naughty children to be summoned for dinner.

"We can't put up with this, Vance," I said, peeping in to see how he was doing.

He nodded, but didn't reply. He knew as well as I did that we'd be too busy preparing for our first shows to search for anywhere else to stay. Like it or not, this would be our home for the foreseeable future.

Eventually, our hostess called us down to dinner. She served our food in virtual silence – food that was adequate, but nothing compared to Ida's. But, then again, what could be?

By the time we'd finished eating, both Vance and I felt jaded and depressed. We dispiritedly climbed the stairs for an early night, reassuring ourselves that the day had been very long and tiring. Maybe things would seem brighter in the morning.

Then again, maybe not.

75

I was dreaming.

A distant voice crying out. Calling, then weeping bitterly.

I stirred in my bed, dragged from a leaden slumber – then realised that this wasn't a dream.

Somewhere, far away, the disembodied voice continued to wail. I pushed back the heavy eiderdown, propped myself on an elbow and listened.

Silence.

Sixty seconds.

There it was again. I sat up.

Faint cries. But from where? Outside the house? Inside? Above me? Below me?

Silence again.

I squinted through the pitch-blackness of my room, listening.

Nothing more.

Perhaps a dream after all.

Sleep beckoned, and I fell back on my pillow.

❦ 76 ❧

Next morning, I was awakened by something rigid prodding me in the back. Still half asleep, I rolled over to see a silhouette hunched around the bedroom door, brandishing a walking stick – the object that had so rudely wakened me.

"Breakfast in ten minutes," the silhouette said, then closed the door.

Ten minutes later, Vance and I were sitting at the large dining table, waiting to be fed.

"Do you know how she woke me?" I whispered.

"With a big stick," Vance grinned.

"Yeah... how did you...?"

So, she'd done the same to Vance! I felt better already, and couldn't help laughing.

Then, breakfast appeared: two plates of slimy undercooked ham and a slippery-looking mound of boiled onions. A wave of nausea hit me, but before I had chance to complain, our hostess had scuttled off back to the kitchen.

"What the heck's this? It's horrible!" I moaned.

Vance stared at his plate, lips curling in revulsion. "It's bloody strange, to say the least."

Pushing my plate towards him, I gave him a pleading look. "Do you want mine?"

"You must be kidding – I don't mind onions, but not at six-thirty in the morning."

Leaving our breakfasts uneaten, we set off early for the

dolphinarium. As I drove through the park gates, I asked Vance if he'd heard anyone crying during the night.

Frowning, he shook his head. "No... didn't hear a thing. Mind you, I was so knackered after yesterday, I'd have slept through an earthquake."

"So, you're sure you didn't hear anything?"

"No. Why... what's the problem?"

"No problem – doesn't matter."

Perhaps I'd imagined it. Either way, I didn't have time to worry about it now: Vance and I had a lot to do today. Not only did we need to familiarise ourselves with our new surroundings, we also had to sharpen up Duchess and Herb'e. Their shows were due to open in two days' time and they just weren't ready – we'd lost too many training hours during those early days at North Liston.

At the pool, we were greeted by two still-excited dolphins, enjoying the expanse of their new home. *"This is absolutely fantastic – look how big it is!"* Duchess chirped.

Not only was the pool large, it was twelve-foot deep – perfect for spectacular tricks such as the highball and, later down the line, somersaults. Double somersaults were the jewels in the crown for any trainer, especially the double forward somersault, which, to my knowledge, had never been achieved. This was my eventual goal.

As the fish thawed, we rehearsed the show routine, Vance compèring and me presenting. The trick list for the first shows read: three opening bows, handshake, tail slap (applause), retrieval of one to three rings, retrieval of hat, retrieval of sunglasses, tail walk, hurdle, toothbrush, singing, highball, wave and closing bows.

"Fab... well, maybe not so fab..." It could hardly be described as the greatest show on Earth, but it would have to do for starters, because I didn't intend to introduce any new tricks until Duchess and Herb'e had mastered these. Training sessions would take place after the daily shows had finished, which meant we'd be in for some very late nights.

After rehearsals, we scrubbed everything down, then embarked on playtime – something Duchess and Herb'e always enjoyed. Underwater tag was especially popular, mainly because there were only two winners

– them! (Not quite true – they *did* allow us the occasional victory, just to keep us interested.)

They also enjoyed flip football – in human terms, beach ball – the game they'd played at North Liston, where they'd used the unfortunate Smelly and Worse instead of a ball. Smelly and Worse… I wondered which poor sod was lumbered with them now!

Playtime over, we begrudgingly said goodbye, then headed back to our newly-acquired digs.

"Wonder what's cooking tonight?" I said.

Wrinkling his nose, Vance replied, "Probably next door's cat!"

❦ 77 ❧

Darkness.
Heavy, disturbed sleep.
A voice, crying out.
Then weeping – muffled, distant… gradually fading into silence.

❧ 78 ❧

Next morning, our stick-wielding hostess again roused me from sleep. I didn't like being wakened this way – in fact, I found it intensely irritating – but I resisted the urge to complain, and sought comfort in reminding myself that Vance was getting the same treatment.

After breakfasting on yet another queer concoction, Vance and I made our way to the park.

"Vance, why can't she give us cereal or something? I mean, it's not hard, is it? Just plain cornflakes would do."

Vance nodded longingly. "Yeah, cornflakes – I could murder a bowl of cornflakes."

"Plus, while I'm at it, I can't put up with all this screaming and crying when I'm trying to get some kip."

"What screaming and crying? I haven't heard anything."

I threw him an exasperated glance. "Well, next time it happens, I'll just have to wake you up so you do, won't I?"

"God, you got out the wrong side of bed, didn't you?" he retorted coolly.

I didn't speak, but Vance's snappy answer made me determined that next time I'd investigate – *after* waking him, of course.

To add to my woes, at the dolphinarium, Herb'e spoiled the morning's training by bullying Duchess. I found this surprising, as Duchess had always been the dominant partner. Maybe Herb'e had got out the wrong side of bed, too.

But, as we progressed into the afternoon, the bullying grew ugly.

Each time I brought him and Duchess into the stage, he head-butted her, driving her away.

"Behave yourself, Herb'e – I won't put up with this! It's not a one dolphin show: you work together or not at all."

"He's been like this all morning," Duchess complained, *"thinks he's the big boss."*

"I know, Duch. Try to ignore him."

But Herb'e persisted, and I realised that I'd have to take firm action or his bad behaviour might jeopardise the opening shows. *"Please, Duchess, come back to the stage – I'll sort him."*

Tentatively, she swam in, only to be again head-butted out of the way.

"Right, Herb'e, that's it!" Blowing my whistle, I threw Duchess a piece of fish.

Herb'e's eyes narrowed.

"Clever, aren't you, Herb'e? From now on, each time you hit her, I feed her... but you get nothing."

He was furious but, far from discouraging him, my tactics only made him worse.

"That's right, Herb'e, carry on – the more you hit her, the more food she gets," I taunted, showering her with fish. *"Oh, my beautiful Duchess is going to grow into a fat little girl, isn't she, Herb'e? Especially now she's getting your share of the food."*

Herb'e screamed his displeasure, shaking his head violently.

"Scream all you want, Herb'e – no one's listening."

This training session was literally the birth of the 'mind games', where I would pit my wits against those of my dolphins in a battle for supremacy. These conflicts would take many forms: on this occasion, I was protecting Duchess; but, at other times, Herb'e would be the one in need of my support. I'd often feel like a marriage guidance counsellor, mediating between my dolphin couple.

The mind games were similar to the special *connections* that I shared mainly with Duchess, although much more intense – psychic battles without that reassuring calm. Yet, somehow, the two were inseparably linked. Here, I'd embarked on a new form of training, where hand signals acted only as a backup to transmission of thought. And, throughout it all, my main objective was to keep my dolphins working as a team: individualism was not an option.

By late afternoon, Herb'e was still misbehaving, though his enthusiasm had waned somewhat. The sight of Duchess eating his share of the fish was obviously having the desired effect.

An empty fish bucket signalled a badly-needed intermission. By now, I was feeling headachy, drained and mentally exhausted – symptoms that would always accompany these encounters – yet I already firmly believed that this thought-based training method was the best way forward.

Only one question: at what cost?

❦ 79 ❧

"Tough session?" Vance remarked as he walked into the kitchen to find me slumped across the table.

"You could say that."

An understatement: Vance might have watched the training session, but he'd no idea *what* he'd actually witnessed. It had been like *The Clash of the Titans* out there; yet, to him, it had all looked so ordinary. Little did he know…

At some point today, we were expecting Gerry. He was bringing us two new presenters to relieve the workload and help open the shows. I was just about to embark on *Round Two* with Herb'e, when I heard his car pulling into the back yard of the dolphinarium. Moments later, he entered the kitchen, followed by two very pretty girls. "Hi, everything okay?"

Vance and I muttered a half-hearted greeting, interestedly peering over his shoulders at the attractive newcomers. "They're a bit of all right," Vance whispered.

"Your new colleagues, lads," Gerry grinned knowingly, "Kim and Joyce."

Following the usual exchange of pleasantries, an already besotted Vance wasted no time in whisking the girls away for a tour of the dolphinarium.

"Didn't take him long, did it?" Gerry laughed.

"I'll say — won't be seeing him for a while. Anyway, it'll give us chance to talk." I started to fill the kettle. "How's training going at North Liston?"

He answered sharply. "It's not! Stumpy's making no progress at all, and blind Scouse is holding Baby back. I just don't know what to do with Scouse." A note of desperation entered his voice. "How do you train a blind dolphin?"

Mental pictures, that's how, I thought. After all, if a dolphin can't see, there's no other way. The thought-based training technique I was developing with Duchess and Herb'e had already shown me that a dolphin needn't rely on eyesight alone. But I didn't say this to Gerry: assuming his question was rhetorical and my advice unwelcome, I remained silent.

"Are you ready for tomorrow?" he said, abruptly changing the subject. "Big day."

He was right there – days didn't come any bigger. In only twenty-four hours' time, we would perform our first show for the public: the culmination of months of hard slog... and the excitement made my head spin.

"Oh, by the way," he announced, grinning impishly. "I've got something for you." He beckoned me outside to his hatchback, lifted the door, then stood back. "Da-daaaa!"

I looked inside. "Oh, no!"

There, paddling in a pool of dirt and frantically trying to saw through the bars of their cage, were Smelly and Worse.

"You've got to be joking – why do we have to have them?"

"Well," Gerry gurgled, "Head Office think they'll be good for the shows. So... what do *you* think?"

"I think I need a drink," I groaned. "And poor Vance is going to need a double."

"A double – why?"

"Because he's the one who'll be looking after them."

❦ 80 ❧

As we drove back to our digs, I broke the news about Smelly and Worse to Vance. He wasn't too pleased. "Why me? Why do I have to look after them?"

"Because there's nobody else, that's why."

He couldn't really object, because he knew I'd have my hands full with Duchess and Herb'e's punishing show schedule. Head Office wanted the dolphins to perform a minimum of five shows a day, rising to eight or more on bank holidays. It seemed they were more than happy to throw us in at the deep end if it meant clawing back some of their investment. I'd already complained to Gerry that the schedule would be too demanding for Duchess and Herb'e, but he'd insisted that it wasn't up for discussion.

That evening, after doing battle with yet another appalling dinner, Vance and I both hit the sack early. I quickly fell into a tranquil sleep – which was unusual for me – but it didn't last long. As the clock struck two, I was again disturbed by the distant sound of crying. Uncertain what to do, I listened uneasily as the cries grew louder, eventually turning into screams.

Suddenly, an agitated Vance burst into the bedroom. "Can you hear it?" he whispered hoarsely.

I nodded, reminding him that I'd heard it for the past two nights.

"So, what do we do?"

"Well, really we should investigate, but it sounds like it's coming from the second floor, and that's out of bounds."

Vance chewed his mouth thoughtfully. "We'll leave it tonight," he decided, "but if it happens again, I think we'll have to say something."

When the noise eventually subsided, he retreated to his room, leaving me unable to sleep. I awoke in no fit state for our grand opening.

"I hardly slept a wink last night," I complained, as we struggled through breakfast. "We're expecting all the top brass today, and I'm shattered."

"Me too," Vance replied, looking annoyingly chirpy.

I rubbed my eyes. "Better keep Smelly and Worse locked up. We'll have enough on our plates without having to worry about them."

"Yeah, imagine if they took a chunk out of some poor kid," Vance replied gleefully. "Wonder what Head Office would say then?"

"They'd say nothing," I growled, "because the men in suits never admit to mistakes. Look what happened with Bobby." I was feeling decidedly hard done to and, to add to my troubles, I still hadn't made a decision about how to handle Herb'e's bullying. After some thought, I decided that I couldn't allow him to take advantage of our première, no matter how important the occasion might be. If he misbehaved, I would continue to give Duchess his reward. Gerry wouldn't approve, because his main concern was pleasing Rogers, but this wasn't Gerry's show – it was *mine*, so it was *my* call.

Throughout the morning, we all worked hard to prepare for the grand opening. After cleaning the stage and auditorium, we changed into our show gear: white tops and red miniskirts for the girls, blue tee shirts and two-tone split-flare trousers for me and Vance. A final microphone check, then we were ready. Nothing more to do, but open the doors to our public.

A nod for Vance and the girls. "Right, folks, let them in." A smile for Duchess and Herb'e. *"It's up to you two now. Give them a show to remember."*

❥ 81 ❥

As the auditorium begins to fill, I wait backstage nervously. I barely have enough tricks to get through a show, so Vance will have his work cut out as compère. It will be up to him to buy me time, to cover for an inadequate trick list with informative and witty chatter. Yet, funnily enough, Vance *isn't* nervous: he is focussed and thoroughly looking forward to the occasion.

I glance at the clock: twelve on the dot… high noon… show time.

"See you in a minute." Vance smiles, then disappears. Loud applause, then he begins his opening spiel. God, he's good… he could talk for England…

"Ladies and gentlemen, a big hand for your trainer, David Capello!" I'm on.

Rapturous applause greets me as I walk onto the stage – a stage that suddenly seems much bigger than I'd remembered. I look timidly across the water at the faces of the huge crowd seated in the auditorium. My heart pounds; my breathing is shallow. I glance fleetingly at a smiling Vance, then turn my gaze to Duchess and Herb'e. I keep well back from the pool's edge, taking a few moments to connect with them mentally. I see their heads bobbing in the water – they are waiting… waiting for me.

A deep breath… two steps forward… a hand signal for them to hold fast. I channel my adrenaline rush directly into their minds.

They are like greyhounds baying to break out of the traps. They're

192

becoming impatient. *"Come on, David, what you waiting for? Come on!"*

Go! I throw up an arm, signalling the opening bows.

Duchess and Herb'e shoot from the stage with the savagery of the unleashed. They dive – twin torpedoes, speeding through the water – circling, building speed. Then, they break through the mirror's surface, leaping into the air in absolute unison.

First bow…

… the crowd gasps…

second bow…

… the gasp builds into a roar…

third bow…

… a tumult of clapping and cheering…

Three bows complete; a loud drawn out whistle, and the first trick ended. *"Good girl, good boy, that's it, that's the way!"*

Back to the stage, where both dolphins lift themselves from the water to touch the palms of my hands, releasing their rewards.

As the shouting and applause subsides, my ears ring. I feel the excitement – not just that of the audience, but of Duchess and Herb'e, too. They are vibrant and gagging to move to the next trick.

I don't look at Vance. I don't look at the audience. I concentrate on Duchess and Herb'e. Only they exist. I hold them in a mental vice.

Handshake next. Duchess first… this is where Herb'e could make trouble.

Duchess rises and places her flipper into my right hand. *"Hello, beautiful!"*

My left hand, rigid like a wall and reinforced by a telepathic instruction, holds Herb'e at bay. *"Stay, Herb'e, stay!"* He thought about having a go at her then – I felt him. *"I'm watching you, Herb'e, don't start!"*

Now it's his turn. *"Hello, lad, nice to see you. Be a good boy."* A shake of his flipper, then release.

Long blow on the whistle, then hold both dolphins at the stage before feeding in unison. Second trick complete.

Next are the retrieval tricks – rings, hat and sunglasses. No problem – they've done these a million times in training. So far, so good.

Duchess and Herb'e are charged by the electricity bouncing around the auditorium, as am I. We charge one another.

"First part of the show complete. Keep it together, you two. Don't look at the audience, look at me – we've a long way to go."

Vance chats away to the crowd, but I barely hear him.

"Concentrate – don't let anyone or anything distract you. Hurdles next. You know the drill: I dip the pole into the water, and that's your cue. Take a good run up. I want two jumps together – nice and high – but make sure you don't touch the pole!"

Up they come, moving as one; but Herb'e touches the pole. Not hard – not even enough to break momentum – just a brush.

I blow my whistle.

Herb'e gives me a clever look. *"I touched the pole, didn't I?"* he smiles. He wanted to get one over on me, and he's succeeded.

I smile back. *"I know you touched the pole, clever clogs. But I'll let you off – this time."*

Mentally, I must maintain the pace: I can't afford to relax. Herb'e's cocky, but he's enjoying the show.

I think about putting the hoops in the routine, but it's risky. We didn't do the trick in rehearsal, and Duchess still doesn't like it. I turn to the ten-foot pole with the two adjoining hoops: shall I or shan't I? I make a decision: I'm going to try it.

Vance gives me a puzzled look and pulls the mic from his mouth. "That's not in the show," he whispers.

"It is now," I reply, "so start talking."

I wrestle the cumbersome prop to the pool edge. Vance continues his verbal build-up. Duchess and Herb'e bob in front of the stage. I look into their eyes. They say, *"That's not in the show."*

"I know, but you can do it."

Herb'e glances at Duchess; but her gaze is fixed on me. I feel her apprehension. *"You can do it, Duch – Herb'e will help you."*

Herb'e pulls his gaze from her and directs it at me.

"You will help her, won't you, Herb'e?"

He knows he is now in control. I have just given him the ammunition to ruin the show.

I concentrate harder. I won't − I can't! − draw my eyes from Herb'e... mentally, I'm at full stretch. *"Come on, come on!"*

A second later, he dives − and, with him, Duchess. I suspend the heavy prop six feet above the water. They circle, picking up speed; then, with one flick of their powerful tails, they leap from the pool and straight through the double hoops.

"Perfect, absolutely perfect!"

In frenzied excitement, I double the decibels shrieking from my whistle. Duchess and Herb'e executed the trick with flawless precision... together as one... a *Perfect Pair*!

My enthusiasm slows the smooth running of the show: this is the start I've been praying for. I try to steady myself... I must cool it... I cannot allow my exuberance to interfere with the pace... I must maintain momentum.

But now, I can afford to relax a little, because next up is the toothbrush − Duchess and Herb'e's favourite.

First for a good mouth tickle is Duchess, her jaws wide open, displaying a set of over one hundred pearly white teeth. My left arm remains rigid, signalling to Herb'e that he must hold and wait his turn. He's like a cat on hot bricks, bobbing impatiently as he waits.

"Thanks, Duch. Your turn next, Herb'e."

Like a shot, Herb'e bolts into the stage, his generous mouth open, inviting the large brush − not just to the roof of his mouth, but also his tongue. He loves a good tongue scratch. *"That's nice − you like that, don't you, lad?"*

We milk the trick for all it's worth, then, before moving on, I crouch over the poolside, arms stretched to give my two friends a reassuring cuddle. *"Keep it up, you beautiful people. So far, so good!"*

The show continues to go well. Up to now, Herb'e is too swept away with the occasion to bully − but it's only a matter of time. A couple of sloppy feeds tell me he's beginning to lose concentration. That could mean trouble, so I've got to keep him hooked.

I tell them, *"After every trick, you must touch the palm of my hand to claim your feed. I want you six feet out of the water − nothing less."*

Approaching the end of the show now, and time for Duchess' only solo trick: the highball. Herb'e's been a good boy so far, but this is where he might make his move. Although this highball is only twelve feet, he nonetheless resents Duchess performing solo.

He moves towards her with intent, mouth open and complaining.

"I'm watching you – if you ruin her trick, no fish."

I signal Duchess with my right hand, my left hand rigidly holding Herb'e at bay. Mentally, I strain. *"Stay, Herb'e, stay!"*

Begrudgingly, he complies, allowing Duchess to make the jump and delight the expectant audience.

"Well done, Duch! Thanks, Herb'e!" I feed both dolphins equally – her for performing the trick, and him for allowing her to perform it. *"This is easy – it's like receiving Danegeld, isn't it, Herb'e?"*

Final two tricks. I feel the pressure lifting but, mentally, I'm tiring… just a little longer, David, concentrate for just a little longer…

Wave goodbye complete. Now the closing bows – last chance for the camera buffs to get that all-important photo.

The thunder of applause signals that Duchess and Herb'e are once more in the air. A final extended blow of the whistle ends the trick, and I hear the voice of an enthusiastic Vance.

Final goodbyes and it's over. The show has gone better than I could possibly have hoped for; but mentally I'm tired – weary, in fact – and this is only the first show. Nevertheless, I fall to my knees, reach out my arms and offer a final cuddle and unspoken message to my two stars: *"Thank you, thank you – we did it!"*

But Herb'e's eyes sparkle mischievously. *"You owe me,"* he whispers with a smile, *"you owe me big time…"*

❧ 82 ❧

After the audience had departed, Rogers came backstage to offer his congratulations. By his side was Gerry – smiling, but disquietingly silent. He'd obviously clocked my insistence on maintaining the high feeds. Nor would he be pleased that I'd included the double hoops – I'd gambled. However, we had four more shows to perform so, if he had anything to say, he'd have to wait until the end of the day when he didn't have the head man by his side. He couldn't afford to rock the boat.

The remaining shows all went well enough but, towards the end of the day, Duchess and Herb'e were clearly very tired – too tired to be asked to work on night training sessions. I decided to leave it.

Whilst Vance and the girls busied themselves cleaning the auditorium, I retired to the kitchen to complete the logbooks. Suddenly, the door flew open and Gerry walked in.

"Good show… when did you decide to include the double hoops?" His tone was challenging, his face stern.

"Just before the show," I lied.

"And what's with the high feeds?"

"It maintains discipline, Gerry."

"You think you're the big man now!" he snapped, face reddening.

I held his gaze, but didn't take the bait. Speaking with measured calm, I said, "I don't know if you're aware, but I need more dolphins. There's no way Duchess and Herb'e can handle six to eight shows a day."

Gerry's expression darkened further, but he didn't reply. Instead, he turned on his heel and walked out, slamming the door behind him.

Hendle had only just opened, yet it had already given Gerry a new set of problems to deal with. Firstly, he knew I was right: Duchess and Herb'e couldn't manage such a punishing programme, so he'd have no choice but to provide us with more trained dolphins. Secondly, his star pupil was going his own way – and he didn't like it.

Perhaps I was moving a little too quickly for him.

Perhaps I was becoming a threat.

<h1 style="text-align: center;">❦ 83 ❦</h1>

A full ten days had passed since Duchess and Herb'e's debut show, and the pressure of performing had taken me up a notch. The psychic link that we shared had become stronger and clearer, making our three-way conversations seem almost normal.

Duchess and Herb'e had transported me to a realm where thought and speech merged: a collective consciousness. Think it or speak it, and the other two were aware. I was now in a universe that held no secrets and yielded no hiding place. I had journeyed into the unknown.

However, in the physical world, our predicament hadn't changed: we were still performing six shows a day, Herb'e was still bullying Duchess and Gerry was still behaving coolly. To add to the mix, we had two penguins shitting all over the place, and Vance and I were still hearing screams in the night.

This couldn't go on – something had to be done – so I kicked off by telephoning Gerry. "Tell Rogers that, if he wants six shows a day, he can do them himself, because I'm not willing to push Duchess and Herb'e any further."

To my amazement, Gerry agreed wholeheartedly. "I understand your predicament, David, so I've decided to send you Baby Dai and Scouse as a support team."

"Thank God," I said, a mixture of relief and excitement sweeping over me. "What can they do?"

He hesitated before replying. "Not much, I'm afraid – but they're better than nothing. Rogers wants eight to nine shows a day over the

July bank holidays, and they're only five weeks off."

My euphoria evaporated. "Impossible! How can I present a show using untrained dolphins?"

"I'm sorry, but it's the best I can do. I don't have anyone else – which is why I'm leaving for the States next week to collect a third shipment."

"Any good news?" I asked sarcastically.

"Yes, Baby and Scouse should be with you in three days' time, along with another presenter to lighten the load."

"And any hope of a cleaner? Or should I just stick a brush up Vance's arse?"

"Nothing that drastic," Gerry laughed. "A cleaner starts tomorrow. Her name is Beryl."

❦ 84 ❧

The day's shows were mostly up to standard – except for Herb'e occasionally misbehaving – but I couldn't complain because we were working both dolphins hard.

After the shows, Vance and the others cleaned up whilst I moved on to training – always a great opportunity to share some quality time with my dolphins. And after training, of course, came the team's playtime swim – something we all loved.

On the way home, Vance and I once again got around to discussing the screams in the night. We both agreed that we'd had enough and would definitely investigate if we heard them again.

After dinner, we retired early but, despite my best efforts, I found myself rolling about on my pillow with one ear cocked, unable to sleep. I heard the grandfather clock strike every hour... but it was on the stroke of two that it began...

Screaming.

Wailing.

I climbed out of bed and crept along the hallway to Vance's room, where I quietly opened the door. There he was: a large, snoring bundle, buried beneath a mound of bedding.

"Wake up," I whispered, tapping his shoulder. "It's happening again."

"What... what's happening? Go away, tell me tomorrow."

He turned over, muttering under his breath and snuggling further beneath his covers.

"No chance – we sort this tonight," I insisted, shaking him vigorously.

A few minutes later, a half-comatose Vance and I found ourselves creeping up the stairs to the forbidden second floor.

"Are you sure about this?" Vance whispered.

"Yeah, I'm sure – we've got to get it sorted."

By the time we reached the second floor landing, the crying had grown considerably louder, and seemed to be coming from a room at the far end of the corridor.

"What now?" Vance whispered.

"Keep going," I told him, pushing him firmly forward.

"I don't know about this…"

"Don't be so soft – we're almost there!"

As we neared the room, the cries grew louder and clearer and, all too quickly, we found ourselves dithering outside the door. Taking a deep, determined breath, Vance leaned towards it, pushing it just far enough open for us to take a furtive peep inside. There, we saw the strangest sight: a frail old woman, wielding a heavy stick from her bed, and, beside her, the sobbing figure of our hostess, Miss Crouch. We had at last encountered the second lady of the house: her mother, Mrs Crouch.

"I'm off," Vance hissed, taking a step back.

"No you don't," I retorted, blocking his way. "You're not going anywhere till we find out what's going on." Another push in the back propelled Vance fully into the room. Seeing him, the old woman suddenly stopped beating her daughter and stared.

"Is everything all right, only we heard crying?" I asked, innocently popping my head over Vance's shoulder.

"Yeah, we heard crying…" Vance repeated.

Miss Crouch remained by the bed, head bowed and weeping softly. But, to our amazement, Mrs Crouch placed her stick carefully on her eiderdown and began smiling. "Hello, who are you?"

She looked as old as Father Time and as frail as a butterfly, but nonetheless delivered her enquiry in a calm, confident manner. Here she was, addressing two strangers who'd invaded her bedroom at two o'clock in the morning... and doing so as if it were the most normal thing in the world.

"We're your new lodgers," I explained.

"Oh, that's nice... pleased to meet you. Can't you sleep?"

Bizarre.

"Not really, we heard a noise and thought someone might be in trouble."

"Oh no, everything's fine. You two stop worrying and get on back to bed."

"Well... if you're sure..." I hesitated uncertainly. "It's been nice meeting you."

"It's been very nice meeting you, too," she replied, smiling sweetly.

Bewilderedly, we returned her smile, then retreated, still not quite believing what we'd just seen.

"Vance, we've got to get out of here," I pleaded.

He gave me a concerned look. "You're telling me – it's a madhouse. Tomorrow, I'll get the papers and look for somewhere else."

Amen to that, I thought – amen to that.

❦ 85 ❧

Baby and Scouse were due today. We were expecting them around mid-morning, which meant we'd have just enough time to install them in one of the holding pens before embarking on the run of afternoon shows. It would be a busy day.

Vance spent the early part of the morning coaching the new girl presenter, whilst I gave instructions to our new cleaner, Beryl.

"Right, Beryl, your main duties will be cleaning the auditorium and looking after Smelly and Worse. You must make sure that those two don't get near the audience. We don't want people suing us for missing fingers."

"Smelly and Worse?" she repeated, giving me a puzzled look.

"Yes, Smelly and Worse – our adorable resident penguins."

"The man at the labour exchange never said anything about looking after penguins."

"Didn't he? Well, he was told," I lied.

"Hmm…" She gave me a measured look.

"Don't be alarmed, Beryl. *You* won't have to worry about Smelly and Worse, because *you'll* have a secret weapon."

She raised an eyebrow, and I thrust a deck scrubber into her hands.

"Let me introduce you to your most trusted ally – your prickly persuader – not just good for shifting penguin dirt, but also excellent for shifting penguins."

"I knew it sounded too good to be true," she commented drily. "Where do you want me to start?"

Yes... a major problem solved! Now I could relax and wait for delivery of our new charges.

As I meandered around the pool, I couldn't help thinking about our surreal experience with the two old girls. Poor Mrs Crouch, confined to her room, basically waiting to die; and her poor daughter, confined herself, in a way, basically waiting to live. I felt sad for them both and the tragic lives they were leading. But I also knew that Vance and I couldn't stay there any longer, and even though we didn't have anywhere else to go, we'd served notice that morning.

Suddenly, my thoughts were interrupted by Vance shouting. "Dave, Baby and Scouse have arrived!"

Within minutes, we were outside the dolphinarium, greeting Gerry as he walked towards us from the transport van. "How was the transport, Gerry? Everything okay?"

"Fine," he smiled. "They've both been very quiet – even Scouse. Philip's with them now."

"Right, let's get them in," I ordered. "Scouse first... he's the most likely to cause trouble. I'm putting them in a holding pen for now, because I don't want them disrupting this afternoon's shows."

In no time, Scouse was on the poolside, lying on a foam mattress whilst Philip checked him over and took the usual blood test. As I looked at him, I couldn't help thinking what an ugly dolphin he was: large head and stunted body, covered with black air burns – permanent scars from his botched transport from the States. His dorsal fin was missing a half-moon (probably a shark attack), and now, of course, he was blind.

Suddenly, I was overwhelmed by a feeling of compassion towards him: this poor, unlucky fella would be my greatest challenge to date, and I was determined to give him my all. I beamed him a message of encouragement. *"They've consigned you to the scrapheap, Scouse, but don't worry, we'll show them... we'll show them all..."*

Next came Baby Dai: a perfectly-formed infant dolphin whose tiny size made him a natural for somersault training – something I intended to exploit. Within a few short minutes, he had undergone the same routine medical and been deposited safely in the holding pen alongside

Scouse. Gerry handed me their logbooks, which – amongst other things – would tell me what they could and couldn't do. I wasn't expecting much.

"I have some good news for you," he told me, as I absently flicked through the pages. "I'm leaving for the States in a couple of days to pick up another dolphin shipment and, while I'm away, you'll be getting a new manager."

"That's terrific news," I enthused. "Not having to worry about the dolphinarium means I'll be free to concentrate on training."

"Thought that would make you happy," he smiled. "Well, see you in a month!"

He was clearly looking forward to his break abroad – lucky sod! "Okay, Gerry, enjoy – don't do anything I wouldn't do," I told him.

But, as he left, my thoughts turned to the disastrous last shipment.

I prayed that this time he'd choose his dolphins more carefully.

❦ 86 ❧

Duchess and Herb'e performed badly that day, repeatedly abandoning the stage to engage in conversation with their new neighbours.

It soon became clear that the arrival of Baby and Scouse was going to cause problems. Firstly, they'd cause a distraction for Duchess and Herb'e and, secondly, they'd steal much of their valuable training time. Then there was the logistics of housing four dolphins.

Only two dolphins could perform in the main pool at any one time, which meant that the other two would need to be penned until required. We'd have to establish a gating system, whereby once a team had finished performing, the other would take its place. Easier said than done. Nevertheless, such a system would be vital to the smooth running of the dolphinarium.

Training a gating system would take some considerable time: Baby and Scouse were still pretty raw in training terms and therefore less likely to comply; and Duchess and Herb'e would resent giving up the freedom of the main pool. So, it looked like Vance and I would be burning the midnight oil for the next three to four months.

That night, I worked Baby and Scouse in the cramped confines of their holding pen. Both were useless – in fact, it looked like Scouse had only just got used to taking dead fish.

"I don't know what the trainers at North Liston have been doing," I moaned. "These two can't do anything – they're virtually raw. We've only got five weeks before the bank holiday shows, so God knows what they'll be like… I'm not a miracle worker."

"They can't be that bad," Vance reasoned, peering into their pen.

"Believe me, they're worse than bad."

It was pointless to continue with any further training, so I released them into the main pool with Duchess and Herb'e. The two little dolphins dashed around excitedly, relishing the expanse of water.

"Better than North Liston, this, isn't it?" I told them.

Vance looked on, smiling. "Well, there go two happy little dolphins – they're having a ball."

"Yeah, our only problem now is how to get them back into the pen before tomorrow's shows. Still, they deserve a treat – life's not been good to them so far... especially poor old Scouse."

When I referred to Scouse as 'old', I did not use the word metaphorically, because everything about him suggested that he was indeed old – except his small size. Even Philip had found it impossible to assess his age. But one thing I did know, the little fella was tough – his scarred body was testament to that. In fact, he reminded me of a low-grade prizefighter.

As I watched him swimming with Baby, I recalled Gerry's words: "How do you train a blind dolphin?"

I believed I knew the answer, and couldn't wait to get started.

I was going to make this dolphin see again.

❦ 87 ❧

I found it impossible to sleep: my mind raced frenetically, a kaleidoscope of activity and imagery. Neither Baby nor Scouse had learned much up to now: each was literally a blank canvas and, as we shared no emotional ties, their training should seem clinical in comparison to Duchess and Herb'e's.

In training, I had originally planned to concentrate on Baby, because he could see. However, I suddenly realised that Scouse needed to be independent: total reliance on his infant guide was no longer an option.

This strange little dolphin fascinated me. I felt strongly that he was different from the others – not because of his handicap or looks, but because of *something*. There was a *connection* alien to any I'd encountered before: an emptiness. This lonely dolphin was lost in the dark and needed leading back to the light. That was my job... and if I failed, I'd have the perfect excuse... people would simply say, "How do you train a blind dolphin?"

My close relationship with Duchess and Herb'e had opened doors in my psyche that I hadn't previously known existed, propelling me off-world, so to speak. This higher state of consciousness had become the norm, giving me the ability to create pictures of the mind – illustrations that had an almost physical feel to them. These images were generated from behind the eyes, rather than from before them. The only thing required to access them was a receptive and willing mind.

The doors were already there; I only had to knock for them to be opened.

I knew exactly what to do. No one expected much of these two misfits, so if I could turn them into something special, I would have the training world at my feet.

No, I wouldn't sleep tonight… because I couldn't wait for tomorrow.

❧ 88 ❧

Over the next four days, both dolphin teams worked on gating… and, as feared, neither wanted to end up in the holding pen. You couldn't blame them: the cramped pen must have felt like a prison cell.

I could have used a net to shepherd them in, but this was dangerous, as a panicking dolphin could easily become entangled and drown. I instead resorted to good old-fashioned hand catching, physically swimming them in. Extreme as this might seem, they had to learn that non-compliance was futile. We couldn't operate without a proper gating system – it was literally that important.

Duchess and Herb'e proved to be the more reluctant pair, which surprised me, because I'd always believed that Baby and Scouse would pose the bigger problem. But these tiny dolphins craved attention and demonstrated a refreshing willingness to please. For the first time, they seemed to feel that they actually belonged. As if – at last – they had found someone willing to listen – and I was all ears.

That morning, I'd been so wrapped up in training my precious gating system that I'd failed to notice the lone figure sitting high in the auditorium. I'd no idea how long he'd been there so, when I finally spotted him, I naturally felt concerned. "Hello, can I help you?" I called.

The stranger jumped from his seat, beaming the broadest smile I'd ever seen and running towards me with an outstretched hand. "Hi! Will Chadderton – your new manager."

So, he'd arrived at last.

Will was a smallish man, with short blonde hair and a well-trimmed, ginger beard. But his most striking feature was a pair of thyroidy looking blue eyes: they bulged like organ stops, giving him an appearance of irrepressible joviality. In fact, his entire presence seemed to radiate laughter, and I couldn't help but immediately like him.

"Hi, I've been expecting you," I smiled, "you should have come down."

"No way… I've been enjoying the floor show with your cleaner and the penguins," he grinned, "it's better than going to the flicks!" Then, lowering his voice, he added, "I hate penguins, all they do is shit everywhere."

"Well, I won't argue with that."

"What do you need those bloody things for, anyway?" His question was delivered with such comic benevolence that I just had to laugh – he was a born comedian.

No doubt, I was definitely going to like him.

❦ 89 ❧

As morning broke, Miss Crouch again woke me with her customary dig in the ribs. "Breakfast in ten minutes…" But, thankfully, this would be the last time: Vance and I had found an apartment some miles away in Hendle city centre. Not ideal, but we were desperate to escape 'Munster Mansion', and beggars can't be choosers, as the saying goes.

So, after picking our way through a final bewildering breakfast, we bid our hostesses goodbye, then walked along the overgrown pathway for the final time. That night we would be sleeping in a new apartment, owned by an impressive sounding Joseph Michael Rorke.

At the dolphinarium, the day began as always: greeting our four aquatic friends, thawing fish and seeking out the nightly contributions of Smelly and Worse. The dolphins seemed to be getting along fine – no fighting or biting, just four friends having a pleasant game of 'flick the penguin'. This game was nothing new to Smelly and Worse – it had been a great favourite at North Liston – yet they still chose to remain in the pool with the dolphins rather than seek sanctuary in the holding pens. Perhaps they actually enjoyed being catapulted through the air – who could tell? I didn't profess to understand the workings of a penguin's mind.

Whilst waiting for the fish to thaw, Vance and I invited Will to join us for an early morning cuppa. As we sat around the kitchen table, he told us that he would be managing Hendle for one season only – just long enough to learn the intricacies of running a dolphinarium. Then, he would take up his permanent position at Welby Park, which was closer to his home.

His replacement at Hendle was to be a newly-appointed general manager, who would supervise the running of all Company dolphinariums from our upstairs office. This surprised me, because Gerry had never mentioned the plan to install a general manager and, as Company head trainer, he must surely have known about it.

Or must he?

Maybe the men in suits had deliberately left him in the dark... and if so, why?

❧ 90 ❧

After the day's shows, it was on to training with Baby and Scouse. Although I'd known that my new dolphins would make heavy demands on my time, I hadn't realised just how badly Duchess and Herb'e would miss their late-night training sessions. But their disappointment was unmistakeable as they dolefully watched us from behind the steel gate of the holding pen.

I'd been working with Baby and Scouse for a week now and, although they still couldn't do much, the change in them was evident. Baby was undoubtedly bolder and Scouse much more confident, giving me a solid base on which to build.

I worked the dolphins as a pair – just as I'd done with Duchess and Herb'e – only rewarding tricks performed in unison. Training wasn't straightforward, of course, because Scouse needed more time to understand; but, nevertheless, basic retrievals were going well. I firmly believed that, given time, I could make a nice little show with these two. Unfortunately, time was a luxury I didn't have.

After training, I released Duchess and Herb'e into the main pool to join their new friends. *"About time, too – thought you were never going to let us out!"*

As always, this signalled playtime, with everyone joining in the swim. This first playtime was undoubtedly a momentous occasion for Baby and Scouse, as neither had previously enjoyed close contact with humans. But, although curious, they kept their distance, and I soon realised that physical contact would take time – it couldn't be forced. I could only hope that they'd be encouraged by observing our closeness to Duchess and Herb'e.

Playtime over, we released Smelly and Worse. As always, they'd have the freedom of the entire dolphinarium for the night, but I had a feeling that when we greeted them in the morning, they'd once again be in the main pool and involved in a game of 'flick the penguin'. And, if so, it would merely prove something I'd long suspected – they were thick, absolutely thick!

Forty minutes later, Vance and I were sitting in our new apartment, accompanied by our landlord, Joseph Michael Rorke. Our luxury pad was in fact the second floor of an old semi-detached house situated deep in the heart of Hendle. Although spacious, it was furnished sparsely with just a few odd chairs. However, on the upside, it had two separate bedrooms and a bathroom so, since our social life wasn't exactly booming, it would do for the time being.

JMR was a larger than life character who seemed to find it impossible to sit still. A bachelor, he'd inherited the house from his late father, and rented rooms to help with its upkeep. Unfortunately, he lived on the floor below us, so would never be far away.

He stayed with us for over an hour, during which time he treated us to a monotonous, rambling monologue, complemented by flaring hands and violently wagging head. By the time we'd managed to get rid of him, both Vance and I felt drained.

"No wonder he's on his own… he never shuts up," I groaned. "He's enough to drive you potty!"

Vance nodded wearily. "Talk about out of the frying pan… I was struggling to stay awake." He was clearly tired, and he wasn't the only one: all I ever seemed to do these days was work, and I felt shattered. "When did we last have a day off?" I asked him.

"*I've* never had a day off," he replied, "and neither have you. We've worked late into the night, seven days a week since North Liston. If we carry on like this, we're going to get ill."

He was right: things had to change. For starters, my jealous possessiveness of Duchess and Herb'e had to end, especially now I had Baby and Scouse to train as well. Plus, I was being unfair to Vance and the girls: they'd always wanted to work the dolphins, yet I'd never given them the chance.

"Okay, new rules!" I said determinedly. "From now on, you and the girls will take over Duchess and Herb'e's shows. That way, you'll all get chance to present, and I'll keep fresh for night training."

He raised his eyebrows in surprise. "About time, too! And, while we're about it, why don't you try working the mic?"

"The mic?" I hesitated before answering. "I don't think so."

Vance shook his head. "Come on, Dave, you've never been on the mic and people are beginning to notice. What's wrong, are you scared?"

"Am I heck scared," I scoffed. But I was lying: the very thought of compèring a show sent shivers down my spine.

However, there was no fooling Vance: he had identified my weakness and was already formulating a remedy.

My mic-dodging days were coming to an end.

❧ 91 ❧

True to my word, I introduced Duchess and Herb'e to their new presenters. However, this was like handing them tickets to 'Club Chaos', giving them a golden opportunity to indulge in as much mischief as possible. For three days, I tried not to look as the shows began to resemble a sketch from *St Trinian's*. My two marauding stars put me in mind of schoolchildren tormenting a student teacher – with Herb'e taking the lead, of course.

"I'm watching you two – especially you, Herb'e! You're really taking advantage."

Herb'e's eyes twinkled with impish delight: he was quite obviously relishing my discomfort. *"Great this, Dave!"*

"Well, enjoy it while you can," I told him, *"because, from now on, I intend to take the last show of the day. That'll stop your gallop."*

Sensing my frustration and knowing that I was powerless to intervene, both dolphins gleefully continued to turn the screws. But, with the arrival of the final show, a miracle occurred, and I walked onstage to be greeted by two angelic faces, bathed in an aura of sweetness and light. *"You're not fooling me... I know your game... you're just winding me up."*

A picture of pure innocence. I had to smile: when I looked into their eyes, I saw myself. *"You two have done exactly what I would've done – you clever, clever people!"*

My next change was to establish a rota system, giving all staff one day off a week. I also implemented a late-night training system for my two dolphin teams, designed to keep Baby and Scouse on schedule for the bank holidays and give back stolen training time to Duchess and Herb'e.

Everyone benefited – especially my *Perfect Pair*, who delighted in the return to normality and, as a result, began to romp through their training. They were on fire – but their sudden surge of enthusiasm led to them demanding even more training time, so my long working day grew even longer.

Our new manager, Will, was all I hoped he'd be. He didn't interfere with training and promoted a friendly, relaxed atmosphere. His smooth running of the dolphinarium led us painlessly towards the bank holidays, which were now only four days away – financially, a huge period for the Company.

The approaching holidays also heralded the return of Gerry with the third dolphin shipment destined for North Liston. After its delivery, he was due to join us to help in the gruelling task of performing nine shows a day. I was looking forward to seeing him again and hearing all about his adventures in America… plus, I was keen to discuss the little matter of an overall general manager.

Yes, I'd be *really* glad to see him – just as long as he didn't get in our way.

❧ 92 ❧

On the morning of the first bank holiday, Will told us that the Company had confirmed its request for nine shows a day. We already knew that Gerry would be here helping to co-ordinate, but now it seemed that Rogers himself would be attending to oversee the entire operation.

"That's big of them," Vance said sarcastically. "What would we do without them? Strikes me there are too many chiefs and not enough indians around here."

"We already know what we're doing, so just try to humour them," I told him.

We expected only small audiences for the first and last two shows, which would make them perfect for Baby and Scouse – fewer people to complain! The five shows in between would likely be full houses, so would fall to Duchess and Herb'e. My gating system would be imperative to the smooth running of day – we couldn't afford any slip-ups – so this would indeed be judgment day for us all.

When Gerry arrived, we greeted each other warmly. He looked relaxed and invigorated following his break in the States, and clearly uplifted by the successful transport of the third shipment. But when I asked him how he felt about Company plans to appoint a general manager, his entire demeanour changed. Looking first shocked, then bemused, he repeated, "General manager? That's the first I've heard of it... are you sure?"

"Yeah, I'm sure. Will told us all about it."

He didn't reply, but his face – pale and bewildered – confirmed my suspicion that he hadn't been informed. Normally, I'd have pressed him to discuss it further, but the first show was due to start within the hour and I had to marshal the troops.

Besides, the discussion would have been very one-sided: Gerry obviously knew nothing... and, what's more, for the moment at least, he was speechless.

❦ 93 ❧

Thirty minutes before the shows were due to start, I consulted my enchanted mirror. All four dolphins were swimming free in the main pool, but the first to meet my eyes was Duchess, head cocked as usual.

"Hello, gorgeous – big day today!"

She gave me a generous smile.

Next came Herb'e, mouth open, head nodding – an unpredictable bundle of mischief.

"Are you going to be a good boy today?"

He nodded enthusiastically.

Then, last but not least, Baby and Scouse: two little dolphins, eagerly anticipating their day in the sun.

"Do your best, boys, that's all I ask – just do your best."

All four literally radiated excitement; they were ready and raring to go. Nothing left to do now but initiate the most important trick of the day: gating.

"Right, Vance, open the right-hand holding pen!" Now for the moment of truth: would they gate to signal?

I glanced at Gerry, who was watching from the auditorium, then mentally took hold of Duchess and Herb'e. Arms raised, I gave the signal… two claps… wait… two claps… *"Come on, don't let me down – in you go."*

Without hesitation, both dolphins turned and swam into the pen, to be greeted by multiple whistles and an abundance of fish. *"Very well done!"*

Now, only Baby and Scouse remained in the main pool – we were out of the blocks. I looked towards Will, who was standing by the doors at the back of the auditorium, watching me expectantly. "Okay, Will," I shouted, "let them in!"

Minutes later, the first of the bank holiday crowds began to descend into the auditorium; and, with them, Rogers, keen to view the show as a member of the audience.

Backstage again, and one final pep talk to calm Vance's nerves. Who was I kidding? He wasn't flapping – I was!

"Now remember, Vance, these two can't do much, so your spiel will have to get us through."

"No pressure then," he quipped with a smile.

We both knew only too well that I hadn't had sufficient time to get Baby and Scouse up to scratch – but, ready or not, these two little dolphins were about to perform their first ever show.

❦ 94 ❥

As I strode purposefully onto the stage, Vance gave me an introduction fit for a king. Although blinded by stage lights, I guessed the auditorium had to be at least sixty per cent full. Not good news: I had hoped for less. Still, nothing I could do about it now, so on with the show.

Baby and Scouse opened their performance with three successive bows – not performed in unison, but as individuals, which these two little dolphins were... something I'd been forced to accept. Then, it was back to the stage for a well-deserved reward.

"Great start, people – way to go!"

Their eagerness was refreshing, again convincing me that all they needed was time. Both dolphins worked through their limited routine joyously. They performed to the best of their abilities and, even though the public weren't blown away, Vance's superb commentary carried us through. We'd got away with it... just...

Afterwards, Gerry and Rogers joined us backstage. "They're not ready for shows," Gerry commented coolly.

I was furious – a swipe at my dolphins was a swipe at me. "You've just seen a minor miracle out there!" I retorted, turning on him angrily. "Those dolphins did *nothing* till I got hold of them."

Both men seemed taken aback by my snappy response and wisely chose not to pursue the matter any further. In fact, Rogers changed the subject altogether, complimenting me on my excellent gating system and obedient dolphins. Smiling benignly, he commented, "It's just like training dogs, isn't it?"

Gerry returned his smile politely – but I cringed. An innocent remark – but a remark that demonstrated a shameful ignorance of dolphins.

In stark contrast, however, Gerry's observation had been both shrewd and precise. Baby and Scouse weren't ready for shows – we simply hadn't been given enough time to prepare. And that made me angry: I was a perfectionist whose dolphins had to be the best.

I would never allow this situation to arise again…

No matter what the cost, I was determined to turn these two little dolphins into Britain's finest.

❦ 95 ❧

Four heavy days followed that first show of the Easter weekend, the Company extracting as many performances from us as humanly possible. Good Friday's till receipts had already sent an ecstatic Rogers on his way back to Head Office; but Gerry had remained with us to help with the rest of the shows.

Before the start of every show, I always walked onstage and banged a fish bucket onto the tiled floor; this done, I'd simply turn around and walk back into the kitchen. This seemingly innocent act was in fact cleverly manipulative, grabbing the attention of both audience and dolphins alike, and creating an air of excitement that left them bubbling with anticipation.

Today, however, things didn't go quite as planned... as I banged down my fish bucket, the stage lights glared on and the speakers blasted a fanfare of music, heralding the start of the show. I looked around for the compère, but he wasn't onstage yet... someone had jumped the gun, and if I didn't make a sharp exit, the show's opening could be ruined.

I dashed for the kitchen door, thumping into it heavily as it refused to open: it seemed to be locked. Confused and just a little flustered, I turned and made for the filter room door – also locked.

By now, the entire stage was bathed in light, permitting a puzzled audience to watch as I feverishly wrestled with door handles. In a final act of desperation, I flew back to the kitchen door, rattling it violently. Then, suddenly, I heard the low, steady voice of Gerry from the other side. "Get on that mic, Capello – you've dodged it long enough."

"Let me in, Gerry!" I pleaded. "You've had your joke, now open up!"

"No joke... get on that mic... everyone's waiting..."

Other than a humiliating flight into the crowded auditorium, I had no means of escape. My fate was sealed. Tentatively, I walked to the microphone, picked it up and put it to my lips.

I opened my mouth... nothing happened.

I swallowed hard... tried again.

"Good afternoon, ladies and gentlemen..."

My voice was literally shaking with fear. Mouth dry, and feeling faint, I gazed bewilderedly into the first row – and suddenly found myself gazing into the eyes of an elderly lady. Sensing my apprehension, she smiled encouragingly and mouthed, "Go on, love, you can do it!"

And I did – I delivered my introduction, speaking only to her, looking only *at* her, and drawing strength from her as she gently willed me on.

Next thing I knew, loud applause, and a smirking Gerry had joined me onstage. "There, that wasn't so bad, was it?"

I threw him an uneasy glance, then pulled the mic from my lips. "Bastard – you set me up."

What followed was without doubt the longest forty minutes of my life but, eventually, three closing bows and a long blast of the whistle ended the show – and my torment.

Somehow, I'd got through it. I'd done what I feared most: a show commentary.

As the applause died, I floated backstage on a cloud.

"Well, you've done it at last, and about time too!" Gerry smiled.

I felt so drained, I didn't even have the strength to remonstrate; I simply sat in a daze, recovering slowly.

"Not bad for your first show," Vance chuckled, bursting through the door.

"It was awful..." I spluttered. "I was scared to death, and what's more, everyone knew it!" Then, I smiled. "But next time, I'll be better... just you wait and see... believe me, Vance, *you've* got competition."

He beamed me a thoughtful smile: he knew me well enough to know that he would indeed have competition.

As for me, I couldn't wait to get back on the mic...

<h1 style="text-align:center">❧ 96 ❧</h1>

Over the next few weeks, I spent more and more time honing my compèring skills. Show commentaries released me from the mental pressures of presenting Duchess and Herb'e – valuable downtime, as even Baby and Scouse were now proving to be mentally tiring. It was as if my two teams were psychic vampires, slowly sucking the life out of me. There was no doubt that my thought-based training was taking its toll; yet the results were plain for all to see. Baby and Scouse improved with every show, excitedly embracing both training sessions and performances. In fact, the results were little short of miraculous.

Although still busy, we were now down to seven shows a day. With everything running so smoothly, I thought about taking a break: I desperately needed to recharge my batteries, and the last thing I wanted was to fall ill.

Confident that Vance and the girls could manage without me, I jumped into my car to begin the drive back home. And, as this would be my first visit since leaving for North Liston, I thought it only proper to arrive bearing celebratory gifts: two slabs of deep frozen fish for Dad and the cat, and a load of stinky washing for poor Mum!

Even though I appreciated spending time with my family, being parted from my dolphins felt strange, as if a chunk of me were missing. What's more, my sixth sense niggled ceaselessly... I had an overpowering feeling that all was not well with Herb'e.

I returned to Hendle three days later, accompanied by my family, who fancied a day out at the park. On arriving, we found the dolphinarium doors locked, indicating that a show was in progress. Even the ticket desk was closed... but, luckily, I spied Beryl skulking around nearby, sneaking a crafty cig. "Caught you!" I laughed, leaping out at her. "How about free entry to the show?"

She grinned. "You're lucky – we've pretty much got a full house, but there's just a few empty seats left on the back row."

Creeping furtively into the darkened auditorium, we found our places, then settled down to enjoy the show – a first for me, as I'd never before seen a performance from the audience's perspective.

But, within minutes, I found myself drifting away, that familiar, sweet nausea flooding my senses...

The *connection* had kicked in.

❦ 97 ❦

I've almost forgotten what it feels like, but here it is, and what's more, it's stronger... much stronger...

"David? Is that you?"

... it envelops me, overwhelms me...

"It is you! Where have you been?"

... robs me of breath...

"Where did you go?"

... head spinning...

"We've missed you..."

... nausea escalating...

The shriek of a vigorously-blowing whistle punches me back to reality, and I suddenly realise that Duchess and Herb'e have left the stage and are swimming towards the packed crowd. *"Where have you been? We've missed you!"*

They reach the security railings, then rise onto their tails, gazing up into the auditorium, chattering and squealing. What's more, the holding pen housing Baby and Scouse is a cauldron of bubbles. This isn't just two *connections* I'm experiencing... it's *four*...

A distraught Vance struggles to summon my two stars back to the stage; but he is ignored. They are resolute, calling... calling to me... *"We can't see you. Come down! What are you waiting for?"*

The audience watches, perplexed, as he continues to clang the fish bucket and blow his whistle...

And I watch with secret delight...

Obscured from view by two thousand strangers, yet they know I'm here: they feel me, just as I feel them. *"Hello, my beauties… so you've missed me, have you?"*

I am drowning in a torrent of emotion as the *connection* continues to embrace me… draw me in… call me home.

Suddenly, Vance stops banging on the fish bucket, raising his eyes to scan the ocean of faces before him. His confusion dissipates… he begins to understand. Taking the microphone from the bemused compère, he speaks. "Only one thing could cause this sort of behaviour: the dolphins' trainer must be somewhere in the audience. If you are there, Dave, come on down."

Unbelievable – Vance can't possibly see me, yet he knows I must be here. My mum, dad and sister blink at me, wide-eyed, as the implications of what they're witnessing sink in. Even I find it hard to believe… it's incredible, absolutely incredible!

"Come on, Dave – I know you're out there…" Vance repeats his call.

Dizzy with pride, I rise from my seat and begin making my way down the steps of the auditorium. *"Coming, my beauties!"*

Seeing me, the crowd breaks into rapturous applause. I walk slowly, milking their cheers and relishing the moment, my eyes fixed on my two stars bobbing impatiently behind the security railings.

"Calm down, I'm here," I tell them, as they thrust their heads into my waiting arms.

"You're back, you're back! Where have you been?"

I stroll towards the stage, throwing Baby and Scouse a self-satisfied look as I pass their holding pen. *"Have you missed me?"*

They nod their heads enthusiastically, their laughter reverberating throughout the auditorium. By the time I reach the stage, I am drowning in a psychic storm.

Duchess and Herb'e are at my feet: they have followed me, their cries of *"Where have you been?"* still echoing inside my head.

Vance grins and hands me his whistle. "You'll need this…"

The audience waits breathlessly.

But I'm not wearing kit, and the salt water will ruin my new leather shoes... Then, hanging the whistle around my neck, I bring Duchess and Herb'e to order. Never mind the shoes... this is more important. *"Are you ready, my beauties?"*

They deluge my brain with raw excitement...

Then, we begin... and deliver one of our best ever shows – one I wish would never end.

By the time my two stars perform their closing bows, the crowd is roaring. It may never be this good again. *"Just listen to that!"* I tell them. *"Fantastic!"*

Perhaps our audience realises that this show is different. Perhaps the people know they have witnessed something special – something truly magical.

Still super-charged by the experience of a lifetime, I retire backstage to wait for the auditorium to empty. I am immeasurably proud. If ever I have had any doubts about the veracity of the psychic bond that I share with my dolphin friends, today those doubts have been forever dispelled. There is no other explanation for what has just taken place.

Which reminds me, I must call Philip – Herb'e's sick.

❦ 98 ❧

We all arrived early to prepare for Herb'e's catch. Although it would have been far easier to do this in the confines of the holding pen, I decided instead to use the main pool, so as not to compromise my gating system. If Herb'e started to associate the pen with catches, he'd never again enter it voluntarily.

But Herb'e's catch wasn't the only problem… something else had caught my attention: the water condition. The crystal mirror that had always beguiled me was slowly turning green. Water readings had been deteriorating rapidly over the past few weeks, forcing me to work with higher quantities of chlorine – something I preferred to avoid, as it was detrimental to the dolphins' health. But since the arrival of Baby and Scouse, the pool's filtration equipment had clearly struggled to cope. This was puzzling: the North Liston pool had housed six dolphins, yet remained clean, so why couldn't the Hendle pool cope with four?

My thoughts were interrupted by Beryl trying to persuade a reluctant Smelly and Worse back to their enclosure. "Get in, you two, I've got more to do than mess about with you all day!"

Standing behind her, thoroughly enjoying the entertainment, was a smirking Philip, briefcase in hand. "Hello, David, what's the problem?"

"There's something wrong with Herb'e – he's sick."

"Really?" He walked to the poolside, stared at him for a few moments, then gave me a puzzled look. "Are you sure? He looks fine to me."

"I'm sure," I replied firmly. "Something's definitely wrong."

Without questioning me further, he placed his briefcase on the floor. "Okay, let's have him out."

With the foam mattress already in place, we embarked on the catch. As always, I made for the head, whilst Vance took the tail. It all went with remarkable ease, as a subdued Herb'e showed little taste for a fight. *"You don't feel too good, do you, lad?"*

After making a thorough examination and taking a blood sample, Philip administered the usual injection of multivitamins, then speedily packed his briefcase. "I should have the blood results by late this afternoon," he assured me, "so I'll give you a call early this evening."

Not long after he'd departed, we embarked on the afternoon shows. But, as the day wore on, it became more and more obvious that Duchess was carrying a lethargic and off-colour Herb'e, and I found myself anxiously awaiting the vet's call.

When it came, it was as I expected. "Right, David, I've got Herb'e's results. Firstly, he's showing signs of anaemia, so he's going to need some heavy doses of iron. But, more worryingly, the test has detected an infection of some kind, which means he'll need antibiotics as well."

"So, what's the infection?"

"We don't know… but we think it could be waterborne."

I thought about my ever-clouding mirror. "I'm getting some very strange pH readings at the moment, plus I'm having to work on higher chlorine levels. Do you think that might be the problem?"

Philip hesitated before replying. "Not sure. Let's see if the antibiotics do the trick first. Meanwhile, keep monitoring the water."

Wishing him goodnight, I was about to hang up, when he suddenly asked, "David, how did you know that Herb'e was sick? He showed no obvious signs."

My answer was simple: "I just did."

Sixth sense, intuition or a subconscious *connection*, I wasn't sure; but this ability to sense impending trouble would remain with me throughout my training career. And Philip, to his credit, never once doubted my judgment: he always came when summoned.

As for me, I was never wrong.

❧ 99 ❧

Late-night training for my four dolphins continued relentlessly as I pushed for more and more tricks. Herb'e had responded well to his medication, seemingly having recovered much of his energy. However, a continuing and rapid decline in water quality had begun to generate other problems, and conditions for my dolphins were fast becoming intolerable.

Gerry hadn't been to Hendle in over a month, because he'd had his hands full break training the third shipment at North Liston. Nevertheless, he'd continued to mentor me daily by telephone. I'd raised my concerns about the efficiency of the filtration equipment in earlier conversations, but now I formally asked permission to dump the pool. Realising the urgency of the situation, Gerry immediately relayed my request to Head Office, only to be turned down because a pool dump was deemed 'too expensive'.

"It's your call, Dave," he told me, when he rang to break the bad news. "They've refused permission, so if you *do* dump the water, *you'll* have to carry the can."

"Look, Gerry, Herb'e's only just getting better, and now I've got four dolphins breaking out in blisters and swimming with their eyes closed. What do you expect me to do?"

Gerry paused a beat, then said, "You must do what you think is right for your dolphins. But be prepared to accept the consequences."

And so was born my first act of rebellion against the Company: a secret water dump.

Even as dolphinarium manager, Will didn't have the power to defy Head Office and sanction a dump; nevertheless, I felt duty-bound to inform him of my plans. To my surprise, he fully agreed that the ditch was necessary, but reiterated Gerry's warning: if Head Office found out, I could be sacked.

We therefore agreed a compromise: I would dump only *half* the pool, giving myself sufficient time to replace the water before the start of the next day's shows. With no loss of takings, the Company would be none the wiser. It would mean working two days and a night without sleep, but there was no other alternative: my dolphins were burning in their own excrement.

Gathering the team together, I outlined the plan. "Right, everyone, this is what will happen. After today's shows have finished, we lock the doors and gate the dolphins – two dolphins to each pen. Next, we seal off the pens with the waterproof doors. Bear in mind that the doors haven't been tested yet, so we'll have to keep checking the water levels, just in case. That done, we start the dump."

Duchess and Herb'e gated, no problem, but Baby and Scouse refused to enter the unfamiliar left-hand holding pen. So, before we could begin, we had to make two tough catches, physically swimming them in – the last thing we needed. We were now behind time.

After sealing the pens, I approached Will to ask him if he wanted to go home. "If Head Office finds out about this, you can always tell them that you didn't know about it. I don't want you getting into trouble because of me."

Will shook his head solemnly. "You're not getting rid of me that easily – you'll need all the help you can get tonight."

I didn't argue – we had already lost valuable time catching Baby and Scouse. "Right, that's sorted, then. Let's start the backwash."

Backwashing entailed putting the filters into reverse so that, instead of pumping water around the pool, they pumped it into the drains. If all went well tonight, it should hopefully mean good riddance to fifty per cent of Hendle's toxic waste.

It would take many hours to lose that much water, and even longer to refill the pool to capacity, so it was going to be a stressful night for everyone. That included my dolphins: they'd be swimming in pens of stagnant water – pretty dire conditions. On the positive side, whilst they were safely penned, I'd be able to 'shock' the remaining bad water with a huge dose of chlorine, greatly improving its quality and appearance.

I finally managed to ditch fifty-five per cent of the pool before feeling morally compelled to stop backwashing and start refilling – after all, Will and I did have a deal – but the stolen extra five per cent was a valuable bonus.

Throughout the best part of the night and all the morning, Vance, Will and I tirelessly hauled bags of salt, emptying them into the slowly filling pool in an effort to redress the fresh/saltwater balance. We eventually finished at 11.15 am the following day, giving us just one hour before the start of the shows.

By this time, we all three looked like zombies, but it was worth it: Head Office would suspect nothing until the next water bill arrived.

Surveying my weary troops, I couldn't help smiling. "Good work, lads – job done!"

⟨ 100 ⟩

The water looked fresh and clean, with chlorine levels almost back to normal. The filtration problem might not be going away but, for now, I was just thankful to have everything back on track.

All my dolphins seemed happy and eager to work – so much so that I decided to begin back somersault training with Duchess and Herb'e. This trick was the first leg of the thing I craved most: the full somersault routine, which also included the body spins and the revered forward somersault.

But *my* routines would be different from those of any other trainer. I dreamed of two dolphins performing as one: a shadow ballet with two silhouettes rolling through the air in absolute unison – a *Perfect Pair*.

For me, this was the ultimate quest… I had to have it. Little did I realise, however, how quickly my dream would grow into obsession – unnatural, ugly and punishing…

I'd already figured out how to train the back somersault. Firstly, I'd take a seven-foot pole with a beach ball dangling from the end, then get the dolphins to jump six feet into the air and hit the ball with their noses. Critically, the dolphins would have to be facing me when they did this – I would not allow them to approach from the side.

Once they'd achieved this unremarkable feat, I'd then begin pushing the pole forwards as they jumped from the water, forcing them to stretch back their heads to hit the ball, inevitably causing them to fall onto their backs.

To the untrained eye, this would look shabby and pointless. But I knew that, once they'd reached this stage, I could remove the prop and start mind training: transmitting mental images of the somersault proper.

Of course, all this would take a lot of time and effort, but I'd just have to be patient. I didn't want to push my dolphins too hard – there was always tomorrow. But with Duchess and Herb'e's night training agenda now fully mapped out, I hoped to achieve the back somersault in just short of three months.

As for Baby and Scouse, they were still below show standard, but improving at pace.

The most important thing was that both teams continued to progress.

❧ 101 ❧

Later that evening, Vance and I crept stealthily into our flat, trying not to alert JMR to our return – but there was no fooling his bionic ears. "Hello, lads, only just finished work?"

He waylaid us like this virtually every night, keen to gossip about the day's news and leaving us with literally no time to chill. But, tonight, I found him particularly irksome – I'd started with a dull headache and desperately needed some sleep.

"Vance, I'm tired enough without him bending my ear every night. We've got to find somewhere else to stay," I moaned, after he'd left.

"You're right, we're getting no peace. Looks like it's back to the newspaper ads," Vance sighed wearily. "I'll start tomorrow."

Despite my tiredness, the pain in my head stopped me from falling asleep until the early hours. However, by the time we set off for work next morning, it had thankfully gone.

Manoeuvring through the traffic, we made a quick detour to the corner shop to pick up the local newspapers, then Vance hit me with his latest brainwave. "I've been thinking... why don't we include Smelly and Worse in the Baby and Scouse show? It'll add a whole new dimension to the performance."

"You must be kidding," I retorted. "We don't want those two shitting all over the stage while we're trying to do a show."

"No, it'll work, believe me. The audience will be so busy watching them, they won't realise how little Baby and Scouse can do."

I still wasn't keen on the idea, but Vance presented a convincing argument and, as always, I allowed him to talk me round. So, during our next show, we allowed the penguins to wander freely around the stage, at least confident that Beryl would be standing guard with a deck scrubber should they try to escape into the auditorium.

To my amazement, Vance's idea worked beautifully: the shows ran smoothly, and whenever Baby and Scouse messed up, Vance artfully shifted the blame onto Smelly and Worse – much to the delight of the audience. It looked like our irascible penguins were a hit.

But Vance couldn't leave it there: just short of a week later, emboldened by success and oozing confidence, he started to improvise. "Ladies and gentlemen, these are the only penguins in the country who can perform the revered triple forward somersault," he announced.

The audience gaped at him with disbelief – and they weren't the only ones. As he launched into one of his flamboyant spiels, I listened to him, mesmerised. What on earth was he going on about?

"Triple forward somersault? Are you joking?" I whispered.

"Not joking. Watch and learn, Grasshopper… watch and learn…"

It was then that I noticed Smelly standing next to Vance at the edge of the pool, no doubt pondering whether to go for a swim or take a chunk out of his leg.

Still gabbing into the microphone, Vance surreptitiously edged behind the unsuspecting bird and carefully positioned his toe beneath its bottom. Then, suddenly, he flicked it into the air, spinning it into one of the finest triple forward somersaults I'd ever seen. Fantastic – if only Duchess and Herb'e could do that!

The crowd roared with laughter, applauding a smug Vance loudly.

Cockily, he turned to me and grinned. "Did you like that?"

I didn't reply. I wasn't sure that I liked it at all. However, there was no doubt that his trick had been a roaring success. So, why did it make me feel so uncomfortable?

Only time would tell.

❧ 102 ❧

Several weeks passed uneventfully, then, one morning, Gerry rang me with some unwelcome news. "I'm sorry, Dave, but you're not going to like this – I've got a problem and it looks like you're my only solution. West Coast dolphinarium is nearly complete, which means I'll soon be pulling all the remaining dolphins out of North Liston."

"Doesn't sound bad so far," I told him.

"That's the good part. The bad part is that West Coast only has one holding pen, and you've got two, so you're going to have to take an extra dolphin."

"Which dolphin were you thinking of?" I asked tentatively.

"I'm sorry, Dave, but it's going to have to be Stumpy."

"Oh no, Gerry, come on," I wailed. "He's too sick to train, and I've already got my hands full with my four. Where am I going to put him? I can't keep him locked in a holding pen all day."

"There's nothing else I can do – you'll have to take him."

Having a sick dolphin foisted on me was the last thing I needed. It would interfere with training and put even more strain on an inadequate filtration system. But, although I argued my case, I knew deep down that Gerry didn't have any other option.

However, this move meant that we at Hendle would now be placed under enormous pressure to keep the dolphinarium running on an even keel.

Without doubt, life was about to get very difficult.

❦ 103 ❧

I'm standing here, waiting to go on stage, yet all I can think about is Stumpy. What the hell am I supposed to do with him?

"Stop daydreaming – our adoring public awaits." Vance taps me on the shoulder as he strides onstage, laughing confidently. "Another day, another dollar."

This is the first show of the day; Baby and Scouse are in the pool, and we only have a small audience.

I'm still unsure about having Smelly and Worse onstage, but the public seem to enjoy them, so I let them be and tell myself that they're at least earning their keep.

The show opens in its usual spectacular manner, with both dolphins performing their opening bows, accompanied, of course, by the animated intro of a hyper Vance. He's obviously enjoying himself. Being on stage with Baby and Scouse is his high – no pressure, just aimless rabbiting with not a care in the world.

Baby and Scouse seem to be enjoying themselves, too – it's amazing what a bit of confidence can do. In fact, the only bad part of this show is coming up: 'the Smelly and Worse trick', or 'flick the penguin', as Vance likes to call it. But, today, Vance seems to be talking much more than usual...

"Come on, Vance, get on with it. We haven't got all day."

"I can't get them into position," he hisses.

He's right, he can't. Today, the penguins aren't playing ball – maybe they're not quite as thick as I've always believed. They seem to have grown wise to Vance's trick, purposely hanging back and steering well clear of both him and the poolside.

Normally, Vance delivers his spiel from the right-hand side of the stage, but since the two penguins are today sticking to the left, he's forced to swap sides.

"Leave it, Vance, it's not worth the trouble," I tell him.

"No, no, no, it'll be all right – give me a minute." He's shuffling behind them, trying to herd one of them to the pool's edge.

"Vance, just leave it, will you?"

He doesn't answer. He's determined to have his way. After several minutes of distracted patter and complex manoeuvring, he at last manages to get one of the birds into position. Stealthily, he pushes his toe beneath its bottom, then – before it has chance to escape – launches into a hurried announcement introducing the triple forward somersault.

The crowd barely has time to switch its attention to the penguin, before Vance hastily executes the flick.

Today, however, the penguin has a trick of its own…

Instead of squatting amenably on Vance's foot as usual, it clamps its stumpy little legs around his toes. So, instead of being catapulted into the air, the gritty little bird is left clinging to his foot like a limpet-mine.

Vance's previous success with this trick has relied on the comic timing of his delivery, but now all that is lost. The audience sees only a panicking compère with a penguin stuck to his foot.

There's total silence as a frustrated Vance performs what resembles a primitive mating dance, hopping about the stage with one foot in the air. "Let go, you little sod, let go!"

But the defiant penguin doesn't let go. Instead, it rides his foot with gutsy determination, hanging on for a full four seconds before plopping miserably into the water. There's a short silence, then groans emanate from a thoroughly unimpressed audience and, no matter how hard Vance tries, he cannot win back the crowd.

But, to make matters even worse, Smelly has clambered clumsily out of the pool and taken flight in the direction of the auditorium, where Beryl, armed with deck scrubber, now strides menacingly towards him like an Amazon warrior. "Get back, come on, back to your cage…"

The audience watches in disapproving silence as big Beryl bullishly jabs at the diminutive penguin, forcing him back towards the stage. Surely this can't get any worse…

We perform the remainder of the show to stony faces, reaping scant applause – and no wonder. I'm thankful when it ends.

"That went well, Vance. Any more bright ideas?"

Needless to say, that's the end of the penguin trick – thank God. Vance has gone to the well one too many times, and I – like an idiot – have followed.

❦ 104 ❧

I have been working on the back somersault for well over three weeks, and progress is good. So good, in fact, that I'm convinced Herb'e already holds an image of it in his mind. The only problem is getting him to share it with Duchess. This clever and mischievous dolphin won't part with his secret lightly – he'll have to be coaxed, which can only mean more punishing mind games.

I can't help smiling. I only have to close my eyes and visualise his face to know that it's true. If I look deeply enough into my own mind, I can sense his psychic paper trail penetrating the darkness. He's already reserving one of my many dream rooms in joyous anticipation of yet another telepathic chess game.

I am once again stepping into that higher plane of communication with ease. Non-verbal exchanges bounce effortlessly around my head, and I find the intimacy of it all truly rewarding.

Duchess and Herb'e have an uncanny way of invoking powerful feelings, reminding me just how privileged I am to experience things that other people can only dream about. No matter what the heartache, times like this make it all worthwhile... very special. It's just a pity about the headaches; headaches that always accompany our psychic encounters... headaches that are getting worse and taking longer to shake.

"Herb'e, stop moaning and concentrate!" I tell him.

His eyes sparkle as he remonstrates.

"Never mind him, David, I'm listening." As always, Duchess draws

my smile, and I once again fall under the spell of those bewitching blue
eyes.

"My lovely Duchess, you always help me along, don't you?"

Her gaze is gentle, and I feel a *connection* of overwhelming love.

"My beautiful, beautiful Duchess…"

I note Herb'e's narrowed eyes. *"No need to be jealous, Herb'e, I love
you too."*

He doesn't answer, but hides within his silent *connection*.

"Playing hard to get, Herb'e?" I give him a concerted stare, which he
returns in spades. *"You already know what I want, don't you, Herb'e?"* I
listen, but he doesn't reply: old crafty Claude is holding his cards close
to his chest. But he doesn't fool me – we both know that *he* holds the
key to the somersault.

Our mental bond is altogether sharper and clearer than the one I
share with Duchess. She's emotional, whilst he's calculating, and, even
at this early stage, I'm positive he knows what to do. *"You know all
right, but you won't tell Duchess, will you?"*

Again, no answer: Herb'e's aware that he's been rumbled, but he's
smug and won't make this any easier for me. He and I will engage in a
hundred more moves before I win the game and get this trick. *"Clever,
clever Herb'e."*

Suddenly, I hear Will shouting from the top of the auditorium.
"Telephone, David… Gerry!"

This is the call I've been dreading. I already know what's coming:
confirmation that all Company dolphins will be leaving North Liston
by the end of the week.

I am about to take charge of one sick little dolphin. In a matter of
days, Stumpy will be on his way to Hendle.

❧ 105 ❧

Sunday morning arrived all too quickly. Gerry would soon be on the road with his five dolphins – four destined for West Coast, and one for us.

This would be a flying visit, which was a pity, because we hadn't had chance to chat face-to-face for many months. Still, there would be other opportunities – the most important thing now was the well-being of the dolphins.

Whilst Beryl and the girls busied themselves cleaning the walkways, Vance and I set about removing the safety railings surrounding the pen where Stumpy would be kept. Not long afterwards, we heard the sound of air brakes outside the dolphinarium.

"Any problems?" I asked, as a smiling Gerry jumped down from the back of the van.

"No, everything went like clockwork."

Good to see him again, but no time for pleasantries: we had to get Stumpy into the water and Gerry back on the road with the greatest possible speed.

An efficient transfer saw the little dolphin safely penned and Gerry on his way to West Coast in less than fifteen minutes. Then it was time for a team chat.

"Right, everyone, I want you to give this little dolphin as much fuss and attention as humanly possible. He's going to spend a lot of time alone in this pen, because we can't have him in the pool during shows or training. It's unfortunate, but we simply have nowhere else to put him."

I felt bad about leaving Stumpy in this way – this sweet-natured little dolphin needed affection – but I had absolutely no choice.

He was yet another heartache to add to the list – but, sadly, one I didn't expect would be here for very long.

❧ 106 ❧

Despite having dumped over half the pool, I still found it impossible to maintain water quality. I did my best, upping chlorine levels and dumping water in small doses by backwashing the filters every two days. But Stumpy's arrival had inevitably increased the pressure on an already overburdened filtration system and, before long, I found myself contemplating a full pool dump, which would once again put me at loggerheads with Head Office.

As for Stumpy, a full month had passed since his arrival, and the poor little fella was still spending at least seven hours a day in his cramped holding pen. It pained me that I couldn't give him more attention; but the afternoon shows and ongoing training made it impossible for me to include him in anything constructive. Although haunted by his plight, I couldn't sacrifice the important training schedules of my two pairs. They had to come first, no matter what the cost.

Nevertheless, despite the unfailing support of Vance and Will, I began to crack under the guilt and pressure. My moods darkened, my temper shortened and my headaches grew worse.

To add to my troubles, Duchess and Herb'e were becoming ever more demanding, pushing me into more and more mind duels, leaving me mentally and physically drained. It was as if they were trying to move me to an even higher level of consciousness.

"Come on, David, what's wrong? Why can't you understand?"

They were now opening doors to rooms I found impossible to

enter. It was as if my mind couldn't cope, yet access to these privileged places was what I'd always longed for. Why couldn't I pass through? What was wrong with me?

I drifted through the next ten days in a zombie-like state, until everything reached a climax. Standing at the pool's edge, staring into my enchanted mirror, I suddenly felt it tugging at me… drawing me in. The water's glare made me feel dizzy, leaving me reeling and staggering as if drunk. The dull headache that had plagued me for weeks suddenly erupted into a screaming pain…

Next thing I knew, I was on my knees… head about to explode… then, I felt someone gently lifting me to my feet and guiding me back to the kitchen.

What was happening to me? Felt sick… couldn't think… nothing made sense…

I'd totally broken down, and the rest time I'd never allowed myself was now imposed on me, like it or not. Doctor's orders: one month's sick leave with immediate effect.

❧ 107 ❧

It felt good to awaken in my own bed: warm, cosy and at peace, with the reassuring voices of my family drifting upstairs and the pressures of the pool seemingly a million miles away.

I felt a bit spaced out – thanks to the Valium I was taking – yet couldn't shake the glorious feeling of having just escaped from prison. Freedom at last!

During my first week's sick leave, I received only two calls from Hendle; both from Will, keen to check on my welfare and reassure me that all was well at the pool.

During the second week, I received three calls. "Don't worry about a thing, David," Will assured me. "Vance is doing a great job and everything's fine. You just concentrate on getting better…"

By the start of the third week, however, Will's tone had changed.

"Not trying to pressure you or anything, but we're having a bit of trouble with Duchess and Herb'e. Nothing too serious – they're just not performing up to scratch. I think they're missing you…"

Nothing too serious actually meant that Duchess and Herb'e had stopped working altogether, leaving Baby and Scouse to carry all the shows. To make matters worse, it seemed that Stumpy's food intake had fallen drastically and the water was smelling like a urinal again.

My month's sick leave had just come to a premature end.

First thing next morning, I made the short journey back to Hendle, where Will and Vance were waiting to greet me, relief evident on their faces.

"Thank God you're back – the wheels have totally fallen off," Will moaned. "Everything's gone wrong and we're having to cancel shows. Do you think you could maybe do a week until we're back on our feet?"

I sighed. "Look, Will, officially I'm still on sick leave… I shouldn't be here. But I'll strike you a deal: I'll bring Duchess and Herb'e back online, if you allow me to ditch the pool. You know it's the only way."

Poor Will, I'd put him on the spot – he knew that Head Office would never sanction a ditch, no matter how bad the water, which would mean once again resorting to stealth. Nonetheless, he agreed that – whatever the consequences – the water must go.

The full dump would mean the three of us – Will, Vance and me – once again working two days and a night without sleep, plus losing a day's shows. Even worse, three of my dolphins would have to share one holding pen, remaining sealed in stagnant water until it was safe to release them back into the pool – around twenty-six hours, by my reckoning. These would have to be the smallest dolphins: Baby, Scouse and Stumpy.

This was hardly the ideal way to come back from a breakdown, but the seriousness of the situation could not be overstated: the water had to go, and fast.

We began ditching the pool that very night.

And so, as the saying goes, out of the frying pan into the fire… I was back.

❧ 108 ❧

It had been a long, stressful slog, but worth it. Having completely dumped the pool, we now only had to wait for it to fill again. I'd already warned Will that we'd lose all tomorrow's shows, but I just hoped the closure didn't stretch into a second day. He was a good man, and I didn't want to get him into trouble with Head Office.

My thoughts then turned to Duchess and Herb'e, and their refusal to work during my absence. Bringing them back online would be easy: they'd made it clear that their loyalty lay with me, and only me, which threw up some interesting possibilities – especially when it came to dealing with Head Office.

I was still pondering the potential advantages, when suddenly I heard a loud cry from the auditorium, followed closely by a dull thud. Thoroughly alarmed, I dashed through the door and onto the stage area, there to find Will lying prostrate in a pool of penguin dirt, with an irate Worse snapping at his ankles. He'd clearly slipped on the stinky stuff, giving one half of our dastardly duo the perfect opportunity to launch an attack.

Face contorted with pain and rage, Will leapt to his feet, grabbing his tiny tormentor and pinning its flippers flat against its body. "Rotten, lousy, nasty little bastard! I hate these bloody things!"

I remember thinking how temper had clouded his judgment: bad idea, grabbing a penguin like that – I wouldn't do it. "Be careful, Will, it'll have you!"

"Have me? I'll kick the little bastard up the arse if it tries to bite me again!" He held the penguin aloft, shaking it uncontrollably and bellowing into its face. "Look at it, just look at it – dirty, smelly, ugly, useless thing…" So engrossed was he in his tirade that he totally missed the warning signs of an imminent second attack.

With breathtaking speed, the penguin's head twisted around, frantically sawing at Will's hands and forearms with its razor-sharp bill.

"Aaargh! Bloody hell!" Will dropped the penguin like a smoking brick, then stared with bulging eyes as blood began seeping from his torn flesh. "Look at that! Just look at that! Bloody evil thing!"

The unperturbed penguin waddled triumphantly back to its partner in crime, who was standing by, more than eager to provide emergency backup if needed.

Will glared at the two defiant birds, who were now exhibiting attack mode, just in case he got any more ideas. "Aaargh! Gahhh! Bloody awful things!"

"Are you okay?" I asked, desperately trying to hide a smirk.

"No, I'm not okay! I hate them, I hate the rotten things!" he screeched, spinning on his heel and tearing off to the kitchen. "Where's that bloody first aid box?"

It must have been at least an hour before he had calmed down enough to call me into his office to discuss what he so eloquently referred to as 'the Smelly and Worse problem'. Coolly inviting me to join him in a mug of tea, he struggled to light a cigarette with heavily plastered fingers. A couple of deep drags, then he exhaled a soothing stream of smoke. "David, I've been thinking – these penguins are a bloody nuisance. How about we slip them a Mickey Finn? No one has to know, and I won't tell if you don't."

I couldn't believe it – was he actually serious about murdering Smelly and Worse? Surely not! "You don't mean kill them, do you?"

He narrowed his eyes conspiratorially. "That's exactly what I mean."

"Well, I must admit, it's crossed my mind on more than one occasion," I told him, "but I couldn't actually do it… I wouldn't be able to sleep at night."

"Well, *I'd* have no problems sleeping, but if that's the way you feel, we'll leave it. Still, it was worth asking…"

I regarded him as he slumped in his chair, puffing on a cigarette, a look of bitter disappointment etched across his face. Shame I'd only be working with him until the end of the season – I really liked him.

❧ 109 ❧

A week had passed since the pool dump, and the water sparkled, brilliant and clear – I at last had my enchanted mirror back.

My two stars were working with renewed enthusiasm, and Baby and Scouse were at the top of their game. Obviously, they were all glad to see me, as I was happy to see them. I hadn't realised just how much I'd missed them. It was good to be back.

The only downside was the condition of poor Stumpy. The sweet, flowery smell that constantly radiated from his pen was now overpowering, and I had real concerns for the little fella. I rang Philip, but he told me there was nothing more he could do, and I sensed that the worst-case scenario was not far away.

Sadly, I still had to pen him for shows and training, but I always released him into the main pool overnight until lunchtime the next day. The harsh reality was I had just one too many dolphins at Hendle.

My medication was definitely having the desired effect, cutting my anxiety and drastically slowing me down. No doubt, I was calmer; but I was also living in a daze, walking into doors, banging into furniture and collecting bruises like a boy scout collects badges. I grew so wearied by my own clumsiness that I fleetingly thought about knocking the tablets off, but didn't dare. The doctor had compared me to a tightly-coiled spring and insisted that Valium was the most effective method of unwinding.

Still, I was back with my dolphin friends so had a lot to be thankful for – plus there were only two and a half months left until the end of the summer season. After that, it would be uninterrupted training all through the winter – something I was really looking forward to.

One big downer, however, would be saying goodbye to Will, who'd soon be leaving to make way for our new general manager. Shame – he'd be a hard act to follow.

❦ 110 ❧

Another late night with Duchess and Herb'e, working on the double back somersault. Training grew in intensity as I ventured deeper and deeper into their psyches. I now had both dolphins leaping from the water and performing a full half somersault in unison and without the use of a prop. We were almost there – just a touch more backwards momentum, then the weight of their bodies would take them that extra mile. We were now very close to achieving a full back somersault, and I had to strike while the iron was hot.

Tonight, instead of one training session, I intended to push for a second. Duchess and Herb'e were tiring quickly now, so this second foray could last no more than twenty minutes.

We had just twenty minutes more to achieve this trick.

❦ 111 ❧

I stand at the poolside, staring into the faces of my two dolphins. They remind me of soldiers awaiting inspection – standing to attention, rigid and unmoving, their eyes locked on mine. I feel their anticipation as I channel a vivid mental image of the somersault.

Eyes still locked, all three of us become as stone. No movement, just sheer concentration. I feel their minds groping inside my head as they search for the final pieces of the puzzle.

"It's there – look deeper, find the picture! I know you can do it!"

I scan Herb'e. I'm sure I've just detected a wry smile. He knows, he's known for a while – the question is… does she?

"Help her, Herb'e, tell her!"

They turn their heads ever so slightly to face each other, and something passes between them.

Has he told her? I can't be sure.

Then, they turn their heads to look me directly in the eye.

Now I'm sure. He's told her – it's now or never!

"Go – make the somersault!"

Both dolphins leap from the stage, blurred silhouettes slicing through the mirror, building momentum and intent.

"Now, do it now!"

A powerful thrust of their tails catapults both dolphins into the air, spinning them into a perfect double one-and-a-half back somersault.

"Fantastic! Incredible!"

The sound of the whistle cuts through the air as the dolphins re-enter the water.

I shower them with fish. Whistle – fish! Whistle – fish! Whistle – fish! Whistle – fish!

"Yes, yes… you've done it, you've got the somersault! Brilliant, fantastic! You clever, clever people!"

I feel the electricity bouncing off the water.

"We've got it – a somersault, and in our first ever season! We've actually achieved the impossible!"

Whistle still shrieking, I empty the entire fish bucket into their open mouths.

I want them to go again… I *ache* for them to go again, but they're tired, and I can't risk failure. I must leave them on a high… leave them wanting more.

Sinking to my knees, I wrap my arms around them. *"Thank you, thank you – I knew you could do it!"*

I sense exultant dolphin laughter as the event replays in our heads. We're unashamedly wallowing in our achievement.

"I told her!" Herb'e shouts.

"No, he didn't – I knew already!"

"Doesn't matter – a double one-and-a-half back somersault is fantastic!" Then I smile and wink. *"But a double two-and-a-half back somersault would be even better. A double two-and-a-half back somersault would be a British exclusive!"*

❧ 112 ❧

As Duchess and Herb'e's progress accelerated, so did our *connection*. I was now a passenger in a speeding sports car, crashing through established training methods with my two dolphins firmly at the wheel. We were three rebellious teenagers steamrolling everyone and everything in our path. We were a gang of three, bonded by a renewed psychic link, and impossible to infiltrate.

Duchess and Herb'e refused point-blank to work for anyone else without my permission – something a concerned Gerry recognised only too well. Further, in successfully achieving the double two-and-a-half back somersault – a British exclusive – I'd unwittingly undermined him.

I was indeed becoming the threat he'd always feared.

❧ 113 ❧

I hadn't seen Gerry since the day he'd delivered Stumpy and, even though we spoke virtually every day by telephone, I would have preferred to meet him face-to-face. But, that wasn't going to happen – he had too many problems at West Coast.

The third dolphin shipment was well behind in training, and I'd heard rumours that Head Office was considering buying in trained dolphins for the new Welby Park venue. This could only mean that Management had lost faith in the ability of Gerry and Sally to deliver shows on time. Pressure on them was mounting.

My log entries showed that both my teams were progressing rapidly. Even Baby and Scouse were now delivering an impressive show. The water change and my enforced rest had certainly paid dividends. Yet I was gratefully aware that we couldn't have achieved any of this without the help and support of Vance and Will – just one of the reasons why I felt so sad about now having to bid goodbye to one of them. Today, Will would be leaving for Welby Park to supervise the completion of his new dolphinarium – but not before first introducing me to the new general manager…

Although already well known in animal circles, it seemed the new chap had never actually trained a dolphin. However, he had been involved in the running of a large urban dolphinarium – the one, in fact, where Gerry had worked before moving to North Liston. Strangely, Gerry had never mentioned him, which made me wonder if perhaps they shared a past – some history that might one day put me in the awkward position of having to choose sides.

Tommy Backhouse… I wondered how he'd work out…

❦ 114 ❧

Down to two shows a day as the season staggered to a welcome end.
Will had left, and our new general manager seemed to be fitting in
well, allowing training to continue without interference.

My two dolphin teams seemed happy and in rude health;
unfortunately, the same couldn't be said for little Stumpy. When
released into the main pool, he'd taken to swimming alone, keeping
well away from the other dolphins. Whether this was by choice, I
couldn't be sure, but he seemed cruelly ignored and discarded as they
played their rough and tumble games.

As I walked around the pool, I noticed one of the girls leaning on
the security railings of his pen. "Everything okay, Kim?" I asked.

She was obviously deep in thought but, as I approached, she gave
me a weak smile. "Poor little fella." She shook her head. "How can
you bear to be a part of this?"

I joined her in watching the little dolphin swimming aimlessly
around, that overwhelming smell of sickliness still lingering over his
pen. "Don't have any choice, Kim. It's part of the job."

As we continued to chat, I gradually became aware that I'd soon be
losing yet another valued member of staff. Kim had obviously seen
enough of life in a dolphinarium and didn't want to see any more.

Later that day, I called my team together. The message was simple:
the end was very close for Stumpy. His dolphin pals had already
abandoned him. They knew – as I knew – that death would soon come
calling.

That evening, instead of releasing Stumpy into the main pool, I left him in his pen. As hard as it might seem, I didn't want him to die in the company of the other dolphins. A dying dolphin invariably evacuated its bowels, which might traumatise the others.

I found it difficult to sleep that night – and with good reason. When Vance and I arrived at the pool early next morning, we found Stumpy half floating in his pen. The little dolphin was dead.

In need of comfort, I turned my gaze towards the main pool to catch Duchess' eye. *"Hello, beautiful, are you okay?"*

She flashed me her customary warm smile. *"Yes, why wouldn't I be?"*

Her nonchalant greeting shocked me. Stumpy's lifeless body was floating less than ten feet away, yet neither she nor any of the other dolphins showed the slightest sign of distress. It was as if the little dolphin were wearing a cloak of invisibility. It was as if he'd never existed at all.

I found it hard to believe how creatures as intelligent and emotional as my dolphins could accept death without a second thought; how they could discard a companion in such an uncaring, even ruthless manner. Perhaps I was trying to impose human traits onto these decidedly non-human beings. Perhaps I needed to accept that life was life, and death was death, without shackling it in my own moral trappings.

Either way, if I wished to continue journeying ever deeper into the dolphin world, it was *I* who would have to conform – not them.

❧ 115 ❧

Vance and I worked quickly to remove Stumpy's body from the holding pen, then I contacted Philip to arrange a post-mortem.

Strange, but as Stumpy lay on the poolside, he reminded me of a plastic toy: he looked unreal – as if he'd been manufactured. In fact, the only upsetting thing about his appearance was that his once-generous smile had turned into an eerie grin.

Everyone was devastated by the loss of this popular little dolphin – everyone but me. I felt somehow removed: devoid of emotion, filled with a numbing sense of inevitability. Was this down to the Valium, or had I been with my dolphins for so long that I'd become like them? *They* were showing no signs of sorrow, cavorting happily as if nothing had happened.

I'd always compared the pool to an enchanted mirror, my dolphins reflecting my personality. Perhaps there was a more sinister parallel: *The Picture of Dorian Gray*, surreptitiously stealing my humanity.

Or perhaps I was just getting carried away…

Later that morning, Philip arrived to carry out Stumpy's post-mortem. His findings were as I'd suspected: liver and brain fluke, and chronically congested lungs – the cause of his sweet flowery breath. But the primary cause of death was pneumonia.

Stumpy had indeed been a very sick dolphin, one who would have died a lot sooner had he lived in the wild. For once, captivity had actually extended a dolphin's life.

After the post-mortem, Stumpy's body was quickly removed, giving the staff time to prepare for the afternoon performances. The show must go on: Head Office would permit no time to grieve whilst there was money to be made.

But, for Kim, Stumpy's death was the final straw and, later that day, she handed in her notice. In two weeks' time, I would lose another popular member of staff.

The only positive thing to come out of all this sadness was the attitude of our new general manager: Tommy Backhouse had been surprisingly supportive throughout the entire ordeal.

Maybe this was the welcome new face of Management... maybe this was someone who could make a difference...

❦ 116 ❧

Two glorious months of training followed. Duchess and Herb'e were performing all their tricks in unison, and Duchess' highball was now one of the highest in the country, standing at an impressive twenty-three feet. My dolphins were well on their way to becoming the dream team I'd always visualised.

I'd also introduced another highly popular trick, where the dolphins would treat some lucky kid from the audience to a boat ride. But the trick I really wanted was the double forward somersault. This had never before been trained in Europe, and would be the jewel in the crown for my dolphin team. But, eager as I was to begin work on this, I couldn't risk jeopardising our newly-acquired back somersault. So, I decided to give Duchess and Herb'e a two-month break, and switch my attentions to Baby and Scouse instead.

My long-term aim was to have Europe's top dolphins courtesy of Duchess and Herb'e, and Britain's top dolphins in the shape of Baby and Scouse – two titles that would propel me to the top of the unofficial trainers' list. Just one problem: the man who presently held this position was my friend and mentor, Gerry. Nevertheless, I had no intention of allowing my loyalty to him to stand in the way of my ambition. I was determined to be the best of the best.

Little did I suspect, however, that the biggest obstacle to achieving my goals lurked just around the corner…

Tommy called a staff meeting. "Listen up, everybody, I've got some great news: the Company has purchased Europe's most famous dolphin pair, Bonnie and Clyde, to perform the opening shows at Welby." He smiled widely, evidently well pleased by the Company's new acquisitions. "I worked with Bonnie and Clyde in my last job. They're lots of fun, and I guarantee you'll love them – especially Clyde…"

Especially Clyde… that sounded ominous…

What he neglected to tell us was that Bonnie and Clyde weren't just famous, but infamous – well known for being difficult to handle. They were also in their thirteenth year of captivity, making them the oldest – and craftiest – working pair in Europe.

"Even better," he continued, "Bonnie and Clyde will be residing here at Hendle until Welby Park is ready to launch."

I could barely believe what I was hearing. "Residing here?" I gasped. "How can they reside here? We have no room."

His smile quickly faded. "We have plenty of room – we have two holding pens."

"And what about the shows?" I pressed. "I can't have more than two dolphins in the main pool at any one time."

"Well, Bonnie and Clyde can take all the shows until we sort something out. We're only doing two a day, so I can't see a problem."

"Well, I can… I can see lots of problems," I snapped. "Two more dolphins at Hendle will cause chaos."

On hearing this, the conversation stopped abruptly and Tommy's face tightened. There was a sticky silence as we both realised that we'd reached an impasse: the honeymoon was over. I chose not to press the matter further, after all, Tommy had only been here for two months, and he *was* my general manager, so I thought it best not to rock the boat.

But I was now painfully aware that my worst nightmare was about to materialise: a filtration system that couldn't cope, a gating system that couldn't be used and a training agenda that couldn't be implemented. Even worse, I'd be forced to incarcerate my two dolphin teams in small holding pens for God knows how long.

How would I cope?

❧ 117 ❧

Although Tommy appeared to listen sympathetically to my fears, he still insisted that the plans for Bonnie and Clyde couldn't be changed.

"We'll get by if we all pull together," he assured me. "Besides, we'll only have them for a short while."

"But the filtration system can't cope with four dolphins, never mind six," I reasoned. "It will mean pool dumps."

"Pool dumps?" That had grabbed his attention – I'd obviously hit a raw nerve.

"Yes, pool dumps."

Tommy paused before answering. "Have you any idea how much a pool dump costs?" he barked. "It's extortionate. Head Office would never allow it, except on explicit veterinary recommendation, so you can forget that. Any talk of water ditching is out of the question."

I listened to him with a sinking heart. If he persisted with this line of thinking, I'd have no choice but to once again resume late-night ditches.

Despite his superficial charm, it was now obvious that Tommy was a Company man through and through, and would follow policy to the letter. He was ambitious and clearly wanted to impress Head Office.

Under normal circumstances, I would have complained to Gerry but, as he was out of favour, I'd just be wasting my time. Nevertheless, I was determined not to let my dolphins suffer because of a misguided Company policy.

Later that afternoon, the sound of air brakes once again heralded the arrival of a new dolphin shipment: Bonnie and Clyde.

Clearly excited, Tommy hurried outside, greeting the transporters like long-lost brothers. Old cronies, I realised.

I'd already safely ensconced my two dolphin teams in the holding pens, as I didn't want them in the main pool with the newcomers. Bonnie and Clyde were fully mature dolphins and would be quick to begin the task of establishing a new pecking order. When that happened, my four babies wouldn't stand a chance.

First in the pool was Bonnie: a large silver-grey female, about eight feet long and incredibly powerfully built. Her appearance was certainly impressive – a perfect dolphin specimen.

Then came Clyde, the male. He was a little longer – about nine feet – but nowhere near as beefy. What amazed me was that even after thirteen years of chlorine bleaching, his colour was still very dark, which meant he must have been almost black when in the wild – a rarity with this type of dolphin.

As they checked out their new pool, I couldn't help but notice how Clyde immediately parked himself outside Duchess and Herb'e's pen. He drifted ominously in front of the gate, issuing challenges – menaces intended for poor Herb'e, who was currently the dominant male at Hendle.

Herb'e clearly didn't fancy his chances against this older, larger newcomer, and responded by hiding behind Duchess.

I watched apprehensively for several minutes, before turning to find myself suddenly nose-to-nose with the head transporter. "Woah, you nearly gave me a heart attack!" I laughed, stepping back.

He didn't answer, but held his ground, standing menacingly close.

I looked him in the eye. "Is there something you wanted to tell me?"

He flung back his head and laughed dismissively. "Tommy knows all about these two – ask him!" Then, apparently deeming me unworthy of any further conversation, he swaggered back around the pool to join his fellow cronies.

Spying a movement at the back of the stage, I turned to see Vance staring after him, his expression dark and angry. His eyes met mine.

"Cocky sod, isn't he?" he snapped, then disappeared into the kitchen.

I followed him, leaving Tommy to entertain his big-shot guests. They clearly didn't need – or want – us around.

Minutes later, I found myself sitting at the kitchen table, silently staring at Herb'e's logbook. The arrival of Bonnie and Clyde had certainly set my alarm bells ringing. But that wasn't all… there was something else… something darker…

It was as if the coming of these two dolphins had somehow triggered a shift, decloaking a malevolent and envious presence… a presence I hadn't sensed before.

Hesitantly picking up my pen, I began to write the morning's log entry:

15th January 1973, Black Monday… the arrival of Bonnie and Clyde.

The adventure continues… *The Perfect Pair: The Mirror Cracks*.

Coming soon!

THE PLAYERS WHO HAVE LEFT THE STAGE

Bubbles: By the power of her own 'hand', the tormented Bubbles finally won her hard-fought freedom from the captive world she so hated. Once released, she used her considerable strength of character to force entry into the Sea of Light, where, to this day, she powers effortlessly through liquid sky – an ocean without boundaries.

Stumpy: This sweet-natured yet sick little dolphin drifted softly into the Light, where he was lovingly nursed back to full health. In appreciation of his gentle disposition, he was allowed to join others of his kind in joyously surfing the Wave of Tranquillity… as an equal.

Bobby: Due to the previous incident at City Zoo, the Company deemed returning Bobby there too risky, so instead covertly sold him to a well-known safari park. There, he spent the remainder of his life swimming free in a large outdoor lake, where he ruled as lord and master over a harem of twelve attentive females and – to the best of my knowledge – lived the rest of his days in blissful contentment.

THE STORY THAT STARTED
IT ALL...

'Deliver Us from Bobby!' won First Prize in the prestigious *Manchester Evening News* 'A Piece of Your Life' literary competition, despite fierce opposition from "over 500 carefully-crafted entries". The judges consisted of Professor Brenda Cooper, Ursula Hurley and Peter Kalu, with their winning choice headlining in the newspaper on Monday 5th December 2011 as 'David's Sea Lion Makes a Literary Splash'.

The covering feature, written by Deanna Delamotta, quoted Professor Cooper as declaring, "This wonderful piece of life has a beautiful ending."

The winning entry was, in fact, written many years ago, and was the starting point for the writing of *The Perfect Pair*.

This version of 'Deliver Us from Bobby!' has been altered slightly to give it standalone status, so if you enjoyed the first version, here's your chance to read it again.

*"**Down the narrow, winding corridor, he pursued his quarry, galloping clumsily and ineffectively like... well, like a sea lion out of water.**"*

David Holroyd

1st

Deliver Us from Bobby

Manchester Evening News 1971 – David lands 'a dream of a job'. My first taste of fame: I was the lucky lad chosen to represent a leading company working as a presenter of dolphin shows. Little did I realise that this opportunity would set me on the path of training The Perfect Pair – Europe's top performing dolphins. So, it seems strange that the first of my many adventures took place, not with a dolphin, but instead with a huge Californian sea lion, named Bobby.

Bobby and I met by chance after he was stealthily whisked away from his zoo home, following a horrific attack on a member of the public. To avoid destruction, he was transported to the training pool where I was based; and with nothing more than two penguins, aptly named Smelly and Worse, to keep us company, he and I soon became good friends. However, his fearsome reputation always commanded respect.

One morning, I had to pick up a crate of herring from the fishmonger's, and as the pool was situated near the local colliery, I set out early to dodge the morning traffic.

Only one road led from the village to the pit: it ran up a steep hill, passing the pool about three quarters of the way up and, thirty minutes before a shift change, got very busy.

I didn't fancy lugging heavy slabs of fish any great distance, so instead of parking in my usual place round the side of the pool, I found a more convenient spot on the main road, a short way from the front entrance.

After dumping the fish in the sink to defrost, I began to clean up the usual overnight mess left by Smelly and Worse. Filling a bucket with hot water and bleach, I strode into the pool room, calling cheerfully to Bobby, "Hello, lad, how you doing, my son?"

It was important to greet the big fellah properly: God knows, it must have been a bleak life for him locked up in this place twenty-four hours a day with nothing but two stinky penguins for company.

Bobby, messing in the water, responded to my shout by lifting his massive head, snorting a plume of droplets into the air, and solemnly regarding me with those big, green eyes. A blink of acknowledgment, then he dived to continue his sub aqua meanderings.

I picked up the deck scrubber, walked to the far end of the pool room, and started to scrub the floor. Smelly and Worse had been particularly productive overnight, leaving a fair number of stinky white pools for me to deal with.

Suddenly, the main doors to the pool room banged open, revealing a miner: early thirties, becapped and dressed in the usual drab garb of the village men.

"Hello? Can I help you?"

The doors hadn't even swung shut behind him before he started yelling abuse of the most remarkable colour. A potent Shire accent delivered four-letter words with the efficiency of a machine gun, and as I stood there gaping, I managed to grasp something about… my car… HIS space… and get it shifted NOW!

It seemed the man was aggrieved because I'd parked in *his* spot – no small offence in the village, where the ownership of a *spot* was of paramount importance. The village was so small and intimate that almost every square foot was deemed to belong to *someone*: be it a parking space, a lamppost to lean on, a wall to sit on, or a stool in the pub. I'd transgressed seriously, and the man was determined to let me know it.

Like all the miners, he was short in stature, but wide and muscular in build, with a chest that looked solid enough to stop a small nuclear warhead. He rather put me in mind of a vertically-challenged Minotaur. His small, steely eyes flashed beneath his cap, the corners of his mouth twisting grimly downwards, then he pounded towards me across the tiled floor, fists clenched.

"Are yer listenin' to mi, or what? I said, are yer listenin'?"

He was very, very angry.

But he wasn't the only one: the training pool was supposed to be a high security facility, strictly out of bounds to the public. It galled me no end that this guy had had the nerve to even breach the main entrance, never mind intrude as far as the pool room.

"Ay, you – you *******! Get that ******* car out of my space!"

Before my eyes, the red mist started to form, and I struggled to steady myself and speak calmly. "You shouldn't be in here."

"Get that ******* car out of my space!"

"Who do you think you're talking to?" I demanded, throwing the deck scrubber aside and stepping forward.

"I said get that ****** car out of my space!"

"Or what?" So enraged was I by his foul-mouthed assault, I could hardly breathe, never mind speak. Everything around me seemed to fade away as all my attention focussed on this nasty, bullish man, and my overwhelming desire to pound him into the ground. I launched myself at him, determined, dangerous and blinded by anger. He had no intention of backing off, either, and if we'd ever reached each other, I dread to think what might have happened. But we didn't reach each other, because a terrifying thought suddenly popped into my mind and all but paralysed me.

Bobby! Where's Bobby?

Distracted, I turned to see him: his massive, black head in the centre of the pool, immobile and watching. Then, ever so slowly, it swivelled round so that his big green eyes locked onto mine. For the oddest moment, it seemed as though I were looking in a mirror; then I felt all my aggression seeping away, and saw it – actually saw it – filling up in those big green eyes.

Bobby's head snapped back round to look at the man; then he dived.

There was nothing left in me now but panic, blind panic. "Run!" I screamed. "The sea lion! Run!"

The man froze in bewilderment, sensing my terror. "What? What do you mean?"

"Just get out! The sea lion!" My voice had deteriorated into a shriek.

He stood there, jaw drooping foolishly, then whimpered, "Why, does it bite?"

By this time, the torpedo which was Bobby had almost reached the deck, a plume of water in its wake.

"Go, go!" I screamed; but the man was already gone, a pair of swinging doors the only evidence that he'd ever been there.

Bobby shot from the water like a ball launched in a pinball game, a loud, hoarse bark reverberating off the walls. He hit the tiles with a dull thwack, then slid headlong through the swing doors, sending them crashing off their hinges.

As he disappeared into the dark corridor, I grabbed the deck scrubber and chased after him. "No, Bobby, no… come back!"

Down the narrow, winding corridor, he pursued his quarry,

galloping clumsily and ineffectively like... well, like a sea lion out of water.

By this time, the man had made it out of the building, down the steps and onto the road, and might have believed – mistakenly – that he'd reached safety; but the avenging Bobby motored on.

"Stop, Bobby! You can't do this!"

Still bellowing his ear-shattering war cry, he burst through the main entrance, slid down the steps, and galloped along the pavement, oblivious to the crawling traffic and gaping drivers. But he managed only five or six yards before his rampaging pursuit slowed to a half-hearted slither. His prey had escaped, and Bobby just wasn't built for manoeuvring along pavements. He flopped to a stop, then lifted his head to regard me apologetically. Sorry, Dave; he got away.

By this time, the traffic had come to a complete halt as the men intended for the early shift stopped to watch. How could this be happening in a tiny, unrecognised backwater like this? A sea lion? Most of them had never seen a sea lion, except in pictures. But this? A sea lion on a road in the middle of the village?

Bobby ignored them. He was dejected, exhausted.

I blinked at him kindly, as he had so often blinked at me, then gently manoeuvred him round with the deck scrubber. "Come on, Bobby. We showed him. Now let's go home."

Bobby sighed heavily, then began the laborious journey back to the pool, hauling himself up the steps and through the entrance, still maintaining an audience of open-mouthed motorists.

As for the aggressive miner, we never saw him again.